CHANTEL GUERTIN

love struck

ECW PRESS

Published by ECW Press
2120 Queen Street East, Suite 200,
Toronto, Ontario, Canada M4E 1E2
416-694-3348 / info@ecwpress.com

This is a work of fiction. Names, characters,
places, and incidents either are the product of
the author's imagination or are used fictitiously,
and any resemblance to actual persons, living
or dead, business establishments, events, or
locales is entirely coincidental.

LIBRARY AND ARCHIVES CANADA
CATALOGUING IN PUBLICATION

Guertin, Chantel, 1976-, author
Love struck / Chantel Guertin.

Previously published:
Love struck / Chantel Simmons. —
Toronto : Key Porter Books, 2010.

ISBN 978-1-77041-161-6 (pbk.)
Also issued as: 978-1-77090-441-5 (PDF)
978-1-77090-442-2 (ePUB)

I. Title.

PS8637.I474L68
2013   jC813'.6   C2013-902485-9

Cover design: Tania Craan
Cover images: woman © Corbis Photography;
rain ©Lonely_/iStockphoto
Author photo: Steven Khan
Printing: Friesens 5 4 3 2 1

The publication of Love Struck has been generously supported by the Canada Council for the
Arts which last year invested $157 million to bring the arts to Canadians throughout the country,
and by the Ontario Arts Council, an agency of the Government of Ontario. We also acknowledge
the financial support of the Government of Canada through the Canada Book Fund for our
publishing activities, and the contribution of the Government of Ontario through the Ontario Book
Publishing Tax Credit and the Ontario Media Development Corporation.

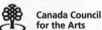

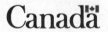

MIX
Paper from
responsible sources
FSC® C016245

PRINTED AND BOUND IN CANADA

chapter one

I t happened on a Thursday, an ordinary Thursday like any other. Except on this Thursday my life was changed forever. And, just like so many things in life, it came when I least expected it. When I had no idea that it could ever happen. At least, not to me.

It was just past eight in the evening and I was sitting at Pretty Nail getting a pedicure. I'd bailed on Parker—he'd called in the late afternoon asking me to accompany him to a prospective client dinner but I'd told him I couldn't cancel my dinner and manicure date with Elin. It was a ritual I'd initiated a few months earlier to give my best friend a reason to come in to Toronto—she'd moved to Jackson's Point a little over a year ago when she and Terrence had found out she was pregnant with triplets—and, more importantly, it got her out of the house and out of her hospital scrubs, which she wore even though she had no plans to return to her nursing position.

Twenty minutes earlier, moments after arriving at

the no-frills nail bar after having sushi and a bottle of Riesling, Elin had gotten a panicked call from Terrence saying she had to come home immediately. One of the kids had a fever and he had no idea what to do. So Elin left, and since I'd already paid for her manicure, I opted for a pedicure, too. I'd just settled into the leather massage chair when my BlackBerry buzzed and I looked down to see a frantic email from one of my newer clients, Lonette, asking what to wear on a first date with a guy she'd just met at the gym.

I mentally drew an image of Lonette, a dark-haired, skittish accountant in her forties who'd won a set of sessions with me in a charity auction. Since my job as an image consultant was, admittedly, a little superficial—helping rich people buy more clothes—I didn't mind occasionally offering advice for free. Besides, the question of what to wear on a first date was always my favourite. Lonette had just gone through a nasty divorce (was there any other kind?), and as a result had lost more than twenty pounds (being incredibly unhappy made most people either incredibly overweight or incredibly thin, and Lonette was the latter) so she was a fairly easy client.

I texted her back to get more info on the date: when, where, who was the guy (age, occupation, likes, dislikes), then mentally went through her wardrobe, finally deciding on a pair of wide-legged, high-waisted dark denim trousers, a slinky, grey-pink sleeveless top, black kitten heels, black leather bucket bag, hair left to air-dry to maximize her natural waves and creamy-taupe and pink makeup. I was just scrolling through the rest of my emails when the girl two seats over from me asked the girl beside me if her sister was still dating that guy on the Blue Jays.

I never understood the appeal of pro sports players. Weren't they all cheaters?

"No. Apparently she wasn't the only girl getting to third base with him," the Sister, who had an enviable British accent, replied, then laughed at her own joke. *See?* I thought. "Now she's fixated on some married guy she works with. She actually just texted me to say she's hooking up with him tonight. Honestly, she has no shame. The only thing that girl cares about is money."

"So what does he do?"

"Investment banker at Feldman Davis."

Oh my God. Parker worked at Feldman Davis. I shifted in my chair so I could catch the names of this scandalous couple and report back to Parker in case he knew them. Gossip was always more thrilling when you knew the guilty parties.

"Feldman Davis? Since when does Sienna work in finance?"

The Sister laughed cynically. "Since she realized those firms were filled with hot, rich guys, and that her commerce degree could actually get her a position as a research assistant. Which has just *got* to be a glorified secretary—if not, she'll probably be fired before her three-month probation is up—but it gives her an excuse to flit around and eye her prey."

Something in the back of my brain triggered when I heard the name Sienna. It sounded somewhat familiar, but I couldn't put a face to it. I pictured last year's holiday party, the summer golf tournament, the partners' annual barbeque . . .

Had Parker mentioned a new research assistant in the office? I couldn't recall. His executive assistant was Barb, a grey-haired grandmother of three who sent homemade shortbread home with him at Christmas.

Sienna . . .

Oh, Sienna Somers! I vaguely remembered Parker mentioning a woman named Sienna Somers. Had he told me she was new? I couldn't recall the context of the conversation, but I did remember thinking at the time, *Who has a name like Sienna Somers at an investment banking firm?* Isn't it more of a porn-star name than an analyst's name? Maybe her parents had other aspirations for her. But now it sounded like she wasn't an analyst at all. Not that it mattered—

"But what's the point of hooking up with a married guy?" the friend was now saying, interrupting my thoughts.

"Challenge, maybe? And it's no-strings-attached sex. Besides, I wouldn't put it past Sienna to believe she could make the guy leave his wife. Anyway, supposedly this Parker guy is super hot."

Parker? Did she just say Parker? My husband's name? My good-looking husband's name? No, I must have heard her wrong. She most certainly did not say Parker. She couldn't have. Or maybe the guy, whose name is *not* Parker, works as a valet, parking cars, in the garage under the Bay Street tower in which Feldman Davis is located. That must be it. So he's the *parker*. Because he *parks* cars. I used all my mental energy to will the Sister to say the guy's name again. Just to be sure that she most certainly, definitely did *not* say my husband's name.

Say his name, I wanted to scream, but didn't. Because even though we weren't in a high-end spa, it just wasn't something I would do.

My heart was beating in my throat, making it difficult to breathe. And so, without thinking, I did the unthinkable.

"Excuse me." I tapped the girl beside me on the shoulder and she turned to look at me, raising her perfectly plucked eyebrows. I wanted her to be in her mid-fifties, which would reasonably make her sister Sienna somewhere in the same decade, and effectively rule her out of being a mistress to *my* Parker. Because surely my thirty-two-year-old husband would not cheat on me with a woman nearly twice my age, right? *Right?*

Of course, what I should've been thinking was that surely my husband wouldn't cheat on me at all.

The girl beside me—the Sister—was not fifty, not even close. She looked to be about my age, or maybe a little younger, and was wearing an adorable floral halter dress and had long blond hair held back with a crocheted headband. She could've been my friend. Except, of course, I would never be friends with someone whose sister would have sex with my husband. Obviously.

"I couldn't help but eavesdrop on your conversation." I paused, hoping she would suddenly smile, shrug and say not to worry, that her sister lived in Atlanta or London or Dubai. Except, Feldman Davis didn't have branches in Atlanta or London or Dubai.

Or maybe she'd tell me I'd misheard the names, that

what she'd said was her sister *Sandra* was having sex with *Peter*. Or that they knew I was Parker's wife and Parker had put them up to it—a belated April Fool's Day joke in May and *ha ha ha*, wasn't that funny?

But Parker wasn't the type for silly pranks.

Instead, the girl beside me stared, a mixture of confusion and annoyance on her face. She raised her eyebrows.

"That guy you were talking about . . ." I fumbled. "What did you say his name was?"

The girl continued to look at me as though I was crazy. And maybe I was. I was sure she was going to tell me to mind my own business (in not-so-polite terms) but she suddenly seemed to have a change of heart. She looked around her and then leaned closer.

"Why? Do you know him? Do you work for *Hello!* or TMZ? Are you an undercover investigator? Are we going to be on some hidden camera show?"

What could I possibly say to that? Actually, those were all really good excuses when you wanted to interrupt a conversation in which you weren't included. Why hadn't I thought of those lines?

She laughed and waved a manicured claw. "Don't worry about it. I'll tell you anyway. It's Parker. Parker . . . Rose. Or Boss. Or—"

Ross. Parker Ross.

My husband.

My husband was having an affair.

And so, I did what I assumed any woman who had just learned her husband was having an affair would do. I stood up mid-pedicure, handed Ming a handful of bills, and shuffled, in my yellow sponge flip-flops, out the door onto Yonge Street, only to find that the sky was dark with miserable clouds and it was starting to rain. I turned right and made my way, umbrella-less, the five blocks home to figure out what the hell I was going to do.

Whenever I'd heard about women whose husbands were cheaters—on *Tyra* or in *Cosmo*—I always thought in exasperation: *How did you not know?* Late nights at the office, early-morning meetings, hang-ups on the home phone, unexplained charges on the joint credit card statement . . .

But I'd experienced none of that. Sure, Parker had early-morning meetings, but what Bay Street banker didn't? And he often had to entertain clients at night, but he always came home to me. Of course, he didn't really ever get any calls on our home phone, since he made most of his calls on his BlackBerry. And while we both had our own separate bank accounts—which I'd agreed to so I'd never have to justify a second pedicure in one month or another silk tunic from French Connection—it had always been that way.

Nothing out of the ordinary had ever happened to make me suspect that Parker could possibly be having an affair.

Nothing.

Except . . . now that I thought about it, there *was* the condom incident a few weeks ago. I'd been transferring a load of wash into the dryer when I'd discovered a grape-flavoured condom in a purple plastic packet, which must have fallen out of the pocket of his jeans. "Gag from Eric's bachelor party," Parker had explained, not missing a beat, when I'd asked him. And I'd believed him. After all, the condom was still nicely tucked into its unopened packet. If he'd been having an affair, there wouldn't have *been* an unused condom in his pants. Besides, Parker would never use something as tacky as a flavoured condom. I simply wasn't worried.

And then there was the time Elin had sworn she saw Parker coming out of the Hilton on Richmond in the middle of a workday a few months ago when she'd been downtown taking the triplets to the pediatrician. I hadn't even asked Parker about this one. After all, I knew the Hilton had a restaurant and bar at which he could have easily been having lunch. There was nothing to be suspicious about, and asking would've only made me look like a jealous, neurotic, paranoid wife. Besides, aren't cheaters supposed to have lipstick on their collar, smell of strange perfumes, or receive mysterious phone calls and emails?

Except Parker kept his BlackBerry on vibrate so I had no idea if he was getting mysterious phone calls or emails. And Parker's office had a no-scent rule, so if he was having sex with someone in his office she wouldn't be wearing fragrance either. And who kissed a married man on the neck while wearing lipstick anyway? That cliché was so *Days of Our Lives* really, wasn't it?

Come to think of it, how on earth was any woman supposed to know if her husband was cheating on her? I had no clue.

Oh my God. Oh my God. Oh my God.

"Mrs. Ross, are you okay?"

I looked up to see Amir, our doorman, standing over me. For some reason, I was lying on the sidewalk. Amir leaned over and put a hand on my forehead.

"What happened?" Amir asked.

"I don't know."

"Did you slip on the pavement? Let's get you inside."

He put his hands in mine and pulled me up to my feet. "Where are your shoes?"

My cute little cream-coloured Betsey Johnson wedges with sky-blue ankle ribbons were still at Pretty Nail.

I shuffled into the lobby. I was having difficulty seeing. Everything looked blurry, but I pushed on toward the elevators, telling Amir I was sure I'd be fine. Inside the black and silver mirrored elevator I looked at my reflection. My face was blotchy and my eyes were red and filled with tears.

I unlocked the door to our condo.

I felt like an idiot.

How could he do this to me? I couldn't understand it. He wasn't a horrible womanizer who treated me like crap. And I wasn't a bad wife—at least I didn't think I was. We'd been happy for the past three years of our marriage and the three years we'd been together before we tied the knot at a lovely 150-guest spring wedding at the Four Seasons. (My parents had hoped to host it at their cottage-turned-home on Lake Muskoka, but Parker's mother thought a country wedding would require everyone to wear galoshes or something equally déclassé and Parker refused to stand up to her. And I didn't want to make a big deal of it, or have Parker think I preferred a country-bumpkin wedding to the swanky hotel wedding we had instead.) It had worked out fine and now we were *happy*. Happy people didn't cheat.

Which was why this was so unfair.

I dropped my cobalt-blue leather Marc Jacobs bag—the one I'd bought myself on our third anniversary only weeks earlier (after Parker's assistant had screwed up and bought me a crystal vase, forgetting that we commemorated with the traditional gifts rather than the modern ones, meaning she should've been shopping for leather)—onto the white marble floor and slumped down beside it.

I don't know how long I sat there before I realized what I would do.

I would kill him.

I envisioned myself dressing all in black leather (though my leather collection consisted solely of shoes, belts and handbags), knee-high boots (would navy Hunter rain boots do?) and a mask (would an organic corn and oatmeal facial masque work?). Never mind the outfit. It was all about the weapon. But what would I use? The kitchen knife? We'd barely used our knives in the time we'd been married and I wasn't sure they could slice a bagel, let alone break skin. A candlestick? I'd put a ban on candlesticks when I moved in with Parker after he'd declared my whimsical candles-in-Chianti-bottles not only collegial but messy. Instead, I'd learned to love tidy tealights. Maybe a gun? Except the only gun I owned was a glue gun for making my own thank-you cards. Perhaps I could strangle him with my bare hands, I thought. Only I didn't have much upper-body strength—I tended to avoid any sort of exercise regime that employed free weights (I certainly wasn't the kind of girl who wanted bulky upper arms busting out of her pretty cap-sleeve blouses).

And then I realized: I couldn't kill Parker. I'd have to go to jail and I'd look absolutely horrible in the regulation orange jumpsuit.

But it wasn't just that.

I couldn't kill Parker because I loved him. I loved him more than anyone.

Which is why none of this made any sense at all.

I sat slumped on the floor, my head in my hands.

And then my BlackBerry buzzed.

I rummaged around in my bag, pulled out the pink device as it rang a second time and looked at the number.

It was Parker.

I stared as it rang a third time, knowing if I didn't answer it on the sixth it would go to voice mail.

But what would I say? Would I tell him I knew? Would I channel a soap opera heroine and coyly ask him if there was something he wanted to tell me? Or would I just tell him I was leaving him and let him figure out the rest when he got home to an empty condo?

But I'd grown to love our condo—and more importantly, what it stood for. The person I'd become living here. I didn't want to leave it. Maybe I'd pack *his* things and leave them outside the front door. Yes, that's what I'd do. Then again, packing up someone else's bags and leaving them outside the door in the middle of the hallway was hardly as dramatic as leaving them on the front steps of a suburban home for all the neighbours to see, was it?

The phone rang a fourth time.

Besides, why did I have to be the one to pack up his stuff? Shouldn't he have to do that? No one *likes* packing. Shouldn't that at least be part of his punishment for committing adultery? I'd tell him to pack his own things, while I called my lawyer.

Except our lawyer was Parker's friend Eric. No matter, I'd call my father. He'd find me a lawyer. Yes, that's what I'd do. But then I'd have to tell my parents that Parker had cheated on me and that was the last thing I wanted to do.

My parents, of course, would love that I was finally opening up—they themselves were total open books, whereas I was the opposite. A closed book, if I was going to use clichés. Or one of those empty cases furniture stores put on bookshelves to show you what your living room would look like if you bought the various pieces on display. Once my parents got over the initial shocking joy that I had shared something personal with them, though, how disappointed would they be that their only offspring had failed at her marriage—after only three years?

I clicked the Talk button and took a deep breath.

"Hello?" said a breathless female voice before I could say anything at all.

"Hello?" I said back.

Oh my God.

Was it her? Was it Sienna Somers? My husband's mistress? It had to be her. Who else would be using my husband's phone? Maybe her sister had called her and warned her. Except I hadn't revealed my identity to the Sister. Or maybe she sensed, using her evil temptress powers, that the jig was almost up.

"Is this Poppy Ross?" The woman's voice was filled with panic, but I could still hear her smooth British accent.

"Yes," I said slowly. My right hand, the one holding the phone, went numb, as though paralyzed.

"Poppy, this is Sienna Somers. I . . . I work with your husband. There's been an accident."

chapter two

I arrived in the emergency room at Mount Sinai minutes later, only to learn that Parker had already been
whisked through the double doors to the ER and up to
ICU. Surely that couldn't be a good sign. Wasn't he supposed to still be sitting in the waiting room, like the other
eighty-three people, while the life-threateningly injured
parties got priority?

I wasn't positive I was breathing anymore. My lungs
felt like they'd been clogged with spare cotton balls from
the stash that was sitting in a jar on the triage desk, in
front of which I was standing.

"What happened?" I managed to ask the triage nurse,
willing myself to be prepared for her to say the worst: that
he'd been in a car accident, had a stroke, a heart attack
or been shot by some delinquent teens while crossing the
street to catch the subway home.

"He was struck by lightning," the nurse said noncha-
lantly, as though he'd twisted his pinky.

Struck by lightning? Was she joking?

"Don't worry. He's going to be okay."

Okay? Were people *ever* okay after being struck by lightning? Lightning never struck twice because it killed on the first bolt, didn't it? Or was the nurse actually channelling her inner Mother Teresa, and what she really meant was that he was going to be okay when he got to heaven?

No, he wasn't going to die. He was only thirty-two. Thirty-two-year-old husbands didn't die. Not even if they'd been having an affair. An affair. My God. I felt sick thinking about it, but my priorities had turned upside-down since Sienna's call. Now I just wanted to know that Parker was okay. But what did the triage nurse really know about the situation? She was sitting out in the waiting room, sticking thermometers in people's ears and taking their blood pressure. Was she even *allowed* to make that statement when she wasn't in the same room as Parker?

"Go through the doors to the end of the hall, up the elevator to the third floor and ask the nurse at the desk which room he's in." The nurse stared at me, and then leaned dramatically to her left to look around me to the person standing behind me, who probably *had* twisted a pinky.

I backed away from the desk and looked for the double doors, then pushed through them, following her instructions. My thoughts were jumbled, so I held on to the one thing I could control: putting one foot in front of the other. Step by step.

Moments later, a nurse on the third floor directed me to a semi-private room directly across from the nurses' station. I entered and saw Parker in the first bed. He was lying on his back, eyes closed, perfectly still. He looked like he was taking a nap, except that Parker was the world's most fitful sleeper. My fair skin was marked with war wounds from sleeping beside him. He would never lie still on his back like this. And it was clear he wasn't just having a nap, because there were wires and tubes running in all different directions, and they were all attached to him like he was some sort of string puppet behind the curtain, ready to go on stage and amuse little children.

"Don't be alarmed," the nurse at his bedside—whose nametag read Abigail—said, while pressing round silver stickers all over my husband's clean-shaven chest, which was not at all clean-shaven this morning when he left for work since he was an investment banker, not a cyclist or some other extreme-sports addict. "This is an EKG to monitor his heart." She grabbed a handful of multi-coloured wires and clipped them on to the silver stickers, then punched some buttons on a machine that was connected to a screen that suddenly beeped and came to life, showing a series of three lines that went up and down, just like on all those medical TV dramas when the patient had a heart attack and they had to make sure that he wasn't going to suddenly flatline.

Not be alarmed? How could I not be alarmed?

"What's that?" I asked, pointing at another tube, as she fed it through his nostrils. What was wrong with Parker and why was he not noticing that two Slurpee-size straws were being shoved up his nose?

"Don't worry."

Why was everyone telling me not to worry? How could I not worry?

"It's a ventilator. To help him breathe while he's

unconscious. He's going to be fine, and even better once we get his blood-alcohol level back under control."

"Unconscious?" My husband was unconscious? No. I must have heard her wrong. She must have said un-conscience. Like, he didn't have a conscience. As in, if he did have a conscience he wouldn't have cheated on me but now that he had, he was having an anxiety attack and these tubes were just helping him breathe. That must be it. Except I wasn't supposed to be thinking about the affair. Because that wasn't important at the moment. "Are those keeping him alive?"

"Of course not. They're just letting us monitor him to make sure that everything's in working order until he wakes up."

Wakes up? So she must have said *unconscious* after all. And what did she mean, "that everything's in working order?" *Like what?* Like his heart? Like his brain? What if he stayed like this forever? What if he never opened his lovely blue eyes again?

"Don't some people stay in a coma for years?" I whispered, crumpling into the mud-coloured vinyl chair in the corner. My husband of three years was in a coma. And he might not come out of it.

"He's not in a coma, dear. He's unconscious."

Fine, correction: He was unconscious. Apparently, there was a difference—though I had absolutely no idea what it was. But the nurse must have sensed my confusion because she patted my hand and said that being uncon-scious was likely temporary and that he would, in all like-lihood, come out of it. That his body was shocked and that he just needed a bit of time to unwind—"like after a hard day at the office"—and that when he was ready, he'd wake up.

I knew her words were meant to be comforting, but I didn't find them so. Still, her touch made me feel a bit better. Suddenly I had this overwhelming urge to ask her to give me a hug, but I didn't want her to think I was weird. I knew I should be calm, collected. And so, instead, I asked in my best calm, collected voice, "When?"

She shook her head and said she wasn't sure. It could be a few days, or it could be a few hours. "I've seen this happen quite often. Some of the other ER girls call me the lightning nurse because I always seem to treat the ones who get struck by lightning"—she laughed but I couldn't really see the humour. Was I supposed to be comforted by the idea that my husband was just one of a million?—"and of all the ones I've seen, this isn't that bad. He's going to be fine. You don't need to get excited." I got the feeling she thought I was going to lose it at any moment. Like some crazy yo-yo, spinning out of control.

I knew I was supposed to feel comforted that Parker's shock wasn't as big as other people's shocks but it wasn't very comforting at all. Did that mean they weren't taking it as seriously? And how could they not? He was still unconscious. Wasn't that serious enough? I nervously wrapped a short lock of blond hair around my finger.

"Do you know what happened, exactly?"

"From what I understand from the woman who was with him, the lightning struck his umbrella. It seems like he was smart enough—or startled enough—that he dropped the umbrella before, hopefully, any real damage could occur."

My chest felt tight and I gave the lock of hair I was gripping a little tug.

"The woman . . . who was with him . . . do you know her name or what happened to her?" I could feel my voice getting tight and high, which tended to happen when I was anxious.

Nurse Abigail raised her eyebrows, as though she just assumed I knew. As though Sienna and I were *friends*. As though I looked like the type of woman who'd be friends with a tramp who had affairs with married men. "She's in the ER, being monitored. She must've been holding his hand or his arm and got a touch of the current."

She must've *what?* Oh God, no. They couldn't have been holding hands. Part of me knew it was ridiculous that I felt this upset to hear they could've been holding hands when I already knew they were having sex, but there was something about holding hands that made me want to throw up.

Holding hands was special.

"Maybe they were both holding the umbrella?" I said accusatorily.

Almost as though she realized what she'd just implied, Nurse Bad News shrunk up a bit in her flowery cotton scrubs. "Of course. Or she could've just bumped up against him at the wrong moment. Just enough to give her a bit of a shock." She nodded for emphasis.

A moment later, in a gentle tone that made me *sure* that she knew what was going on, she added. "You should sit with him. Sometimes, we find that talking helps. He might hear your lovely voice and wake up just so he can see his pretty wife's face." She smiled sympathetically, and leaned down to put her arm around my shoulder.

I didn't think my voice was one of my best features—I always sounded younger than I looked—and I knew my tear-streaked, blotchy face had to be a fright, but it was nice of Nurse Abigail to say so and I smiled and nodded at her as she turned to walk toward the door.

I looked over at Parker from my chair a few feet away. At his dark blond hair that was slightly tousled on top, his thick eyebrows that always had a few longer hairs that he refused to trim, saying they'd just grow even longer, his five o'clock shadow that scuffed my chin whenever he kissed me, his lips, slightly parted, as though waiting to be kissed, even though I knew, sensibly, he probably wasn't thinking about being kissed. Still, I wanted to kiss him, to hold him, to turn back time . . .

"What should I talk to you about?" I whispered to him.

This wasn't how things were supposed to play out at all. Parker and I were supposed to be together forever, just the two of us. No one else. That's what we'd promised each other when we got married. So how had everything suddenly changed? The tears that had welled up in my eyes spilled over.

"You could talk to him about something happy," Nurse Abigail said gently. "Tell him the story of how the two of you met."

I waited until she left the room, then pulled my chair over to the bed, wedging myself between two machines, and took Parker's hand in mine. But I couldn't help wondering if it was the same hand Sienna Somers had been holding only an hour earlier.

~

I met Parker in the summer of 2004. Elin and I had decided
to spend our last summer of bliss before our final year of
university (after which point we'd be forced to get grown-
up jobs) as lifeguards at Sunnyside Park. We were set for
a summer of tanning, tankinis and unbridled romance
(Elin with the male lifeguards and I with guys in bands I
planned to meet with my evenings free to go to shows).
But while Elin was studying for the lifeguarding exam, I
was busy planning my summer wardrobe (clearly, the first
sign of my true calling as an image consultant). When it
came time to resuscitate the dummy, I asphyxiated him.
(Note to aspiring lifeguards: kissing is *not* the same thing
as giving mouth-to-mouth.)

So while Elin got a blue Parks bathing suit that showed
off her golden Croatian skin and long legs, a whistle and
a job at the pool, I got a no-frills apron and a summer
schedule from hell as the newest waitress at Cleats, a popular guy's guy kind of sports bar whose only saving grace
was that it was near the pool so I could spend my after-
noons before work suntanning and complaining to Elin
how much I dreaded slinging pints.

But it was at Cleats where I met Parker Ross.

Actually, first I met Diesel Cartwright, who was a night
bartender at Cleats, and the lead singer in an all-guy band
called Wonder Woman, which I deduced, after going to
my first show, was thus named so they could ensure their
female groupies would dress up like the sexy heroine herself. What guy didn't love a bunch of girls in blue panties,
red bustiers and knee-high pleather boots? But after I

found Diesel in the backseat of his car with one of the Wonder Woman groupies I switched all my shifts to the daytime—when Diesel was still dead to the world—so I wouldn't have to see him ever again. It was hard on my tan, but easier on my heart.

And *that* was how I met Parker.

His uncle owned Cleats and Parker worked in the office, learning the business before starting his MBA in the fall. Although he was the most perfect-looking human I'd ever come in contact with—especially in such a grimy pub—I wasn't at all attracted to him. He wasn't my type. With his short blond hair that gleamed slightly, due to his meticulously applied hair gel, clean-shaven face, sparkling blue eyes and straight white (but not too bright) teeth, not to mention his freshly pressed blue Oxford shirts tucked into his khakis, he lacked all the qualities I typically seemed to look for in a guy, including, but not limited to, shaggy, unwashed hair; stubble (whether intentional or a result of sheer laziness); baggy, ripped and wrinkled clothes; tattoos; pierced ears and the reek of cigarette (among other types of) smoke.

Parker was sweet and funny and made the task of serving people greasy fries during my never-ending day shifts not only bearable but actually enjoyable whenever he came out of the back for a break.

We were complete opposites, though. While I read *NME*, he read *The Economist*. I lived on Queen West above a video store, and would finish my undergrad in fashion marketing at Ryerson in the fall. He was in Toronto for the summer, staying in one of two places his parents owned in the city, before going to Cambridge to do a twelve-month MBA. My parents were happily married—even though they squabbled constantly. His were happily divorced, several times each, and never spoke to each other. My parents lived on a lake in Muskoka. His parents owned an island off the coast of Fiji, where his mother lived between marriages.

We had nothing in common but Cleats, but he was sweet and kind and made me feel happy whenever I was around him, and I thought nothing more of our friendship until one rainy day when Elin came to visit me at work—and practically swooned.

"Why have you not mentioned *him?*"

"What do you mean?" I remember saying.

"He's totally into you."

I was sure the chlorine had gone to her head. "He's not at all my type," I told her with confidence.

"Exactly. That's why he's perfect for you."

Her theory was that, since I'd had zero luck dating guys I thought *were* my type, I needed to date the complete opposite.

"He probably just dates Rosedale girls who went to Havergal or Branksome."

"Don't be ridiculous. And you want to be an image consultant. So prove yourself. Dress the part and see what happens."

But obviously, I couldn't dress the part. I was stuck in my apron, black pants and white Oxford, day after day. And yet he still asked me out.

Instead of taking me out of one bar and into another, Parker packed a picnic and hired a water taxi to take us across to Centre Island where we found a quiet spot on the beach and spent the afternoon drinking white wine from a Thermos. And the entire time, I couldn't figure out why I'd been so against someone who had manners, an impeccable sense of style and an abundance of ambition. Not only did he use a napkin and chew with his mouth closed without burping (and then laughing), he talked about interesting things and asked interesting questions and then listened to the answers. It was a strange feeling, like I was either watching myself on a date or finally being myself. I wasn't sure. But I liked it, and I wondered if this was what I'd been missing my entire life.

I decided that Elin was right. I was done dating losers. And if that meant showing only the mature, refined side of myself to win over Parker, I was willing to do so. I was done with guys who lived for beer and sports and guys who were interested only in bars and bands and I made that quite clear to Parker. He liked jazz, so I learned to appreciate music without words (even though it mostly put me to sleep). He liked art galleries, so I learned to be quiet and appreciate art. He liked fine wine with dinner, and so I learned to sniff and swirl before I sipped.

And before long I couldn't remember what I liked about going to dingy, smoky bars and drinking watered-down gin-and-tonics with dehydrated lime wedges.

Near the end of the summer, he left for Cambridge and I stayed in Toronto with Elin and looked forward to Thanksgiving and then spring break when I got to play the sophisticated girlfriend I longed to truly be.

As the end of our last year of school drew closer, Elin and I decided that we'd propose a combined vacation to our boyfriends before finally getting grown-up jobs. Since Parker wouldn't be done his program until the end of

August, we even agreed to put the trip off until the fall, rather than going in the summer. But even with that concession he wasn't very receptive to the idea. For one thing, he didn't like Elin's boyfriend, Geoff. I could understand why Parker didn't feel he had much in common with her hippie boyfriend of three months, who was "practising" to become a specialist in alternative therapy, though he didn't seem to take any actual courses for this specialty (instead, opting to home-school himself by smoking as much pot as he possibly could, whenever he could). Still, I was disappointed that it didn't seem as though our foursome trip would work out.

Parker had already secured a job in Toronto that started as soon as he finished school, and couldn't take two months off, which was understandable, but just highlighted the reason I wanted to do a big trip before I had to settle down and get a real job that would give me only two weeks vacation and a few paid sick days—if I was lucky.

Elin said I could come solo with her and Geoff. But while I'd envisioned a month-long trip that included stops in all the major fashion capitals of the world (I was considering it research)—Milan, Paris and London—before heading home, Elin and Geoff were proposing to go to Vietnam, Myanmar, Sri Lanka, East Timor and Brunei. It seemed a bit *rustic*, but I figured there'd be beaches, which was always a good fallback plan when I couldn't shop. When I'd looked up Myanmar on the Lonely Planet website, though, there was a comprehensive list of reasons not to go, which included, but were not limited to, the cyclone that had hit just months earlier, killing thousands and rendering most of the country a disaster zone, and the fact that the government had asked tourists not to visit, but Geoff claimed that it would be cheap and deserted, since no one else would be there. "Our own private Idaho . . ."

Parker thought Idaho, USA, seemed like a safer option. Still, I tried to be optimistic. It would be an experience I'd never forget (if I made it back alive). It would make me cultured (about places I knew nothing about). Until Elin and Geoff announced it was time we went to Mountain Equipment Co-op.

"What on earth for?" I remembered asking, appalled.

"You don't plan on lugging a regular suitcase through the jungle in an open-air jeep, do you?"

To be honest, I hadn't realized we'd be riding anywhere in an open-air jeep, and when I'd thought of our trip, I thought it was going to be more beach than jungle, and that I'd be lying on white sand, wind in my hair, a Jackie Collins novel in hand, a Mai Tai by my side . . .

"There *will* be wind in your hair. In the jeep. On the way to the ruins," Elin teased me.

But while Elin and Geoff were buying matching backpacks, Parker surprised me with a pink Chanel suitcase and an itinerary for a two-week trip to Geneva, Florence and Venice to celebrate the one-year anniversary of our first date. It wasn't exactly the month-long trip I'd been planning, but how could I say no to a romantic anniversary vacation with the man I loved (even if the itinerary *had* been decided by work meetings Parker needed to attend in each city)? And to the very man who, under a bridge in Venice, in a very *My Best Friend's Wedding*-type of scene, gave me a beautiful princess-cut diamond pendant and asked me to move in with him.

By the time Elin returned from her trip I'd already moved all my belongings—minus the Chianti candle-holders—out of our shared apartment and into Parker's King West apartment.

I didn't regret my choices, though I did sometimes wish that I'd spent at least part of my final summer of singlehood with Elin. Sometimes I wondered why, after Parker and I had returned from Europe, I hadn't repacked my bags and met up with Elin and Geoff, even for just a couple of weeks. But at the time I was caught up in the excitement of being in love and cohabiting and I didn't want Parker to think I felt like I'd missed out on some-thing after he'd treated me to such luxury and indulgence. Besides, Parker's place cost more than double what Elin and I had been paying for our Queen West apartment, and although he had insisted it didn't matter to him if I couldn't afford to give him *exactly* half the rent every month—he reasoned he'd been paying it (or rather, his trust fund had been paying it) on his own before he asked me to move in—it felt wrong to spend what little savings I had jetting off to the middle of the jungle instead of con-tributing to condo fees. Besides, as soon as we returned, Parker gently suggested I should start looking for a job. Within a few short weeks—and with the help of a phone call from his mother to the head of merchandising at Holts—I had a job in the personal shopping department, which, six months later, turned into a client specialist position in the Chanel boutique inside the store.

I was finally happy.

And then, on a repeat business-vacation to Venice, under the very same bridge as the previous year, Parker presented me with another diamond, only this time it was nearly twice the size of the pendant, and was secured on a platinum band that he slipped on my ring finger while asking me to marry him. And I said yes because I had no doubt that he was the one. I loved him more than anything. He promised that he would love me forever, and I promised the same.

We got married almost a year later, then moved into our newly built condo in Yorkville, which we purchased together (although I really wasn't able to chip in as much as Parker, given that I was still a personal shopper at Holts and building my own business—Perfect Package Image Consultants—at nights and on weekends).

Our new place looked like a tribute gallery to *Miami Vice*. It was a South Beach cliché: white walls, white tiles, white curtains, white cupboards. I remember thinking it felt like an insane asylum. (I'd been hoping we'd buy a cozy little brick house with a fireplace and carpeting but Parker didn't want to cut a lawn, clean an eavestrough or figure out what to do if the furnace stopped working.) Parker loved the condo because it was clean, and so I pretended to love it because it was everything I wasn't. Because if I was going to start fresh, I needed the type of apartment that was the opposite of anything I'd ever had before. Besides, it would look good on my business cards to have a Yorkville address, Parker reminded me.

I grew to love our place—or so I told myself. And somehow the past three years of marriage had flown by with nothing but happy moments and memories in the making. Although, I supposed, having your husband cheat on you didn't exactly count as a happy moment.

Which made the affair even more puzzling.

I thought I made him happy. He was always telling me I was the perfect wife for him. Sure, I didn't cook, but he'd never said that was a problem. He'd wanted me to spend my time building up my business, so while the rest of my friends were learning their way around the kitchen I was learning my way around other people's closets, and then we just sort of fell into the habit of ordering takeout or eating out. Besides, he grew up with a live-in chef. It wasn't like I was married to a guy who'd lived off hoagies for years and thought my tuna surprise was a delicacy. How could I compete with beef bourguignon and crème brulée, the Ross family's typical Monday-night dinner?

And although I wasn't the tidiest person that ever lived, I'd made a conscious effort to clean our place when we first moved in together as a way to repay Parker for covering my share of the rent until I could scrape together the extra money. But within a few weeks Parker had hired a weekly maid service (he said it was a housewarming gift to me, though I think he just didn't like the way I mopped or swept), so how was I supposed to get better at cleaning when I never got to practise?

And it wasn't as though I was one of those naggy wives who was always telling him to pick up his baseball cap or socks (though I suppose there was no need since Tildy, the cleaning lady, did that and besides Parker didn't wear ball caps, ever since the time that I told him I thought they made guys look like slobs and were really just an excuse not to groom, and how would he like it if I wore my hair in dreads so that I didn't have to brush it, or worse yet, white cotton Jockeys for Her every day, simply because they were comfortable?). And I never complained that he was playing Xbox or watching sports and not helping out with the yard work (we didn't have a yard, but if we did . . .). Actually, Parker didn't really do anything that typical husbands seemed to do that made wives upset. He didn't own any sort of video game system and didn't like to watch sports. In fact, Parker was quite content to come home after a twelve-hour day at the office and read a book or listen to his iPod in bed.

I supposed there was a downside to not marrying a guy's guy. Whenever we got invited to a Super Bowl party or to watch the Tour de France or March Madness, he never wanted to go. It's not like I enjoyed basketball or football (though I did enjoy the occasional *Entertainment Weekly* photo with a sweaty, shirtless Tom Brady) or understood the thrill of a race that went on for an entire month, but it wasn't really about the sport as much as it was about hanging out with my friends and their husbands. But Parker didn't see the point in wasting his time doing something he didn't enjoy with people he barely knew.

So instead, we spent our time with his friends—who tended to be investment bankers, with stay-at-home wives who lived in Forest Hill and drove SUVs, even if they didn't yet have kids.

And we still travelled—to vacation locales that were usually dictated by Parker's business meetings, but that was okay, because it was always somewhere exciting and cosmopolitan.

Although, sometimes I wished we could just go camping. I grew up camping with my parents, spent my pre-teen summers at sleepaway camps and went on annual end-of-school-year camping trips to Sandbanks with my high school friends.

I felt comfortable with a cold hot dog and a mug of hot cocoa for sustenance.

But Parker had never been camping and the one time I suggested it, back when we'd first started dating, he planned an elaborate weekend in the woods, where we stayed in a deluxe cabin with three bedrooms, three bathrooms and a hot tub in the living room.

There was a general store a few steps away that carried prepared homestyle foods, and a pizzeria down the road where you could eat in and get ice cream cones to go.

I'm not saying I didn't love it. But I never suggested camping again. How could I tell Parker that no, I didn't want to go on an all-inclusive holiday; that what I really wanted to do was rough it and wear the same clothes for three days straight? It was like saying, "Thanks for the Prada boots. Do they come in a pleather knock-off version at Payless?"

I could hardly complain—although I *was* sort of longing to add an "outdoor chic" section to my walk-in closet ever since I'd spotted an adorable pair of pink plaid hiking boots that I otherwise had no excuse to purchase.

Besides, Elin would kill me if she heard me wallowing. Since having the triplets, Elin couldn't afford to go back to work because she didn't make enough to pay for daycare. So she was stuck at home all day every day and hadn't been on a real vacation since her Southeast Asian adventure with Geoff.

I felt bad for her, but that was precisely the reason I

was never getting pregnant. Because you just never know what could pop out. Like three babies instead of one.

Just then my own cellphone rang. It was Elin.

"I was just thinking of you!" I told her.

"I must have known! Power of thought. That's what Dr. Phil says." Elin was obsessed with Dr. Phil and TiVo'd every episode to ensure she didn't miss a single word of wisdom. I couldn't stand Dr. Phil's nasally counsel but I wondered if Elin had a point. Did someone really know when you were thinking about them? In which case, I really shouldn't have thought of my old boyfriend Diesel— especially not now. Especially when I hadn't thought of him in years.

"I just got home from the grocery store and got your message. What happened?"

"Parker got struck by lightning. He's unconscious." I realized a moment later how blunt that was. Because, of course, if that was all that had happened, it would be a big deal. And it still was a big deal. But compared to his infidelity it was merely a detail.

"What? Are you kidding?"

I wanted to say, *Yes, I'm kidding. He broke his toe mowing the lawn*, but we were still yardless—and didn't have a simple suburban life either. Although I had thought our life was fairly drama-free until three hours earlier.

I considered not telling Elin the entire story because I knew what she would say—that I had to fix my marriage. But Elin was biased. Although she loved Terrence, a real estate agent whom she'd met online about three years ago, she didn't love her life at the moment. And although she had a big backyard where the kids would eventually play, right now they were stuck in the house. And if she did want to get out of the house, it was a 45-minute hike to the nearest grocery store because they had only one vehicle. If she wanted to use the minivan she had to strap all three babies into their car seats at half-past six in the morning so that she could drop Terrence off at the train station.

And while my life with Parker wasn't the life everyone wanted, right now, with our condo in the city and our disposable income thanks to our childless lifestyle, it was pretty attractive to Elin.

Then again, Elin had a strict no-cheating policy. So did I. We made a pact when we were teenagers to never put up with it. But this was different. This was my husband, not someone else's. And how could I even think about leaving him when he was lying in bed, unconscious?

Elin was my best and oldest friend—how could I *not* tell her? She would help me figure everything out. I took a deep breath.

"There's something else. Parker had an affair—"

"What? *Now* are you kidding?"

I was practically finished my story when I felt a tap on my shoulder.

"You can't use that in here." I turned to look at an intern. She glared at my BlackBerry and then gave me a reproving look as if to say, *Shouldn't you be talking to your husband, not your cellphone?*

I decided I liked Nurse Abigail much better than the intern, even if she was just doing her job.

"I'm sorry. I thought that was just around babies." Which was the truth. I really *did* think that. Although, come to think of it, I suppose there could be babies in the ICU.

"It's disruptive to our patients who are trying to sleep."

Disruptive? Wasn't I supposed to be trying to wake Parker up—wasn't that the goal? What did she know? Where was Nurse Abigail? I stood up and walked into the hall.

"Not out here either."

"Okay! Elin, I have to go." I clicked off the phone.

I turned to go back into the room, but the intern told me to wait outside since she had to check his catheter.

"His *what?*" I shook my head. "Parker doesn't have a catheter. He's only thirty-two," I added, realizing milliseconds later that, that was a ridiculous comeback. Still, *typically*, healthy thirty-two-year-olds didn't have catheters. Surely she had the wrong patient.

"Of course he does. He can't exactly get up and walk to the bathroom on his own." She clucked her tongue as though she were eighty-five (and not twenty-five) and I were a blithering moron.

I wanted to slap her for being so insensitive, but then Nurse Abigail appeared out of nowhere. "Why don't you take a break, sweetie." She put a hand on my back. "Go get something to eat or drink."

"I shouldn't leave."

"He'll be fine. I'll watch over him. Come back in ten minutes or so."

Ten minutes? A lot could happen in ten minutes. He could wake up. What if I wasn't by his side?

"If he wakes up, he'll still be awake when you get here," she said, as though reading my mind.

I was about to protest, but Nurse Abigail followed the snotty intern back into the room and closed the door. I supposed I didn't have a choice.

But what on earth would I do? *Perhaps I should go to the gift shop and buy a little something for Parker, for when he wakes up*, I thought. Except, he didn't like tchotchkes. He didn't play board games. He probably wouldn't want to read about the stock market after being unconscious for hours. Perhaps I should just buy him a drink. I could use a drink. Or a new lip gloss, so I'd look pretty when he woke up. And then it dawned on me.

What if Parker didn't think I was pretty?

What if that was the entire reason he had the affair? What if Sienna was ten times prettier than me? What if that was the reason he'd strayed?

She's in the ER, being monitored, Nurse Abigail had said. And how many rooms could there really be? It wouldn't be that difficult to find Sienna, and I'd just sneak a teensy tiny glimpse of her. She wouldn't even notice me. I'd be in and out in a flash. And if she *did* notice me, well, I'd just pretend I was looking for someone else and was lost. She'd never know it was me, Poppy Ross, Parker's wife. I had to see what she looked like. Just a tiny glimpse.

I pressed the down button on the elevator. *Sienna Somers, here I come.*

chapter three

The elevator door opened on the ER floor and I stepped out and walked over to the nurses' station. "Hi," I whispered to the middle-aged woman at the desk.

"Hi," she whispered back, leaning forward. "Why are we whispering?"

"Oh, um . . ." I shifted into what I hoped sounded like a regular voice, even though I was still whispering. "I didn't want to wake anyone."

"Most of the people here could use a little excitement. Don't worry. They're not sleeping. Just waiting for medical attention."

"Well anyway, I was looking for a woman named Sienna . . ."

"Oh yes, Sienna Somers," she practically hollered and I wanted to hide, or die or both. "She's in that room over there." She pointed at the closest door to her right.

"Oh, um . . . is there something I could perhaps drop off?" I asked her.

"I don't understand."

Why hadn't I thought to pick up flowers so that I'd have had an excuse to enter Sienna's room?

"Never mind."

I stepped away from the desk and prepared myself for the walk to her room, wishing it was at the end of the hall, not ten steps away.

I took a deep breath and pushed open the door to room 3B. Two steps later I was far enough in to see the bed by the window. It was empty. I leaned forward and peeked around the corner to view the bed that was closest to the door.

I breathed a sigh of complete relief. She wasn't in the room.

I turned around and my eye caught the name at the top of the chart that was in the holster on the wall beside me.

Sienna Somers.

Maybe she had already been discharged or moved to another room. (Though, wouldn't her chart have gone with her?)

It really didn't matter, because honestly, it had been a ridiculous idea. What good would it do me to see what she looked like?

And what if she'd caught me? I could hardly lie. What if I saw her at the Christmas party and she remembered me? *Weren't you the one who snuck into my room in the ER?*, she'd say, and then what would I do? Total mortification in a little black dress.

A moment later, a worse thought entered my mind.

What if I wasn't *at* the Christmas party with Parker this year? What if *Sienna* was his date instead of me?

No, I *had* to see her. I turned to leave the room so I could hunt her down.

"Can I help you?"

I froze, not letting myself turn toward the sound of the voice.

A sultry British voice, on the other side of the room.

"Hello? Hi. Over here." As if I didn't know.

I turned to see the most beautiful woman ever standing in the doorway of the bathroom. She was a goddess: caramel-coloured, flawless skin and long, thick, wavy, dark hair with buttery highlights that matched her amber eyes.

Why?

I wanted to cry.

To be perfectly honest, I wasn't expecting her to be that gorgeous.

Sure, in made-for-TV movies the mistress was *always* this young, hot, sexy girl that the tired, overweight old wife and mother of five couldn't compete with. But this was reality, not Lifetime. And I wasn't a tired, overweight old wife and mother of five. I was only twenty-seven. My near-daily raw lunches ensured I was still a size two, and thanks to thrice-weekly Pilates classes I was a quarter of an inch taller than I was when I met Parker. My blond hair was always shiny and perfectly coiffed into its pixie cut with sideswept bangs that highlighted my defined cheekbones, my tailored clothes were always minimally accessorized and my nails were always (today's catastrophe of a pedicure aside) perfectly manicured. I wasn't trying to be smug— after all, I knew my shortcomings, and could rattle them off effortlessly: cooking, baking, knitting (or any other sort of happy homemaker craft), politics, gardening (though I had a knack for choosing fake plants that *looked* real), finance (aside from sales tax, which I could practically calculate in my head on any purchase), sports and karaoke.

But making a good impression—as superficial as it seemed—that, I was good at. My job as an image consultant was to make others seem perfect—or as close to it as possible—so it just went without saying that it was my job to always look as close to perfect as possible. And it was my firm belief that anyone, no matter what unfortunate genes they were given, could impress even the most discerning critic. I was proof: in grade school, I was nicknamed Poppycock. I had horrible acne, abominable eyesight, a lack of curves and too many cowlicks to count. But it was nothing a round of Proactiv, laser eye surgery, a pixie cut, a padded bra, a set of etiquette lessons and a positive attitude couldn't fix.

It wasn't that I thought looking good was the be all and end all, it was that if you looked good, then you'd feel good and you could stop thinking about your appearance and get on with the stuff that really mattered to you (like being a good mom, or a good wife, or being good at your job or, say, gardening with real plants). In reality, I was the equivalent of a maid you hired to clean your house so you didn't have to do it. I cleaned, defined and refined others' appearances while wearing pretty shoes. I had done it to my own life when I'd met Parker and now I helped others get the happy life that they dreamed of. Just like the happy life I had (until this whole affair debacle, that is). So it was a rare instance when I felt intimidated upon meeting someone for the first time. But *intimidated* was exactly the word that I would use to describe how I felt looking at the part Angelina Jolie, part Megan Fox creature who was passing in front of me as she strutted from the bathroom to her bed. I might have been pretty and perfectly put together, but this woman exuded raw sexiness—and she was still in her hideous hospital gown.

I was demoralized.

This woman worked in finance? Shouldn't she have had a conservative bob and tight lips, not long flowing locks and a perma-pout?

Then I remembered she was a research assistant, with a degree in Mrs.

"Are you all right?" Sienna asked, bending down to pick up a white Gucci handbag with tacky gold lamé Gs from the chair by her bed. As she stood up, she flipped her long dark waves over her tanned shoulder, exposed above her gown. "You look a bit woozy," she added, not unkindly, which made me feel slightly guilty.

But I wouldn't fall for her charms. It was probably just the British accent. Brits always seemed so polite and caring even when they weren't. Look at Simon Cowell. Or Jack the Ripper—he was hardly a goody two-shoes, was he?

"I—I'm fine," I stuttered.

Sienna nodded. "Okay . . . so then . . . are you looking for someone?"

"Actually, I'm just, uh, a sociologist, doing a study on the types of events that land people in the ER." Did sociologists even *do* things like this? I had no idea, but I had to assume Sienna didn't either. Confidence first, knowledge second. That's what I always told my clients. I reached into my handbag and pulled out the spiral notebook I always kept in the inside front pocket, and reached for my fountain pen. My fingers ran across something smooth, and I pulled out a coffee-coloured eyeliner. It would have to do.

"Would you mind just telling me a bit about what happened to you, to land you in the ER?"

"Oh, um . . . is this protocol?" Sienna asked, and I couldn't help but notice just how perfectly aligned and white her teeth were. I bet she drank red wine through a straw.

"Of course," I said with confidence while doodling a lightning bolt on my pad—wishing one would strike her down before my very eyes.

"Well, I'm hoping they're about to discharge me," Sienna announced. "You don't mind if I get changed in front of you while we talk, do you?"

I shook my head. This was a nightmare. I was about to see my husband's mistress naked. The way he saw her. Sienna untied her blue gown and let it fall to the tile, revealing a tacky black-and-red leopard print satin lingerie set that was fit for a cougar of the New Jersey species, not a twenty-something vixen. I studied her as though she were an animal in the wild that I needed to better understand.

"You know . . ." Sienna said slowly, placing her hands on her bare, curvy hips, which balanced her large C-cup breasts. "I feel like I've met you before . . ." she said, squinting her eyes critically and I froze, horrified. *Of course*, I thought. *She's probably seen my picture on Parker's desk. I'm caught.* But I shrugged, trying to act nonchalant.

"You've probably seen a lot of people this evening. I bet we're all starting to blend together."

She didn't look convinced, but then nodded. "I suppose you're right. Everything's a bit fuzzy. I was hit by lightning, you know. Can you believe it?"

I wanted to say, *Of course you were struck by lightning. That's what happens to women who steal other women's husbands!* But I didn't. Instead, I put on my most surprised look.

"Lightning! Gosh, that must have been quite a scare . . ." I scribbled on my notepad some more.

"Yes, it was," Sienna said thoughtfully and then paused as though considering saying something else. "It's been quite a day."

Sienna picked a slinky piece of fabric off the chair and tossed it over her head, then slithered into it. Although the colour was lovely—a deep plum that made her caramel skin glow—the top looked like a cheap polyester blend and was at least two sizes too tight, making her breasts look like they were trying to escape the purple restraints. Then she slipped on a tight black skirt that was four inches too short and was pilled around the hem, and a three-quarter-length black blazer that barely buttoned up, but at least helped rein in her bosom. Finally, as I stared in wonder, she stepped into a pair of purple Gucci patent leather pumps with two-inch soles and four-inch heels, leaving the rose tattoo on her ankle exposed.

I was too stunned for words. This was the type of woman my husband liked? I stared, mesmerized, as she slipped on a dozen gold-plated bangles. She added an oversized black and gold ring that spelled out *Sienna* over three fingers, and slipped a large slate-grey plastic link necklace with a Gucci logo over her long dark waves, flipping the ends over the back of her neck like a Pantene commercial. She grabbed her bag, reached inside and pulled out a piece of bubble gum, unwrapped it and stuck it in her mouth, completing her image. "So what did you want to know?"

I looked down at my pad to compose myself. "Um . . . what were you doing when it happened?"

"Well, we'd gone to Frites for dinner . . ."

Frites? They went to *Frites* for dinner?

Parker and I had been planning to go to Frites together. It had just opened the week before, and Parker and I always tried out new restaurants together, especially high-end ones, and especially if he was considering taking clients there for dinner. It was tradition. Sometimes, though, I wished we could go for a simple date. Something that cost less than a bottle of San Pellegrino at one of those restaurants. Popcorn and a movie. A burger and fries. We were so busy we rarely went to movies, and the only fries we tended to eat were those called *frites*.

We were adults. We ate at adult establishments. Like Frites.

Or—we used to, anyway.

Now Sienna and Parker did. But then I realized. That's it. They had dinner. Maybe nothing more. Parker had said it was a business dinner, so surely there were others there. Still, what was Sienna—a research assistant—doing at a client dinner? Of course I couldn't let on that I knew anything about the dinner. "So that's it? And then you went outside to head home and the lightning struck?"

Sienna shook her head. "No, *then* we left and went to Le Germain." She raised her eyebrows for effect.

My heart was pounding and my hands were numb.

They went to a hotel? A boutique hotel with 600-thread-count sheets and down-filled mattresses. But why?

Of course I knew. But I couldn't stop. I had to get her to say Parker's name to my face.

"Sorry, it was you . . . and . . ." I suddenly regretted what I was doing.

"Parker Ross. My boyfriend."

Her *what*? My stomach clenched and my mouth went dry. My arms felt frozen but a trickle of sweat escaped my underarm. My eyes filled with water and I tried to blink back the tears but there were too many. My legs felt weak, like I might collapse at any moment. How dare she call my husband her *boyfriend*. I wanted to slap her.

What was I doing here, in the same room as my husband's mistress, listening to her tell me where they'd gone for dinner and where they'd gone to have sex? This was torture. I didn't deserve this. Perhaps I wasn't the perfect wife or even the perfect person, but this was too much.

"So, do you have any other questions for me? Because I want to try to track down a nurse and get discharged so I can go check to see how my man's doing."

Her man? She was calling Parker *her man?* Who was she, a character in a Spike Lee movie?

"I have to go," I said abruptly, backing toward the door. I had to get away from her.

"Sorry, I didn't catch your name," she called to me before I could escape.

"Uhhhh . . ." My name. I hadn't thought of an alias.

"What was that?" She laughed, mocking me.

I felt sick. I was always so composed. This woman was ruining me.

I couldn't let her.

"Uhma." I said, suddenly mustering a burst of confidence. I would not let her get the better of me. "Like Uma but a short 'U.'"

Sienna studied me, then nodded. "Uhma. Interesting."

I had to get out of the room. I had to get back to Parker before she did.

~

I arrived back at Parker's room slightly out of breath after running up three flights of stairs in three-inch wedges. Parker was still lying in bed, his eyes closed, body still. I collapsed into the chair beside his bed and stared at his serene face.

I suddenly had the overwhelming urge to slap him. I wasn't usually a physical person, but looking at him lying there, so peacefully, as if he'd done nothing wrong, while I was forced to deal with the results of his actions, forced to watch his mistress dress in front of me and describe the details of their evening together . . . it just made me crazy.

I didn't want him to die. All I wanted was for him to wake up. But then what?

I leaned over and took his hand in mine and squeezed it, wishing it were a time warp button that would send us back in time.

Why couldn't things go back to being perfect? To this morning, when I still thought I had the perfect husband. The perfect marriage. The perfect life.

Why couldn't he just be asleep? When he woke up it would be just like when we were at home, when he rolled over in the middle of the night, kissed me on the tip of my nose and whispered, "Love you, Popsicle," before pulling the covers over himself and going back to sleep.

What if he never called me Popsicle again? What if I never even heard his voice again? I shook my head, tears welling up in my eyes. That couldn't happen. He *had* to wake up. Even if he went back to Sienna. Even if he left me—*God*, a divorcee at twenty-seven—he had to wake up. Just to give me a chance to fight for him. Or for me to give him a second chance. For us to work this out. If he would just open his eyes.

And then he did.

He opened his eyelids to reveal his sparkly blue eyes. He looked at me and smiled. This was the man I loved. This was my husband. I had to fight for him.

"Poppy?"

I squeezed his hand as tears formed in my eyes.

"I—" He tried to cough but no sound came out. "Wha—?"

"Don't move. I'll call the nurse."

"Don't go." He squeezed my hand back.

Tears streamed down my cheeks. I nodded. The nurses could wait. My husband was awake.

"What happ—?" he tried again.

"You were hit by lightning."

His eyes widened. "What?"

I instantly regretted my words. It was a traumatic statement to tell someone who'd just awoken from a coma. But it was too late.

And it wasn't like he wasn't going to find out soon enough. As soon as Sienna returned to work, everyone would know. Any minute, Sienna could even show up at his door.

But for now, it was just the two of us.

"Don't worry. You're awake now. That's all that matters." I squeezed his hand even tighter. Even with all the tubes he looked perfect to me as his eyes crinkled up into a smile.

~

I'm not sure how long I sat there staring at Parker before I realized that, even though I didn't want to leave him, I should probably tell someone—a nurse, intern, doctor, anyone—that Parker was awake.

"Could you call my mom and dad and let them know, too?"

I told him I already had and that I'd left a message on his father's voice mail, but gotten through to his mother, who'd requested I call again if his condition worsened, since she was at a detox spa in Fiji and didn't want to make the trek if he was just going to wake up in a few hours anyway. Her self-absorption no longer surprised me, so I wasn't concerned that Parker gave a half-shrug when I told him, and said he'd call her when we got home.

"Can you call Ray, too? Tell him I guess I won't make the game tonight."

I stared at Parker. "Ray?"

Parker nodded as best he could. "Isn't it Thursday?" He wrinkled his forehead.

It was, but I had a sudden feeling that it was a lucky guess. He hadn't gone to a basketball game with Ray in two months, since his best friend had moved to Vietnam at the beginning of March.

Didn't he remember? Maybe it was post-traumatic stress.

"Do you think you could get me some orange juice? I'm so thirsty. But only if it's fresh. No pulp."

I let out a breath. Parker loved orange juice (and was very particular about it). At least he hadn't forgotten that.

Out in the hall, I told Nurse Abigail that Parker was awake and she sent the intern in to check on him.

"He seems to have lost his memory a bit," I said worriedly to Abigail.

She nodded. "That sometimes happens—especially if something is particularly traumatic. Not to worry. After he's had a chance to rest for a bit, and we monitor him, we can ask him some questions." She patted me on the shoulder.

That made sense. Besides, it was just one little thing.

I turned to go back into Parker's room, but stopped immediately when I caught sight of *her*. Sienna. She was walking down the hall straight toward me. I slipped into Parker's room. The curtain was drawn around Parker's bed and I could hear the intern talking to him. I ducked into the bathroom, closing the door so that it touched the frame, but didn't shut. My heart was pounding. A moment later I heard that familiar, deceptively friendly British voice say, "This room here?" And then the click of her plastic-soled heels into the room.

"Oh, Parker," I heard her say. "How are you, sweetie?"

Sweetie? She called him "sweetie"? I wanted to die. Or punch her.

"I'll come back in a minute," the intern said.

No! Stay! Don't leave them alone! I wanted to scream.

Would she straddle the bed like some sort of cheap hooker and start making out with him? *Oh God, please no. I'll do anything,* I silently prayed. *I'll be the most perfect wife ever. I'll be the perfect woman for Parker. I'll . . .* I bit my lip. *I'll go to church?* Maybe that was a bit much. *I'll wear leopard print. I'll forgive him for cheating on me.*

"I heard you were unconscious." I interrupted my list of promises to listen in. "I would've come sooner but I was trapped in the ER. Are you all right?"

Silence.

I felt my throat close up. Were they *making out?* Didn't God hear me vowing to wear leopard print? I wedged the door open a crack and tried to see the two of them through the slit in the curtain. What was happening?

Finally, Parker said, "I'm . . . fine." Pause. "I'm sorry. I just—do I know you?"

"Parker, it's *me*," Sienna said, her voice full of confusion. "Sienna. Si-en-na," she said even more slowly, as though he were stupid.

"I'm sorry," Parker said again. Was his subconscious talking? "I just don't remember you. Do we work together or—?"

"Are you being serious?" Sienna said. "Oh—is your wife here?"

"Oh, yes . . . are you a friend of hers?" Parker sounded almost relieved.

"Of your wife's?" Sienna sounded appalled and I felt a tiny glimmer of hope.

That's right, I thought. *Be afraid. Be very afraid that Mrs. Parker Ross is right around the corner, about to catch you.*

Only, I couldn't very well catch her, since I was supposed to be Uhma the Sociologist. And since, well, I was crouched on the bathroom floor, frozen with fear. Part of me wanted to open the door and catch the two of them, but the other part wanted to see how far this charade—if that's what it even was—would go.

"No, I am *not* a friend of your wife's," she said, sounding genuinely confused. "Parker, it's *me*. I was with you when you got hit. Remember, we had dinner together, and then we went for more drinks and then we . . . *hooked up*. How can you not remember something that happened, like, five hours ago?" She sounded exasperated.

I couldn't move. It was over. Who was I kidding? Nurse Abigail had said Parker's memory loss would be temporary. Any minute now he was going to remember everything. All it would take was a few minutes to let Sienna's words sink in and everything would be out in the open. My marriage would officially be over.

My hand slipped away from the door handle and I curled up on the floor and listened to the silence reverberate off the cold tiles.

"I'm sorry, I think maybe we should call a doctor. Maybe you have the wrong room?" Parker said, his voice full of concern. "I just—I really don't know what you're talking about. But maybe if we call someone in here they can tell you where you're supposed to be. I think maybe you're confusing me with someone else."

I sat up. Was he being serious?

"Don't worry. You're probably quite exhausted. Why don't you get some sleep?" Now she sounded annoyed.

"That's probably a good idea, if you think you'll be okay. You should probably sleep too. It was nice to meet you."

Parker sounded relieved, but sincere.

Did he really have no idea who Sienna was?

I wedged the door open a bit to see what was happening. Sienna emerged from behind the curtain looking confused and slightly put-off as she walked out of the room. I counted to ten, then stood up, opened the bathroom door and walked over to the edge of the room, then pulled back the curtain.

"Popsicle," Parker said as soon as he saw me. He smiled.

I wasn't sure what to do. Should I pretend I hadn't heard a thing or should I say something—but what?

"There was a strange woman in here," he said before I had a chance to say anything. "I think maybe she got hit on the head or something. She was acting like she knew me." He looked at me questioningly.

"Oh?" I wasn't expecting this turn of events. Maybe it was better to play dumb and just see where this all went.

"Was I in the accident with someone—a woman?" His brow was furrowed, as though he were trying to put together a bizarre mystery.

I didn't know what to say. But if he didn't remember that Ray had left, then was it possible he didn't remember Sienna either?

It was one thing to pretend he hadn't cheated on me, but it didn't make any sense that he would pretend not to know her. Maybe he really didn't remember her.

I nodded. "Sienna Somers. Dark hair? Kind of plump?

Dresses a bit tacky?" There was no reason I had to play up all her assets, like her gorgeous flowy hair or lovely skin or suspiciously perky C-cups. "You work with her," I added bluntly.

"I do?" He looked at me, confused.

I wanted to believe him. After all, if he'd been cheating on me for months shouldn't he have had all his excuses worked out?

I nodded. If I hadn't known about the affair I would've believed that he really didn't know her and I wouldn't have given it a second thought. But it just didn't make any sense.

"Maybe she's a new client . . ." he said thoughtfully, as though he were really, truly trying to figure it out.

"No," I said firmly. "You *work* with her. In your office. I think she's an assistant."

He looked at me, slightly taken aback. "Oh. I—I just don't remember." Then his face flushed. "Oh, geez. I feel like an idiot. I just told her she had the wrong room." He laughed and put a hand to his forehead. "I guess she was just trying to get me riled up. She told me we had dinner together and then *hooked up*," he said, as though it were the most preposterous thing he'd ever heard. "Kind of an odd joke to make to someone you barely know." He shrugged. "Oh well. I'll apologize to her when I see her at work, I suppose."

I stared at him. If I'd just met him I might wonder if he was messing with my mind, but I knew Parker. He was a terrible liar. He wasn't lying.

He didn't remember Sienna.

He didn't remember that Ray had moved away.

And then I considered the awful truth: maybe he didn't remember anything.

Maybe he has amnesia. Maybe he doesn't remember me, I thought. For all I knew, he thought I was a nurse, or his sister, or . . .

"Who am I?" I demanded.

"Poppy, don't be silly." He laughed. "You're my wife."

I breathed a sigh of relief. "How long have we been married?"

"Three years." He paused. "Give or take a few days," he added with a smile.

But it was more like a few months.

"What month is it?"

"Poppy, it's February. Tenth. Or maybe eleventh. Can we go home?"

It was May seventh. Ray left in March. I tried to remember when Parker had first mentioned Sienna—and why. But I couldn't recall. And if he had mentioned her, it had to be well before this affair started. Before I would suspect anything. Had it only been a few months? I tried to think of anything else that I could test him on that had happened since February to see if he remembered, but the past few months had been a blur. The transition into spring was always my busiest time, with myriad trade shows, and new and past clients wanting to revamp their wardrobes. I'd barely seen Parker.

So if he'd lost his memory of the last three months did that mean he'd honestly lost his memory of the affair? Elin had once told me about a *Dr. Phil* episode where this super-horrible woman got hit by a car and lost her memory of all her negativity, and all of a sudden she was

Little Miss Sunshine, baking people cookies and singing or something. At the time I totally didn't believe it could happen, but here it was, happening before my very eyes. Could he really have completely, totally, forgotten about his God-awful affair and that evil bitch Sienna? I stared at him, looking for any sign that he was faking, but all I could think was, *He doesn't remember her. He has no recollection of his affair. It's like it never happened.*

And then it occurred to me: If he didn't remember, could I give him a second chance, no questions asked?

chapter four

The doctors discharged Parker on Friday afternoon with a clean bill of health. Except for the burn on the palm of his hand where the lightning bolt had entered, another on his foot where apparently the bolt exited, and, of course, the partial memory loss—which they clearly did not think was a problem.

I felt concerned, but what could I say? *Don't you under- stand? My husband does not recognize the woman with whom he's having an affair.* It wasn't as if I *wanted* him to recall that part of his memory, and he didn't seem to see the problem with not knowing someone with whom he apparently worked. "She must be new," he'd said off- handedly when I'd tried to ask him about her again. Part of me wanted to celebrate that he'd forgotten her, but the sensible part of my brain knew it was too good to be true, and that pretending it hadn't happened was going to only prolong the inevitable.

But just before we left the hospital Nurse Abigail handed

me a pamphlet about memory loss, with a list of things you could do and foods you could eat to help trigger the brain to remember. Then she pulled me aside. "He might never get those three months back. If there's nothing terribly important, I wouldn't push him to remember. It'll only frustrate both of you."

We walked the three blocks home from the hospital to our Yorkville condo. The weird thing about recovering from getting hit by lightning (so I was witnessing) was that Parker didn't really have any injuries. It wasn't as if he'd gotten appendicitis or tonsillitis and had to have one of his non-vital organs removed (so maybe tonsils weren't actually organs, but whatever). He said he felt completely fine. Still, I cancelled all my appointments to spend the rest of the day and weekend with him. A long weekend with absolutely nothing planned, no obligations, no work to do. Nothing but nearly sixty hours of relaxation. Pure bliss.

My phone buzzed and I recognized it as a client, but I silenced it.

"Don't you need to take that?" Parker asked as I slipped my phone into my handbag.

I shook my head and squeezed his hand.

"I can't believe you cancelled all your clients to be with me."

"Of course, sweetie," I said, then cringed inwardly. I *definitely* could not pull off "sweetie." It just wasn't me. I cleared my throat. "It's going to be great."

I felt slightly offended that he seemed so surprised that I would cancel my appointments to be with him. He'd nearly died. What kind of wife did he think I was?

Besides, if he felt I worked too much, he was to blame. I hadn't always been like this. Although I always knew I wanted to be an image consultant, I'd just imagined it as an extension of the rest of my life as I'd known it for twenty-two years. But when you fall in love with someone who's never home and encourages you to put your career first, you reevaluate your own priorities. And rather than risk being a disappointment for having some semblance of work/life balance (or however we thought of it before we were forced to label it as such), you decide to create a career that's as enviable as it is exhausting, and weekends suddenly look like extra days to work on everything you couldn't get done in a five-day work week.

I couldn't think of the last time either of us had taken a full weekend off work. Since most of my clients had regular jobs, my busiest hours were before work, lunchtime and after work during the week, and all day on the weekends. Long weekends tended to be even busier than regular weekends, as clients who stayed in the city took the extra day to treat themselves, something that often included an appointment with me to assess their wardrobe for a special event or revamp their closet for the upcoming season.

I supposed we were less busy back in our early days, before we'd really launched our careers. Back when I was at Chanel and still dreaming up Perfect Package Image Consultants—the business I would start—and fantasizing about surprising Parker at work to take long, luxurious lunches between clients. Back when Parker was still putting in long hours, but insisting they'd decrease once he made managing partner at Feldman Davis, and he could actually take those luxurious lunches. Or lunches at all.

But our long hours became longer and, well, we got on with real life.

And I didn't really miss the alternative. Or I didn't let myself consider it. Now I couldn't recall what we did on those long weekends when we didn't have to work. Maybe they never really existed.

Maybe that was an indication that we really could use a weekend of nothingness. Not a care in the world . . . except of course, the affair. But there was nothing I could do about that right now. All I could do was take care of Parker.

"Would you like me to make you some chicken noodle soup?" I asked Parker as we got in the elevator of our building. I let the doors close without pushing a number, just to test whether Parker remembered where we lived.

Parker put his free arm around me and pushed the 17 button on the wall. "Chicken noodle soup always makes me feel like I'm supposed to be sick, and I don't feel sick. Poppy, you don't have to take care of me."

"Oh." I wasn't sure what to say to that. Didn't he *want* me to take care of him? I wanted to take care of him. I wanted to show him what a good wife I was. But maybe that was the problem. Maybe I was supposed to be a *bad* wife.

I could be naughty.

If that's what he really wanted.

Maybe I should've been offering him . . . Oh God, was I really going to have to start dressing up and dancing around to Usher in the bedroom? Hadn't I earned my right as a wife to have nice, normal sex? It just wasn't me and, anyway, I couldn't even think about *sex* of any kind (not even the nice, normal type) after what had happened.

Parker stepped out of the elevator, and I considered just

letting the doors close behind him and riding the elevator back down to the ground floor. I could rush out onto the street and just run. Keep running until I couldn't run anymore. I'd literally run away from everything: Parker and Sienna. My entire failed marriage. I'd run until it was all a distant memory.

Except I wasn't a very good runner. And I was still wearing my espadrilles. I'd have a blister by the time I reached Bloor.

"You coming?" Parker put his hand out to stop the closing elevator door.

I stepped out.

"Besides, you don't know how to make chicken noodle soup," he said.

I felt slightly offended, even if it was true. Maybe I didn't know how to make chicken noodle soup, but who did? I knew how to open a can and dump the contents into a pot on the stove. What, did he think I was offering to make him noodles from scratch? Sometimes he could be so high maintenance. No wonder I'd stopped trying to cook for him—even if I wasn't Julia Child reincarnated.

Once inside our place, Parker called his mom to let her know we were home and that she didn't need to stop detoxifying, then his dad, while I first left Elin a quick message so she wouldn't worry, then called my parents and let them know that everything was fine (everything but the affair, of course, but I could *not* tell my mother about that because she would tell everyone she knew and I really did not need all of cottage country knowing that I'd failed as a wife. Besides, she'd have enough news to share, what with the lightning and the whole unconscious thing, to keep her going for a while. And even if my mother wasn't a tell-all, I couldn't tell my dad, period, because that would be like admitting that I had sex. And of course, I did not have sex, in his mind). Before we hung up, I asked her if she knew how to make chicken noodle soup.

"Sure I do. And so do you. I taught you when you were seven. Don't you remember?" she asked, and though I didn't doubt that she had tried to teach me, I didn't remember at all. "I could've used a refresher course in my teens."

"Ha! You try getting a teenager to make soup on her weekends with her mother. I'll show you next time you come up here."

"Thanks, Mom."

By the time I got off the phone, I found Parker in bed, still fully dressed, fast asleep.

He looked so peaceful, and part of me wanted to curl up next to him, to erase the past twenty-four hours.

But I knew it wasn't that easy.

On Saturday morning, Parker suggested we stay in bed all day.

All day? I felt panicky.

Of course. That was what normal people (and by normal, I really meant couples on sitcoms with nine-to-five jobs) did on Saturday mornings, but even they didn't stay in bed *all day*. And we never even stayed in bed for an entire morning. The old Parker would never even suggest it. We didn't have time. We had things to do. We were Motivated People.

"What do you think?" he asked.

"Sure," I agreed, because clearly he thought this was a fantastic idea. But inside I was thinking, *What? What on earth are we going to do in bed all day?*

Of course. The obvious. Clearly. Which wouldn't have been a problem a few days ago, but now . . .

There was no way I could have sex with him. I just couldn't. As Parker moved over to me and nuzzled my neck, I cringed and shut my eyes tight. All I could see was Sienna's face, Sienna's lips, Sienna's hips. I didn't look like her, I didn't act like her (from what I could deduce in five minutes), and I was sure we were *very* different in bed. If she was the girl he'd chosen to cheat on me with, then she had to be better in bed than me. You didn't have sex with someone because they were a nice person who visited old people in nursing homes and put spiders outside rather than killing them. You had sex with someone because you were turned on by her, pleather shoes or not.

Parker moved from my neck to rolling me over on my back, but I had to stop it.

"Is that the phone?" I said, jumping up.

Parker looked at me with raised eyebrows. "I don't hear anything."

"I'm sure it was. I'll just go check." I raced out to the kitchen in my taupe silk Vera Wang nightie that Parker claimed washed out my skin tone, but which I thought was pretty and delicate, and dialed Elin's home phone number.

She answered on the first ring.

"I can't do this."

"Do you need me to come over?"

"No." Of course I wanted my best friend nearby, but I knew it was an empty offer—even if Elin didn't mean for it to sound like one. Our monthly dinner and manicure date was one of Elin's only guaranteed trips into the city on her own. With the triplets, who were less than a year old, she couldn't commit to a regular trip in from Jackson's Point any more often, and we both knew it. I was just going to have to get used to getting by without her.

"Have you talked about it?"

"He doesn't remember."

"What? What do you mean?"

I filled her in.

"So you're not going to say anything?"

"I can't. I just can't. Could you? What if I say something and that's all it takes to trigger his memory?"

"I suppose you're right." One of the triplets wailed in the background. "So what are you going to do?"

"I know what you're thinking. That he's fine now and I should leave him. Or make him leave. But . . ."

Elin interrupted me. "Why do you think that?" she said softly.

I reminded her of our pact. That we didn't stay with cheaters. "I can't even believe I'm saying that I'm considering it. I feel like the biggest loser."

"You're not a loser, Poppy. You're the strongest woman I know. You're determined and smart and savvy. And that pact? We made it when we were seventeen. And actually, as I recall, you made it. I just agreed to it because you said you'd give me your Seven jeans if I left Rocco."

I didn't mention that part of the reason I was glad

she left Rocco DiRocco was his name—not just his habit of sleeping around. "And just so you know, I ended up sneaking out to see him for weeks after that pact. Until I realized you were right."

"See?"

"There's a difference. We're not talking about Rocco DiRocco. We're talking about Parker. Your husband. You have the perfect marriage. This is just a blip."

I knew Elin liked Parker. But I also knew that right now Elin saw my life as easy. I didn't blame her. She probably saw anyone's life as easy. She and Terrence didn't live in the suburbs by choice. Terrence had changed jobs because they couldn't afford a house in commutable distance—not the size they needed with three kids—and now they had no reason to come into the city. She didn't go on vacation, she didn't eat out. She didn't even order in. I knew that she thought what I had with Parker was good. But good enough to accept that he'd cheated?

"What should I do?"

"You can do what it takes to make sure he never remembers that he had an affair. Hang on a second, okay?" I heard muffling in the background as Elin instructed Terrence on something. "Whoever decided to promote swim lessons for babies should be shot. It's like hell in water. With dozens of babies grabbing at whatever breasts they can get their tiny little hands on."

"Sounds like a teenage guy's dream."

"Listen, it's going to be okay. It is. Dr. Phil says the most critical choice you'll ever make is about what you're going to do next. The past is over. The future hasn't happened yet. The only time is now."

I wanted to believe Elin. I had to believe her. I just wished I didn't have to also believe in Dr. Phil.

I hung up the phone and slowly began to walk back to the bedroom.

What had been wrong with our sex life that had made Parker look elsewhere? Oh sure, we didn't have it every single day, but at least every other day. Definitely twice a week.

And when we did have sex there were no problems. Of course, now I couldn't help wondering whether he really liked the sex we'd been having or whether it was too boring, too dull, too . . . quick?

It was sort of quick, I supposed.

I just wasn't a linger-in-bed kind of girl. I wasn't a linger-doing-anything kind of girl, really. But that was me. Although, that wasn't always me, I supposed. But whatever—that was me now. Because that's what Parker was like. Busy. And how could I be expected to change when I wasn't even sure what Parker wanted? All I knew was he wanted Sienna. But I didn't know her well enough to know what that meant.

"Would you like a latte? I'll go to Starbucks." I suddenly needed someone—anyone—to make me a cup of tea. Even if it was in a recycled paper cup.

What I really needed was someone to tell me that it was going to be okay. But was it?

"I'll come with you." Parker got out of bed and pulled a T-shirt on and then slipped into the jeans that were lying askew on the floor.

Ten minutes later, we were back in bed. Since the Starbucks was in the lobby of our building it didn't take very long to pick up two cups and a copy of the *National Post*.

I tried to muster a positive attitude by reminding myself of the facts:

1. Parker had no memory of the affair.
2. He was here, with me. And didn't want to be anywhere else.
3. I'd thwarted his attempts at sex, at least for the next hour or so.

I opened the style section and tried to relax. I scanned the front page, which was a spread of the top ten fall fashions, even though it was only May, made a mental note to look for a new skinny red belt, then turned the page.

Twenty minutes later, I'd read every section. Or at least, the important ones.

I stared at the ceiling for a bit, then sighed.

"Everything all right?" Parker said, leaning over to kiss my ear.

"Oh yes, fine, thanks," I replied, as though he were a waiter and all I wanted was the bill.

"Sure? Do you want another section of the paper?" he asked.

"I'm done."

"Oh, well then maybe you have a book you want to read?"

Of course! A book! I never had time to read books. I leapt out of bed and went into the alcove where we kept our books. I eyed *The Time Traveler's Wife*. Elin kept telling me I just *had* to read it, but it was so long. I mean, sure we had the whole day, but it wasn't as though I could finish the Bible-size tome in eight hours. Besides, given the title, it was clearly about a couple and I didn't have the energy to focus on other couples' problems. I had my own problems. I scanned the shelf.

The Slow Seduction.

Maybe that was just the book I needed. I'd learn how to seduce Parker *slowly*. After all, I might not have wanted to have sex with Parker at the moment, but if I was going to win him back I was going to have to have sex with him at some point, wasn't I? I grabbed the book from the shelf, slipped off the dust cover and headed back to bed.

"Found something good?" he asked, then leaned over and kissed me, but all I could think was, *When I was meeting with clients, was this how you were spending your Saturday mornings, with Sienna, in her bed?*

I felt like I might throw up.

One hour and thirty-four tips into *The Slow Seduction*, I was done with the whole slow sex thing. I clearly didn't have the patience for it. Besides, how did I know that was what Parker wanted? I had no concrete evidence about what Sienna and Parker were like in bed together. Maybe they weren't slow at all. I mean, would you be taking your sweet old time if you only had an hour for lunch or had to get home for dinner *with your wife?* Maybe they had five-minute sex. Maybe Sienna kept her leopard-print lingerie on. Maybe she had matching leopard-print stilettos. Who knew?

I slammed the book and got out of bed. "I'm going to rearrange my closet."

For me, touching fabric was therapeutic. Soothing.

But twenty minutes in, I was even more disconcerted. I had the prettiest clothes—or so I thought. But now I was doubting my well-established style. All I could think of was Sienna's slutty outfit and how maybe that was what Parker preferred. That perhaps my conservative, classic look wasn't what Parker liked at all.

Maybe it turned him off.

I crumpled into the carpet and stared at the wall.

The truth was, I didn't know what had attracted Parker to Sienna. I'd spent only five minutes with the woman. I'd witnessed one outfit, in all its tacky glory. I knew she had full lips and silky hair, but what colour gloss did she wear? Did she tie her hair back or leave it loose all the time? Did she always wear plastic shoes, or did she ever wear pretty little flats?

Just then, my BlackBerry buzzed. I grabbed it off my dresser.

It was Cheryl, a new client I was meeting with the following week.

"I thought of my inspiration!"

The first exercise I did with any new client, before our face-to-face, was get them to think of their soon-to-be-lookalike inspiration. For most, it was a celebrity.

"Jennifer Aniston."

Of course it was. Half my clients wanted to look like Rachel Green. I reassured Cheryl we'd make her look as close to Jennifer as we could, and then hung up.

And then it hit me.

If I could turn my clients into the celebrity they most wanted to resemble, why couldn't I make over myself into the woman my husband lusted after?

It was possible. Sure, I looked absolutely nothing like Sienna Somers. She was Angelina Jolie and I was Gwyneth Paltrow. But I could change that.

I went to my laptop and logged on to Facebook. First, I would become her friend. Or rather, have Uhma become her friend. I'd get access to all her photos, which I could use to transform myself into her, one detail at a time. It was perfect.

The first step was as easy as typing her name into the search bar. Only one Sienna Somers in Toronto appeared on the list. I clicked on it to get a better look at the image. There, in a tight, white, practically transparent T-shirt, her long wavy hair barely covering her visible red lacy bra, was the culprit.

Now all I needed to do was figure out Uhma's last name, create an account, find her some friends so she didn't look like a total fake, add Sienna as a friend and then hope that she accepted.

And Project Sienna would be underway.

By Sunday night I felt much better. I'd managed to erase Sienna's phone number and any history of calls to and from the number from Parker's BlackBerry while he was in the shower, then added her number to my own phone, just in case I needed to use it. I'd been hoping to find text messages, saved voice mails, *something* that would give me more information about their relationship, but there was nothing. But it didn't matter. I had a plan. And it would all launch into action as soon as Sienna accepted my friend request.

I logged on to my Facebook account for the fifth time that weekend.

Login: uhmarudimaker
Password: sociologist

Just so I didn't forget.

I scanned my friends list, which had increased to nineteen thanks to the myriad publicists who I knew accepted any friend requests they received. I scrolled through the list then felt my heart skip. Sienna had accepted my friend request—which meant my first goal, to get access to her photos, was a success.

Except, as I discovered when I clicked on her name, she'd put me on a Limited Profile—which meant I wouldn't be able to see all her photos. Actually, she'd left me with access to only one photo: her profile pic. *The nerve.*

To be fair, what did I expect? If some strange sociologist added me as a friend after meeting me for five minutes, wouldn't I put her on Limited Profile too? Uhma, on the other hand, didn't discriminate. But then again, she didn't have any photos to share. I studied the tiny picture. Sienna had changed her picture since I'd first logged on. In this one she was wearing low-cut jeans and a tight black T-shirt with diamond bejewelling on the front. One outfit. And I couldn't even see her shoes. That's all I got for my efforts. I probably deserved it for being conniving.

I'd been hoping to see her interacting with other people. To get a sense of her personality. Or at least how many boyfriends she had. But this twist meant I needed a new plan. But what?

"Poppy?"

I slammed the lid on my MacBook and turned to face Parker, who was standing in the doorway in a navy T-shirt and plaid shorts. He raised his eyebrows at me in amusement.

"Everything OK?"

"Yes! Why?"

He smiled.

"I just wanted to tell you that Ian called. I'm going to go back to work tomorrow."

"Tomorrow?" I felt panicky. That meant he would see Sienna. "Are you sure?"

He nodded. "I feel fine, and the longer I'm home without my laptop the further behind I'm going to be when I do go back, so I might as well just bite the bullet. Ian wants me to come to an all-day meeting, so it'll be pretty easy anyway." He moved a lock of hair off my forehead. "You look worried. Are you okay?"

Of course I knew he had to go back to work eventually, but I was hoping I'd have a few days to kickstart my makeover before Sienna attempted to lure him back into her toned, tanned arms.

What if he saw her and everything came rushing back to him? Or what if he still didn't remember, but she reminded him, reciting every tiny detail until he remembered it all?

By tomorrow, everything could be different. He could return from work and tell me it was over. That he was leaving me for Sienna.

I had to do something. Sure, if he was in an all-day meeting tomorrow there was a chance Sienna wouldn't get to talk to him. But by Tuesday, I couldn't be so sure.

What I needed was an intervention.

~

I awoke at five minutes to six, before the alarm even went off. I got up, had my shower and put on my favourite outfit—grey bubble skirt, pink champagne blouse with French cuffs, thick grey belt with flower buckle and grey slingbacks. I brushed my hair and slipped a headband behind my ears. I might be posing as a boring sociologist, but I was going to be a stylish one. Especially if, to save my marriage, I wasn't going to get to wear some of my favourite clothes anymore.

"You have to go already?" Parker said as I leaned over the bed to kiss him on the cheek. He hadn't gotten out of bed yet, which was weird, because on a typical workday he'd already be at the office by seven. Hopefully that meant he'd arrive at work with just enough time to get to his all-day meeting.

I nodded.

"I'll miss you."

I wondered if it would be the last day he would say that.

"Me too," I told him honestly. Because by the time he got home what we had right now—whatever our marriage was—could be gone.

"What time will you be home?"

Parker never asked me that. We just weren't *that* couple. We did our own thing. We always had—or at least, until I made the mistake, when I first moved in with him, of asking him that very question and getting a mini lecture about how his hours were unpredictable and us living together wouldn't change that.

He'd asked that I be understanding.

So I was. And I found my own ways to keep busy.

Now, I didn't need to find ways.

I looked at my BlackBerry, distracted by the volume of emails from clients. "I'm not sure. Maybe seven thirty," I said.

"Perfect," he said as I slung my grey leather handbag over my shoulder. He said something else about dinner, but I was already halfway out the door.

After a quick meeting with one of my clients at Starbucks, then a three-hour closet organization session with another, I made my way to the financial district. It was eleven thirty. I had cleared my schedule for the next two hours, and I was ready for action.

My plan, in essence, was simple but effective. I was going to wait for Sienna to go out for lunch, and then follow her.

Which, on further reflection, sounded a bit like I planned to stalk her. But I wasn't going to do *that*. Stalkers were crazy. I wasn't crazy. I was dressed like a professional. I *was* professional.

Feldman Davis was located on Bay in a building that thankfully wasn't connected to the underground PATH system, where I knew most people who worked in the financial district disappeared to at lunchtime. It was an inconvenience Parker complained about routinely, particularly in inclement weather. But for my purposes, it was fortuitous. It was a warm, cloudless day, perfect for getting out of the office for a bit of sun and a bite to eat.

Now, I just hoped Sienna wasn't the type of girl to pack a lunch and work straight through the day.

I selected a stone wall a few yards from the main entrance of the building and positioned myself so that there was no way Sienna could exit the building without me noticing.

And so I sat, and told myself it was time well spent. Not only for the obvious reason: that when Sienna came out, I'd be practically doubling my knowledge of her—the way she dressed, the way she walked—just by seeing her in the flesh for a second instance. But aside from that, I was also exploring my career opportunities as both a sociologist (okay, wearing the outfit didn't *really* count) and a private investigator.

Not that I needed another career.

I continued to sit.

For a very long time. While dozens—no, hundreds—of people came and went from the building. Men in Zegna suits, women in Prada pumps. Guys in blue Oxford shirts and khakis. Girls in Banana Republic trousers with Coach handbags. But no sign of Sienna.

My BlackBerry buzzed every few minutes, indicating a new email, but I refused to take my eyes off the entrance for fear I'd miss her.

Two hours later, I'd almost given up (and was coming close to being late for my next appointment) when I saw her emerge from the building.

Her long brown hair flowed in perfect waves. Her skin was bronzed and glowing. I took in her outfit as she paused for a moment, reaching into her bag and pulling out a pair of oversized sunglasses. She was wearing a tight red sleeveless blouse with ruffles that made her chest even more prominent and a tight black skirt that was definitely not office-appropriate length. A gold chain, which drew even more attention to her appearance, draped her curvy hips.

I stared. And then suddenly she turned to her right and I realized if I didn't do something, she was going to see me.

I hurled myself over the stone wall I'd been sitting on. Thankfully, it was only a few feet high.

"Are you all right?" a male voice asked and I looked up to see a salt-and-pepper-haired man in his fifties leaning over the wall, peering down at me. I waved a hand to shoo him away and remained crouched. He gave me a bemused look and kept walking. I peered to the left to see Sienna only a few steps away. She was staring straight ahead, so I counted to ten and then got up, stepped over the stone wall onto the sidewalk and started to follow her.

I expected her to be only a few steps ahead, but she was walking at an extremely quick clip, despite what appeared to be four-inch red pleather stilettos, which threw my approach, since it wasn't at all how I'd envisioned the situation playing out. I thought I'd be able to dodge behind buildings and get ahead of her, snap a few pictures, hold back as she passed and then catch her again at another intersection. But at the pace she was walking it was all I could do to keep up with her. A minute later she approached an intersection and as she waited for the light to change she turned to look behind her. Thankfully, I was beside a large oak tree, and I slipped behind it. I held my breath and shut my eyes so that no one would speak to me, and then, after what seemed like forever, peeked around the side of the trunk to make sure she'd started to cross the street.

I merged with the pedestrians once more and within moments she was back in view. I picked up my pace, worried that she was going to arrive at her destination and this whole endeavor would've been pointless, and a minute later I was only a few steps behind her.

But just then Sienna stopped walking and reached into her bag. I stopped and quickly looked around but there were no trees to hide behind. I had nowhere to go. I felt someone slam into me.

I yelped without thinking. "Well, don't stop in the middle of the sidewalk then!" the woman who'd bumped into me huffed. And then, almost in slow motion, Sienna turned.

"Uhma?" She stared at me, confused.

Now what?

I gave a half-wave and smile.

She took a step toward me, pursing her lips and narrowing her eyes. "Are you *following* me?"

"Following you!" I let out a loud laugh. "Of course not," I said. My heart was pounding.

"I could've sworn I saw you a minute ago, too. Are you *sure* you're not following me?"

I tilted my head. "Well actually," I said, folding my hands in front of me in just the way I thought a sociologist might, "I saw you and remembered you from the hospital, so I thought I'd just make sure you were okay."

"Really?"

I nodded.

She eyed me skeptically.

"So . . . you're back at work then? Feeling okay?"

"Yep."

"And um, how's your . . . *boyfriend?*" Just saying it made me feel sick.

Sienna sighed dramatically. "Oh *him*. I haven't spoken to him."

"What do you mean? Is he all right?"

"I guess. I don't know when he's coming back to work."

Thank God for all-day meetings. She didn't know he was already back.

"Oh? You work with him, too? That's not really an ideal scenario for a relationship, is it?"

"Well then you probably won't think the fact that he's married is ideal, either," she said as though it were a *total* drag.

"Your boyfriend is married?" I asked, feigning confusion.

Sienna looked around as though wondering if anyone was listening to our conversation. "Yeah, it kind of sucks, but it's fun, too. There's something different about married guys . . ."

"Yes. They're married. They have wives," I said bluntly.

Sienna looked at me in alarm.

I managed a fake laugh. "I'm kidding. But aren't you worried you're never going to get married if you only date guys who can't commit to you?"

"I'm only twenty-nine. Besides, I'm not looking to settle down."

Twenty-nine? My husband was cheating on me with a woman older than me? Wasn't he supposed to be leaving me for a younger model? So age clearly wasn't the attraction.

Sienna checked her watch, and as she did I caught sight of her nails. *Oh my God.* They were two inches long and blood red, with a single tiny crystal on the end of each.

Fake nails? Parker liked plastic nails with goth-like polish and bejewelling? This was what I was going to have to do to win my husband back? It was so unfair.

"They're Swarovski," Sienna said suddenly, obviously catching me staring.

They're appalling, I thought, but nodded and smiled, then looked down at my own nails, which were short and lightly coated in gel and then light pink polish so they looked professional and perfect at all times. I loved my nails. I didn't want long red claws. But my nails *were* a bit predictable and boring, I supposed. And this wasn't about me. I was revamping my image for the sake of my marriage, and although I had no clear proof that Sienna's fake nails were what wooed Parker, I could leave no detail out.

Just then, Sienna's phone rang, and she reached into her bag to search for it. I quickly reached into my own bag and pulled my BlackBerry out of the inside pocket where I always kept it. Sienna was still rummaging around. Now was my chance. I quickly held up the phone, clicked on the capture icon and it made a snap noise.

Sienna didn't notice. "Hello?" She looked at her phone and shrugged, then started typing on the keypad.

I looked down at the screen, but I couldn't decipher the blurry image. I looked up and then back down at the camera. I'd gotten a close-up of her boob.

Hmm. I'd need a few more tries to get this right.

I held the camera up again—higher this time—and pressed the camera button, just as Sienna looked up.

"Are you taking a picture of me?" she asked with alarm.

I could feel my face getting red but I whipped the phone back to my side and tried to keep my composure. "No," I

said defensively. "I was just checking my messages. I just
. . . didn't have very good reception, so I was holding it up
high to try to, um, catch a wavelength or . . ." What had
happened to my cool and collected self? Uhma Rudimaker
was a bumbling idiot. I wasn't making any sense.

Sienna narrowed her eyes at me. "Are you sure . . . ?"

Oh no. What if she made me show her my phone just
to be sure? And then she would see my real name right on
the screen and would know that I was Parker's wife and
. . . oh God, I had to do something . . .

And so I ran. I ran as quickly as was possible in Kate
Spade slingbacks.

"Uhma!" Sienna called after me, but I didn't stop.

chapter five

P roject Sienna was barely off the ground and I'd already almost blown it and I didn't even have time to feel sorry for myself since I'd barely made it to my two o'clock appointment.

Two hours later, I emerged from a three-storey home in Rosedale and walked south on Yonge, pulling out my BlackBerry to study the photo I'd captured of Sienna. I felt annoyed at how good she looked despite the grainy quality, her sexy pout taking up half the screen. As I approached Scollard, I glanced at my own reflection in a store window and saw, stenciled in the glass: Designer Smiles. *You change your shoes, why not change your smile?*

I smiled at myself, baring my teeth.

Not bad, I thought, though maybe it was really all relative. My teeth *were* a bit small, I supposed, but I'd never really minded it. But I suppose they weren't *sexy* teeth. They made me look cute. I didn't want to be cute. Cute didn't work. I needed to be sexy.

Why *not* change my smile? My bottom teeth were small, too, and when I smiled my upper lip tended to disappear. Elin had gotten veneers shortly after university when she'd dated a dentist, and while I wouldn't let her tell me all the gory details, she had much fuller lips afterward because her new teeth had pushed her lips forward, or something like that. "Like a free lip implant!" she'd exclaimed. In fact, I'd always thought her fuller lips explained her impressive dating career in the two years between university and meeting Terrence.

I'd never really considered veneers, but that was because I didn't like the dentist. In fact—let's be honest—I was deathly afraid of the dentist. The real problem harkened back to my university years, when I didn't want to pay to go to the dentist, so I'd go to the student hygienists in the school's dental program. They may have been near-hygienists but they had not mastered the art of using that pointy tool without making your gums bleed. And they tried to blame it on me—telling me I had gingivitis. Really. Even though I now went to a qualified dentist, I only showed up for the absolute bare minimum of appointments—and only after taking a handful of Advil.

Well, maybe I could think about veneers, down the line. Sometime.

Only, I didn't have a lot of "down the line" time. I had to act quickly if I was going to transform myself into a Sienna lookalike. She may or may not have had veneers, but she certainly had the sexy pout.

Maybe I should just pop in, I thought, opening the door. Just to inquire. What could it hurt?

Going to a cosmetic dentist was nothing like going to a regular dentist and certainly nothing like going to a student dental hygienist.

First of all, the office was all swishy and warm and cozy and sort of looked like the lobby of a mountainside chalet, with a roaring fireplace, which was really quite comforting (it wasn't actually emitting any heat and I was pretty sure it was one of those fake-log-switch-on-switch-off types of fireplaces, a good thing given it was nearly 30 degrees outside).

And over to the right there was a whole bar with various pitchers of flavoured water, lemonade with flower petals and floral teas. I poured myself a glass of cucumber water and sat down on the chic caramel-coloured leather couch. On the mahogany coffee table, right beside the fan of gossip magazines, was a large bowl filled with mini Green & Blacks organic chocolate bars in all sorts of flavours: butterscotch, milk, almond, cherry. I always knew it was an urban myth that sweets rotted your teeth. Although, if everyone who sat on this very couch was in the market for fake teeth anyway, I supposed it didn't matter what they ate. . . .

I picked up two chocolate bars and hesitated before grabbing a third. *Oh what the heck,* I thought. One (or three) mini chocolate bars weren't going to rot my teeth. Besides, I'd chew some gum once I left—everyone knew nine out of ten dentists recommended sugarless gum when you couldn't brush your teeth. And anyway, if my teeth looked really bad, surely the dentist would recommend a cleaning after my consultation. After all, I was already in the office. It was time to stop being afraid of the dentist anyway. Fear was hardly sexy, was it?

I'd made my way through only two of the chocolate bars when the receptionist, a petite blond girl about my age told me that Gretel, the hygienist, was ready to see me.

I wondered if Gretel was her real name, or just a stage name she used to reinforce how you could eat candy, just like the fairytale, and have lovely teeth. It wasn't a bad marketing idea.

Gretel, who was also blond, led me into the assessment room where Dr. Jefferson was waiting for me. He was young—maybe only late 30s—and wore a tailored grey suit with a light pinstripe, and had sandy-blond hair, making him coordinate quite nicely with the rest of his staff and his décor. I wondered if it was planned that way. He smiled at me and gestured to the plush cloud-white chair on the other side of his desk.

"So . . ." Dr. Jefferson said amiably, rubbing his chin. "What brings you in today?"

"I was thinking I might like to have veneers," I said.

"Okay." He nodded. "And what made you consider them?"

Huh. I wasn't expecting that sort of question. I just sort of thought he'd start his sales pitch at that point. After all, didn't he want to veneer the whole world over? It was just money in his pocket.

Perhaps he just wanted to make me feel at ease by asking some simple questions first. Fair enough.

Was now the time to mention that I thought perhaps

my husband's mistress had them and I'd like to look more like her? Maybe not. It was probably a little too *Single White Female*-ish.

"Well, I was just assessing my smile, you know . . ." I said, feeling quite pleased with my natural-sounding answer. Besides, it was the truth. I *was* assessing my smile, just minutes ago, in the window.

He nodded.

"And how long have you been considering veneers?"

Oh. Well. I looked at my watch. *About fifteen minutes?*

"A while. It's hard to say, really. The idea comes and goes, you know?"

"Sure," he said and smiled again. He had very nice teeth. I wondered who put his veneers on. Surely he couldn't do it himself?

"So what we're going to do then is take some images of your teeth, then we'll show you a short video about the veneer process, some before-and-afters of other patients . . . and then I'll give you my recommendation. Then, if you want to go ahead with them, we'll make an appointment for your assessment, your initial appointment in which we'll shave your teeth down to points—"

Shave? What? They had to shave down my teeth to points? Like a vampire?

"Fit you with the fake teeth to go home with while we prepare the veneers, then when they're ready you'll come back in to get them attached."

Like dentures?

Oh God. Suddenly I felt a bit woozy.

"So . . . how many veneers do you think I'd need?" I

asked nervously as Dr. Jefferson led me to the photography room.

"You know, actually, I don't think you need them. You could build up your front teeth with bonding if you're worried about the size."

"Really?" I felt relief.

"We can still go through the process, just so you have something to think about, but all I really think you need is a good teeth whitening session. It's quick and painless. You'd be surprised how white teeth can change your appearance—and if you purchase the take-home kit we offer a twenty percent discount on the in-office service." He handed me a price list.

Teeth whitening? I'd never really thought about it but it *would* be less painful . . . and I could keep my own teeth. Besides, I didn't even know for sure if Sienna had veneers. Maybe teeth whitening was the way to go. It wouldn't give me fuller lips, but at least it was a start.

"How quickly could I get an appointment?"

"We could have you in and out of the chair in an hour, if you're interested."

I pondered this for barely a moment before nodding. It was only Day 1 of Project Sienna and I could already have white teeth. Oh sure, I'd been planning to do some clothes shopping, but I could always do that on my way home. I was here now, and I had the time before my next appointment . . .

"Let's do it!"

The teeth whitening room was not at all what I was expecting. I just assumed it would look like any other dental treatment room. You know, beige pleather chair covered with clear plastic, builder's beige walls, a bunch of machines, a sink to spit out your fluoride . . .

But this room was so posh. The walls were a creamy white with mahogany trim and crown molding, the floor was gorgeous dark hardwood, and the chair in the middle of the room was a souped-up leather La-Z-Boy, with massagers and a heated back and seat. In the corner of the room was a huge entertainment system, complete with a flat-screen TV, DVD player, stereo system and remote control.

"There are headphones if you'd like to listen to music," Gretel said, pointing at a pair of oversized puffy headphones beside the chair. "Or you can choose a movie."

What? Movies at the dentist's office? This was like going to the spa! It really didn't get better than this.

I went over to the DVDs and pulled out season one of *Gossip Girl*, then slipped it into the DVD player. This was going to be so fun!

"Your teeth are so white," I said, admiring Gretel's own perfect teeth. "Did you get that from the White Out X3000?"

She leaned close. "Actually, no," she whispered. "Crest Whitestrips."

Oh. Well, no matter. She probably had to use a million strips every night. And who wanted to go to bed with plastic sheets on their teeth every night for months? That was hardly sexy, and the whole point was to become the new, sexy me.

Besides, this would be instant—and I'd get to watch *Gossip Girl!*

I sat down in the chair and Gretel reclined it slightly as the opening credits began to roll. At least, I thought they were the opening credits. To be honest, it was a bit hard to see the screen at the angle I was sitting. Gretel put a heavy bib on me, then applied a gel to my teeth and gums, slipped a pair of massive plastic contraptions over my teeth and pulled a machine with a blue light in front of my face.

I shifted my head to get a better view of the screen.

"Once I turn the machine on, you shouldn't move your head at all. You'll need to keep it very still, otherwise the light could burn your gums."

Burn my gums? That didn't sound very fun. Or painless.

"All right," I tried to say but instead it came out, "Ow wub." I was so sexy already.

Gretel handed me a pad of paper and pen. "You can use this if you need to tell me anything."

I wondered what exactly I was going to need to tell her, but I nodded.

"No moving!" she said with a smile.

Right. Okay. Keep my head still.

"Ready?"

Why on earth did she keep asking me questions I wasn't allowed to answer?

I kept my head still and attempted to write *yes* on the pad of paper. Only, it was quite difficult to write without looking. Oh well, she'd get the point.

Gretel moved around to the back of the machine—completely blocking my view of the TV—and flicked a button. The blue light shone brightly and she pushed it in toward my teeth.

I couldn't feel a thing. It was perfectly painless.

And then, like a flash of lightning, all I felt was pain.

It started as a slight burning sensation, though it wasn't direct and didn't feel like anything I'd ever experienced before. I couldn't pinpoint where the pain was, it was just an overall pain—in my teeth, my gums, my entire mouth. I tried to ignore it, instead focusing on Serena and Blair on the screen, but it was becoming worse and worse.

Hurts, I wrote on the pad of paper and held it up.

Gretel looked at the paper and then at me. "What hurts?"

Good God, what did she think?! *Teeth,* I scribbled.

"Do you want to stop?"

I shook my head.

"No moving!" Gretel said with alarm.

How long?

"Not much longer. Twenty minutes."

Okay, twenty minutes. I could do twenty minutes. Twenty minutes would probably take me to the end of the episode. I could do it.

Only, I couldn't see the screen, since my eyes were filled with tears.

"Are you sure you want to keep going?" Gretel asked what seemed like years later.

I wasn't sure at all.

Finally, I couldn't take it any longer. I started to write *stop* on the pad of paper when, thankfully, at that moment, the light switched off. "We're done."

Thank God.

"Now we move to the bottom row."

What? The bottom row?

"Do you want to see the difference?"

I nodded, tears spilling down my cheeks.

Gretel handed me a mirror and removed the teeth guards.

I smiled. And froze. The air hitting my teeth hurt. I looked around. Was there a fan on? There was so much *wind*. But there wasn't a fan. It was just the normal air circulating in the room that, when it passed over my teeth, felt like it was burning a hole right through them.

I couldn't go on. I couldn't possibly do the bottom row.

But then I looked at my teeth. The top row really was white. They looked so shiny and gleaming and, well, there was still that goopy gel all over them, but still, they looked amazing. The only thing was, now my bottom row looked awful. They looked yellowed and stained, like I hadn't seen a toothbrush since the '80s, and . . .

I had to do the bottom row. I couldn't stop now. I wiped at my tears, handed back the mirror, and nodded at Gretel to continue.

Within minutes, the pain was so bad that my eyes had refilled with tears. I was going to die. I was going to die.

Why on earth did I think I needed white teeth? Of course, because white teeth would make me look like Sienna.

Oh my God. The pain. Not only did my bottom teeth ache now too, but it felt as though my top teeth were getting worse.

How was I going to breathe? How was I going to eat?

Maybe it was just the gel Gretel had applied to my teeth. Perhaps as soon as Gretel turned off the machine and wiped off the goop I'd be fine. I tried to focus on that thought.

Chuck kissed Blair on the screen. I envied them, with their painless teeth.

A moment later, Gretel turned off the machine and removed the guards.

"All done!" she said happily. Why was she so happy? Her teeth didn't hurt. No wonder she used Crest Whitestrips rather than endure this torture.

She handed me a glass of water. "Swish this around in your mouth to get rid of the gel," she said.

I took a sip and immediately spit the water back into the cup. Oh my God. The pain of the water hitting my teeth. I couldn't do it. I couldn't—

"Is it that painful?" she asked, getting a small cloth and wiping the drool from my chin. I nodded. Great, I was drooling. Very sexy.

"I'll wipe the gel off."

I opened my mouth but the evil air felt ten times worse than it had before, now that all my teeth were sensitive.

The cloth hurt. I shut my eyes tight. *It's going to be okay,* I told myself. As soon as she got the gel off . . .

Only a moment later, Gretel said that the gel *was* off my teeth. And they still hurt. In fact, they hurt even more.

"Without the protective gel barrier, you might find your teeth a bit sensitive."

A bit sensitive? A bit?

Did she have any idea the pain I was feeling? I wanted to ask her how long it would last, but I was afraid to reopen my mouth. The air was just too much to bear.

"It'll go away in a few days."

A few days?

Oh God.

"You probably should've mentioned you had sensitive teeth. We could've given you some painkillers."

What? I had the option of getting drugs? Why hadn't she just given them to me? How was I supposed to know I had sensitive teeth? I'd never had my teeth whitened before.

"Drugs," I said quickly, then shut my mouth again. Hurt. So. Much.

"Would you like some now?"

I nodded.

She went to the cupboard and took out a bottle, then gave me two Advils. Advil? That was her drug? But I didn't care. Anything had to help. Gretel handed me a glass of water. Oh God. The water. I couldn't do it. I'd have to swallow the pills dry.

Then she handed me a mirror. I took it and slowly opened my mouth.

My teeth *were* white. At least, they looked white through my tears.

"They look really good," Gretel said, her hand on my shoulder, though her touch felt more like a push out the door than a consoling embrace.

I nodded, tears still in my eyes. They *did* look good. And besides, surely the pain would go away sooner than a few days, wouldn't it? Maybe if I just kept taking Advils . . .

And what was the saying? No pain, no gain. Pilates could be painful, but it was the only way to ensure the Brie I occasionally indulged in didn't go to my ass.

Come to think of it, I was going to have to rethink both my cheese-eating habits and my workout regime. If I wanted a voluptuous figure like Sienna, Pilates and salad were going to have to be off-limits from now on.

~

Out on the street, I checked my BlackBerry through semi-dry eyes and saw that Uhma had a new friend request. Curious to see who the latest person was to request a woman they'd never met as a friend, I logged on to my account, and after declining the request (Uhma had to be discriminating, at least some of the time), I scrolled through the news feed, then stopped when I saw that Sienna had updated her status.

People are strange . . .

I gasped, then threw a hand to my mouth to shut out the air. Even the gentle breeze coming across Bloor felt like acid on an open wound.

Did she mean *me?*

Just then, my screen jumped and I scrolled to the top and stared at the tiny screen. Sienna had just updated her status again.

Need to find a new guy.

Oh my God. I wanted to yelp with glee, but knew better than to open my mouth again. Instead, I gave a little skip of joy. Now all I could do was hope that she found someone soon, so I could be sure Parker would be permanently off her radar. Just then, I heard someone call my name.

I turned to look over my shoulder. Walking toward me was Diesel Cartwright. My ex-boyfriend. The one who came right before Parker. I hadn't seen him in six years.

His brown hair was just long enough on top to be that good kind of messy. He was wearing a blue T-shirt with the number 76 on the front and white ribbing on the sleeves that made his biceps (ones he'd never had when we dated) bulge, blue-black Rock & Republics and white Penguin sneakers.

"Diesel!" I said as he approached me, an impeccably groomed collie that could've been a Lassie stand-in at his side. I was surprised. I would've thought Diesel was a mutt kind of dog owner, but he himself had also become better groomed than I remembered. Diesel leaned in for a hug and instantly my heart started racing. I inhaled through my nose, trying to calm myself down, but instead I got a whiff of his cologne. He was still wearing Boss. I never forgot a boyfriend/cologne combination and as I breathed in his scent, all the memories came rushing back, unbidden. The first time I met him, when he was bartending at Cleats, the way he smelled after a show, our first date—which had actually been a group outing at a pub, but had ended back at his apartment with me trying to deflect his guitar-string callused fingers inching their way into my jeans as I convinced myself I was in love. And, of course, the way I felt when I caught him in the back of his Geo with a Wonder Woman groupie.

When he pulled away, I took in the rest of him. He was clean-shaven, showing off a dimple in his chin I'd never known was there. It was like looking at someone new but with a familiarity that was comforting. It was an odd feeling that made the hairs on my arm stand on end and clichéd butterflies dance in my stomach. I felt guilty for feeling nervous and excited but I couldn't help it.

"Actually, it's Colin now," Diesel said, his dark brown eyes twinkling. "I changed my name back. You know, now that I'm an adult." He let out an easy, comfortable laugh.

"Mmm . . ." I said to kill time while I mustered my strength to actually use words. "But what about the band?"

I quickly shut my mouth and bit down on my tongue to deflect the pain.

"No more band. I'm actually an assistant producer on *This Morning?*" he said, as though I'd never heard of one of the most popular TV morning shows in the city.

Diesel Cartwright had given up his rock-and-roll life-style for a real-world job in television?

"So, you look great!" he said and I smiled, showing off my teeth despite the pain. "Although, I have to say, I miss your long hair."

He missed my long hair? I didn't know he'd been thinking about my long hair enough to miss it. His own long hair had been chopped, and while his shaggy locks had suited him, his shorter style looked even better. Like when Orlando Bloom went short and slightly mussed.

"It's been forever. What have you been up to?"

What could I say? That my husband had just had an affair and today was Day One in Operation Make Myself Over to Look Like His Slutty Mistress? Why did the day I ran into my ex-boyfriend have to be the one when I couldn't smile without searing pain shooting from my teeth throughout my entire body?

"I'm an image consultant," I said quickly. "Are you living in the city?"

"Kensington. Never left—I've got a great little place there."

I couldn't help wondering if he shared the space with someone: a girlfriend? A wife? I looked at his hands but, where they were once loaded with hardware, they were now entirely bare. "I was just up here checking out a new doggie daycare for Ralph. I've got to go away next week and the place he usually stays at is fully booked." He looked at his watch. "Do you have time for a drink?" he asked with a smile. My heart flip-flopped. That was the smile that had got me into trouble in the first place. "I'm pretty sure I owe you that much."

I looked at him, surprised. Did he mean for cheating on me?

I put a hand on his arm and fluttered my eyelashes, wishing I'd thought to start with eyelash extensions before white teeth.

"So does that mean you're single?" I asked him, looking at his ring finger.

He looked at me in surprise. "Um, yeah. I guess you could say that," he said. He eyed my left hand then raised an eyebrow. Was he looking at my ring? Did that mean he was still interested? Or re-interested? "Why?"

"Oh, no reason. It's just hard to believe, a cute guy like you, still single," I said, playfully pushing a hand to his chest. I felt guilty for misleading him, but my punishment was the pain that was shooting through my entire body every second I kept my mouth open. *That's what you get for being a cheating bastard,* I added to myself. He was a jerk. I just had to remember that. Even if he wasn't acting like one at this moment. He was still a jerk who hurt me by being a player. Which meant he would be perfect for my plan.

"I have to get going, but maybe a rain check?"

He agreed and we swapped numbers, then he leaned in to kiss me on the cheek. My heart, which had just settled back to a post-Pilates workout rate, sped right back up again. "It was great to see you. I'll look forward to your call."

He walked away from me and I watched him merge with the late-afternoon crowd.

It was like fate, my teeth whitening. I had just found the perfect distraction for Sienna.

∿

Twenty minutes later I found Parker standing in the kitchen, wearing my pink apron (I always thought every woman should have an apron, whether she cooks or not, simply because it was a fabulous accessory to have in the kitchen) and squinting at a cookbook. We had cookbooks?

"You're home early!" he said brightly, turning down the burner on the stove and coming over to greet me.

"So are you," I said, then quickly shut my mouth to keep the air out. He leaned in and I realized he was going to kiss me. I couldn't kiss. It would hurt too much to have his lips press into my lips, which would then press into my teeth. It hurt just to think about it. But I could hardly tell him I couldn't kiss him because I'd gotten my teeth whitened so I could have gleaming teeth like Sienna. I kept my lips tightly shut and turned so that his kiss landed on my cheek.

He didn't seem to register my feint and pulled me in for a hug. I tried to breathe in his scent, but because he didn't wear cologne and liked unscented antiperspirant, all I could smell was the oil in the frying pan on the stove.

"So, why *are* you home already?" I asked cautiously.

He pulled me back and looked me in the eyes. "It was

hard, going back to work. There was this project I thought I'd been working on last week, but my team told me we closed the deal months ago. I guess I'm still a little forgetful." He laughed, but I could tell he didn't think it was funny at all.

"It's okay, Parker. It'll all come back to you." I was trying to be reassuring, but inside, I was praying that my words were lies, all lies.

He nodded. "I suppose it will. Didn't the doctor say there were things we could do to help my memory along?"

He did, I thought, *but there is absolutely no way we're doing any of those things.* I had the list of memory triggers tucked safely away in my lingerie drawer, where I could refer to it to ensure we weren't abiding by any of the suggestions on the list. It made me feel terrible, but there was no way I would help him remember Sienna.

"Anyway, I thought we could make a romantic dinner together."

What? Make dinner? I couldn't remember the last time we'd made dinner together. I couldn't remember the last time we'd *made* dinner, period.

I barely knew how to cook.

Actually, that wasn't true. At one point I used to attempt to cook, but when Parker and I got together he was so critical of everything I made (okay, so maybe it was legitimate, since I did explode an entire lasagna when I put the glass pan on top of the gas burner), that I stopped trying and just admitted disinterest rather than defeat. Parker himself claimed "being overworked" as his reason for not cooking, though I'd honestly never seen him even attempt anything more difficult than a piece of toast.

But the more pressing problem with dinner was that, as hungry as I was, I couldn't eat. I couldn't even drink water. It hurt to breathe. I scanned the countertop, which looked like a salad bar. How on earth was I going to manage to bite a bean sprout, let alone endure the pain of chewing a crunchy carrot?

My BlackBerry chimed, indicating I had a new text message, and I walked over to the couch.

Hey babe. Are you free for that makeup drink on Saturday night?

I stared at the message from Colin. I was most certainly *not* ready to see him again. But I *was* ready to pawn him off onto Sienna.

Sounds good. Somewhere in your neighbourhood?

I could always hope that things would go so well between him and Sienna that he'd take her back to his place—particularly convenient if it was right around the corner.

How about Roxy's at 8?

Perfect.

See you there babe.

Two "babes" in one conversation was two too many, I thought, cringing.

Now all I had to do was get Sienna there. A more difficult task, for sure, especially now that she probably thought I was crazy after my ridiculous escape this afternoon, but I had to try.

I went to my laptop, logged on to my Facebook account and clicked on Sienna's profile.

Her latest update was still active—she apparently hadn't found a new guy in the last few hours—and I clicked on my inbox to send her a message.

Hi Sienna,

Funny bumping into you today. Sorry to seem like a crazy woman, dashing off like that, but I realized I was late for a client at the office. Anyway, saw your status update and actually have a guy I think you'd really like. I know you probably don't need a setup, but I wouldn't suggest it if I didn't think he was your type: totally hot and works in TV . . .

　　I've attached a picture. Let me know if you're free Saturday night.

—Uhma

I didn't feel confident about this part of the plan, but I couldn't think of any other way to set her up with Colin that was better than this straightforward request. Still, I had serious doubts she would accept the invite. I certainly wouldn't if I were her and she were a lunatic sociologist I'd met twice. All I could hope was that Colin was enough of a lure.

I opened another browser window and quickly typed "Colin Cartwright" into Google Images. A whole page of photos showed up. I copy and pasted the best one into my message to Sienna then hit Send. Now I just had to hope that she'd agree, stay for a drink (or two or three), fall madly in love with Colin and forget all about Parker.

I had even figured out how to explain my dual names. I'd just tell Colin that "Uhma" was my nickname at Girl Guide camp, which was where I met Sienna years and years ago and that we'd just reunited so we didn't know a lot about each other so he shouldn't bother talking about my job or anything. And I'd add something tragic, like how the word *poppy* made her think of the war and how her grandfather died in it or something so he really shouldn't bring up my real name at all if he didn't want to make her upset. It was totally believable, I was sure. After all, she was British and that was close to Normandy and Flanders Fields and all that.

Except it wasn't believable at all. The first rule of thumb if you're going to lie is keep it simple. But I couldn't think of anything else.

Anyway, it wasn't as though they were going to be talking about me the whole time. They'd be too busy flirting and talking about themselves and then, if I was lucky, they'd get a room. I mean, it wasn't as if it would be unheard of for either of them.

∿

Parker had already started—and was nearly finished—what he was calling Yaki Teriyaki Crunch (whatever that was), so there was nothing for me to do but pray that he lost interest or somehow blew up the kitchen, forcing us to order in soup. Or milkshakes. Instead, his BlackBerry buzzed.

I watched as he picked it up and looked at it. Would I wonder if it was Sienna every time it buzzed?

"Hey, Ian."

That's what he got for leaving work early.

I walked into the bedroom to get changed into the velour tracksuit Parker's mother had bought me two years ago in an attempt to bond. For obvious reasons I'd never worn it, but now, it seemed like the perfect outfit. I clipped the tags and pulled the purple fabric over my body, then looked at myself in the mirror. My ass most certainly did *not* look juicy. It looked . . . juiceless. It made me want to go out and get one of those track suits that actually said Juicy across the bottom, except that I thought they were so tacky and tasteless. Still, wasn't the saying that you were supposed to "fake it 'til you make it"?

Parker wasn't talking, which could only mean the conversation was just beginning, so I slipped out the front door and knocked on Annabelle's door across the hall. Annabelle had a pop culture blog and knew everything about everything. She'd also had more cosmetic enhancements than Heidi Montag. I knew she'd have the answer to my questions.

Annabelle had pale, barely freckled skin, green eyes, defined cheekbones and red hair that reached the middle of her back. None of it was natural, but only I knew, because I'd seen her through her transformations.

"What are you doing? Why are you holding your

hand in front of your mouth?" she asked as soon as she answered her door. She was wearing black leggings and a turquoise Lululemon sweatshirt that was only halfway zipped, revealing the top of her lacy black bra.

"I got my teeth whitened and air hurts."

"You're crazy. Come in here." She opened the door wider. "Why did you do that?"

"I wanted to get veneers so I could get a free lip plump at the same time, but apparently I don't need veneers. I figured you'd know the best doctor in the city to get my lips plumped."

"No way. My cousin Mara got her lips plumped and they ballooned out to here." Annabelle extended her arm and made a face. "She sent me a picture. It was nasty. And even if that doesn't happen, they deflate at different rates so you're all lopsided and shit. Just buy a plumping lip gloss or something. Anyway, what's with the sudden facial makeover?"

"Oh, it's not just my face. I need a bigger butt, too."

"You do?" she said skeptically.

I nodded.

"I think you need a drink. What the hell's going on?" She led me into her cluttered kitchen, poured the remaining contents of an open bottle of wine into a glass and handed it to me.

I wasn't about to tell her about Parker. She was my neighbour but she was also the biggest gossip in our building. I took an instinctive gulp from the glass and then froze.

"No!" The searing pain made me realize what I'd done and I sent the wine in my mouth spraying into the air like a human lawn sprinkler.

"Shit! What are you *doing?*"

"I can't have red wine!" I grabbed a knife on the counter and peered into it. "Are they stained?" I opened my mouth wide to Annabelle and stared at her.

She dumped the wine from my glass into hers and ran to the bathroom, then returned a moment later and handed me my glass, which was filled with a green liquid. "Mouthwash. Rinse."

I took a swig then spit back into the glass. The pain was worse than the whitening itself.

"Ooh, I probably shouldn't have given you alcohol," Annabelle said immediately. "It makes the pain worse." She dumped the mouthwash into the kitchen sink and filled the glass with water, but I was finished with liquids. I sunk to the hardwood floor.

"Now, what's this about a big ass?" Annabelle asked and sat down across from me on the hardwood.

"Right. I need a bigger butt too. But not fat. Just more voluptuous. I figured you'd know some sort of exercise I could do."

"Spinning."

"But I hate spinning." I'd done a spinning class once, but I'd left midway through the hour, discouraged by how thick everyone's thighs appeared to be. If that was the result of religious spinning, I wanted no part of the congregation.

"It'll bulk up your butt. And if that's what you want . . ."

That's what I wanted. "But the seat is so hard," I whined. "It's like riding on a rock. I think I'm still bruised."

"Woe is you with your bony ass," she said shaking her head. "Pick up a pair of cycling shorts. They're padded."

"Really? Who knew there was such a thing?"

She raised her eyebrows, bemused. "Everyone who cycles. Or spins."

I gave her a quick hug then walked back across the hall. I closed the door and locked it just as Parker let out a string of swear words from the kitchen.

"What's wrong?" I asked, coming up behind him.

"I didn't turn the burner off while I was on the phone." Parker looked helplessly at the frying pan on the stove.

"Oh?" I supposed I should've thought to turn the burner off or at least watch things while he was on the phone rather than also disappear from the kitchen, but . . . it hadn't been my idea to make dinner.

"The vegetables are supposed to be crispy. They're mush."

I looked at the pan. He wasn't kidding. I picked up an empty can of mixed vegetables from the counter and stared at it. "Did you put canned vegetables in this recipe when you've got a whole bunch of fresh veggies right here?" I asked in shock. For one, the only time Parker would've ever bought canned vegetables was for a food drive, but why on earth would he purposely choose canned vegetables when he'd clearly gone to the store to buy fresh ones? I looked at the recipe. It definitely called for fresh veggies.

"I figured I'd mix the two. It was cheaper and easier than using all fresh vegetables," he said simply.

Actually, ordering in was cheaper and easier, I wanted to tell him. I didn't mention this, though, since I was singing hallelujahs in my head—there was no way there was going to be a bit of crunch to any of *those* vegetables. I was saved. Of course, I kept my joy to myself. *That* would've been insensitive.

"Oh, that's okay."

"We could make tuna melts."

Tuna . . . something triggered in the back of my brain.

"No!" We couldn't eat tuna. According to Nurse Abigail, tuna was a memory prompt. He could eat it and instantly remember Sienna. Besides, there was no way I could manage a piece of crunchy toast, even if it did have melted cheese on it. "I'm, um, off fish. Too much mercury."

"Oh, well . . ." Parker opened the cupboard and I wondered if Yaki Teriyaki Crunch and tuna melts comprised his entire entrée repertoire, though that was double my own. "I guess we could order pizza."

I felt totally guilty, like I'd crushed some big romantic gesture. It was bad enough that I couldn't eat, but now I had to worry about hurting Parker's feelings too. I leaned my head against the cupboard and sighed. I couldn't do this. I was exhausted.

I knew that the easy out was to tell Parker I'd gotten my teeth whitened, but I couldn't. This nagging voice—which I had to believe was the voice of reason—was telling me that if I started to tell him about any of my plans to change my appearance I'd somehow end up blurting out my whole plan. No, for my plan to work I needed to be stealth-like. My transformation had to be without explanation. A slow, almost subliminal process.

I looked at the Yaki Teriyaki Crunch on the stove. It looked more like Yaki Teriyaki Soup. I lifted my head. Maybe it wouldn't be so bad after all.

"Let's eat the Yaki." Mushy vegetables might be manageable. And they'd save Parker's ego, too.

"Really?"

In actuality, not *all* the vegetables were overdone—because Parker had somehow slipped in some bok choy and broccoli. Not only were they still crunchy, but they were both on the Memory-Boosting (aka The Forbidden) Food List, which meant I had to steal them from Parker's plate when he wasn't looking, swapping them for mushrooms and carrots. Then, I attempted to pass the vegetables from my lips to the back of my mouth without allowing them to touch my teeth, but I wasn't very successful. The pain was awful.

When Parker looked over at me, beside him on the couch, tears were running down my face.

"What's wrong?" he asked, alarmed.

I couldn't tell him. "This is just so nice."

"What?"

"Having dinner together. You cooking. Us both being home at a reasonable hour."

"You act like it's so rare."

"But it is," I said with confusion.

He looked at me thoughtfully for a moment. "It doesn't have to be," he said.

Of course it had to be. Maybe today he was home early, but his boss had already called him, and tomorrow he'd be back to his usual self, and by the end of the week he'd probably catch up on everything he'd been working on. And we'd go back to the way things were. Except for the part about Sienna.

As I cuddled into the crook of Parker's arm, tears kept welling up in my eyes, only I realized that it wasn't the pain of my teeth that was making me cry. The reality of what had happened—that my husband had cheated on me, and was now making me dinner and being incredibly caring and thoughtful—hit me. It could all change tomorrow and I might never have another moment like this with him again.

chapter six

P arker left for work early the next morning, and I inspected my teeth. They sparkled, but now my face looked sickly and sallow. I pulled out my BlackBerry and opened the photo album to study my photo of Sienna (focusing on the physical and trying not to get discouraged by the fact that she hadn't yet responded to my email).

She glowed.

I did not glow.

I normally prided myself on my pale skin—the result of five years of daily SPF 60 (ice storms included) in an attempt to reverse the damage of my summers spent tanning. Some people called it crazy; I called it cautious. And now it was all a waste because my face looked jaundiced compared to my too-white teeth.

What I needed was a peel session. I was always telling my clients that to get glowing skin they needed to invest in at least one full day at the spa every month, getting exfoliated, peeled, waxed and polished.

"Have you ever had a peel before?" the esthetician, Noreen, asked me when I arrived at Flawless Spa.

Truthfully, I hadn't. I usually opted for a deep cleansing facial or a microdermabrasion session, but apparently my safe spa ritual wasn't going to cut it. I needed to glow. I needed a chemical peel, and I wasn't going to get an effective one by getting a starter peel.

"No, but I have very thick skin."

She didn't look convinced, but nodded and led me toward the treatment rooms. "Okay, so here's how it works," she said once I was lying on the table, as she removed my makeup with a cotton swab. "There are twelve levels, so we start you off on the weakest level—level one. You won't feel a thing and it's so mild that you'll barely notice a difference. But what it does is build up a resilience in your skin. It's great because you'll get a nice fresh look but you won't peel at all. Then, in a few weeks you come back again, and we go up to the next level. And we continue like this until you are getting the results that you want. Sound good?"

Sound good? It sounded like it was going to be 2033 by the time I got a peel that made a difference. I needed glowing skin and I needed it now.

"So actually, I've had peels before," I said as she finished cleansing my skin. "I thought you meant here. This is my first time here. But I've had lots of peels. Lots and lots of them," I added for good measure. I could take the pain. I burned my forehead with my flat iron all the time and I barely flinched anymore.

Noreen looked at me skeptically. "Are you sure? Your skin looks very fair."

"Oh, it used to be so weathered," I lied. "Really dark and

tanned and leathery, but then I started getting peels and that's why it's so light now." That sounded *totally* legit.

"So what concentration are you up to?"

Oh, hmm . . . I couldn't very well say that I was already a twelve. That was just ridiculous. Maybe a six? That was right in the middle. But what if the first six were really very mild? I really didn't have time to come back for multiple sessions. I needed instant results. Maybe if I said seven . . .

"Eight," I said firmly.

"Eight?" Noreen shook her head. "The twelve-level system is unique to Flawless Spa. Which spa did you go to?"

"Oh, um . . . it was one in London when I was there," I lied.

"Hmm . . . Perhaps they had their own system. Do you recall how many levels they had in total? Or maybe you recall the acid percentage? For example, most start out with 20 percent and work their way up." She looked at me expectantly. Seriously—people were supposed to remember this stuff? This was more confusing than ever. I wasn't sure what to say. What if I said 80 but the peels went up to only 75 percent?

"How many peels have you had?"

I had a feeling I was losing Noreen's trust by the minute. We really just needed to settle on the percentage and get going. How hard was it to get glowing skin?

"About a dozen."

"Really?" But for some reason, instead of doubting me (as I would've expected—I mean, how many people have had twelve peels and can't recall the details of a single one?), Noreen seemed to believe me. Perhaps it was because she couldn't believe that someone who'd never had a peel before would have had any conceivable reason to lie about it.

Noreen said she didn't feel comfortable giving me a level eight, even if I really had had one before, but she prepped a level seven for my skin, and then began the procedure. As soon as she applied the first brush stroke of peel to my skin, I felt like I was on fire. By the time she'd applied the entire concoction to my face, it was as though I were running through a burning house, the flames melting my skin while I searched everywhere for an exit, or a corner without fire, so I could stop, drop and roll.

I thought I was going to die.

Teeth whitening had nothing on a level seven chemical peel.

Only I couldn't scream or Noreen would stop, and if I'd learned anything from my teeth whitening it was that, well, the pain would eventually subside.

"All done," Noreen said what seemed like an hour later, but was likely only two and a half minutes after she'd started.

"Um . . ." I said, as she walked away. Where was she going? "Don't you think you should take the peel off—or whatever you need to do?" I said through the burn.

"I've already neutralized it. You're all set to go."

All set to go? My face was still on fire. Wasn't the pain supposed to go away at the end of the two minutes when the peel stopped working?

"You're actually quite red," Noreen said when she flipped on the light. "Do you usually get this red after a session?" she asked with concern. I sat up and turned to face the mirrored wall. And stared in horror.

My face was fire-engine-red. As red as Sienna's nails. I was one bright red nail, minus the Swarovski crystal. Oh God. Why did I have to lie and say I'd had peels before?

"Do you have any cream?" I asked through the pain. It hurt to talk. Correction: it still hurt to talk. Except now, it was my face, not my teeth, inflicting the pain.

"Yes, of course. You probably shouldn't make any plans for a few days. You're going to need to stay indoors as the sun and wind will make the redness worse."

"When is it going to go away?"

"The redness will probably subside by tomorrow, and then you'll just be left with the peeling for the next week or so."

I started to cry.

"What's wrong?" Noreen asked.

The tears were hurting my cheeks.

"Do you want to lie down for a bit?" Noreen asked, concerned.

But I didn't have time to lie down. I had to get my butt in gear. Or rather, into cycling shorts, and then to a spinning class.

~

"I'd like to buy some cycling shorts," I told the sales guy at Duke's Cycle. I'd wrapped my scarf around my head in what I hoped was an Audrey Hepburn–inspired look as a way to partially cover and detract from my pomegranate-like skin tone, but I wasn't sure it was working. And the fabric against my skin, although silk, felt like hot coals against my face.

"You came to the right place," he said with a laugh, though I couldn't help wondering if he was laughing at my face as much as his own joke. "What's your pleasure? Castelli, Pearl Izumi, Sugoi, Nalini, Specialized, Louis Garneau, Giardana . . ."

I wasn't sure what he was naming. Cyclists? The only one I knew was the guy with the bracelets who'd dated Sheryl Crow. I tried to remember his name.

"Lance Armstrong?"

"Sure. We've got the Livestrong line."

I gave him a blank look.

"Are you doing indoor, outdoor or tri's?"

"Tri's?" I asked, confused.

"Triathlons," he said slowly, his eyebrows raised.

"Oh." I never understood people who spent their weekends working out. Like it was fun, rather than a means to an end. "Does it make a difference?"

"It affects the chamois and the thickness—mini, medi or maxi. I wouldn't suggest maxi if you're doing a tri. It'll just get soggy. Like a diaper."

"I'm just doing a spinning class."

He raised his eyebrows. "You don't need padding. The seats are already padded," he said. Which I probably would've known if I'd actually been to a spinning class more than once in my life. But I distinctly remembered the seat being rock hard. But I wasn't about to start arguing with him. And I wasn't about to go to a spin class without a padded bum. Period.

"I mean, I do spinning, but I also ride outside," I corrected him. "And my seat is really hard. So I'll take the maximum cushioning you have."

He gave me a funny look, but then turned to head to the back of the store. "Do you have something pink?" I asked as I followed him.

He handed me a pair of Pepto Bismol-coloured shorts and I took them into the change room. Not only did the word *Pirate* run down each leg in huge letters, but once I'd pulled them on and turned around to view myself in the mirror, I realized there was a skull on the butt. And the colour totally clashed with the hue of my peeled face. But then I noticed something else, and slowly turned back to examine my profile. I had a butt.

I actually had a butt.

The maxi padding was so thick it created a lovely round shape.

I pulled my black skirt over my shorts and turned back to the mirror, trying to keep my gaze away from my red face, which looked even darker red under the dim lighting in the change room.

I looked like a new woman. A voluptuous woman with a curvy, sexy ass.

Who needed spinning class when I could just wear padded shorts? I'd just saved myself an hour. Whoever said no pain, no gain had obviously never discovered the world of padded cycling shorts.

∼

I arrived home to find Parker sitting at the dining room table, which was strewn with photographs, various sheets of multicoloured papers in an array of sizes and shapes, scissors, tape and glue. Parker looked up.

"Are you *scrapbooking?*" I asked.

He looked at the table, then laughed, as though his kindergarten art class reenactment could be anything *other* than scrapbooking, then got up and came over to me, pulling me into a hug.

"Yeah, I guess I am." When he pulled away he studied my face. "Are you okay? You look flushed." His voice was full of concern.

"Just hot."

"Got that right," he said playfully and I made a face. Was my husband *flirting* with me? Parker had never called me *hot*. And rightly so, I supposed. I wasn't hot.

At least, not yet. Who knew? Maybe the peel was already working its magic.

"I have some news," Parker announced.

Oh God, I thought, pulling away from him. Sienna didn't take my advice. She went and told him everything. He knew about the affair. He was just buttering me up with compliments so he could tell me he was leaving. I looked past him to see if his suitcases were packed. My hands started to shake.

I didn't want him to leave. I wanted . . . what did I want? I wanted his memory of Sienna to be permanently lost and for him to never see her again. To tell me he loved me. Only me.

"I quit my job."

"What?"

This was not my husband. He didn't quit his job.

"But . . . why?"

"I realized when I was there today that it wasn't worth it. I just wasn't happy."

"You weren't?" This was news to me. Who worked seventy-hour work weeks by choice at a job they didn't like? More importantly, who decided this after only two days back on the job and then immediately took up scrapbooking? I eyed my pink glitter pen on the table.

"I don't know—it's just, ever since the accident, and staying home, I realized how much I like being at home."

"But you were only home for three days. It was like Easter. Without the eggs. Not reality."

"Exactly. And I can't remember the last time I had three days in a row at home. Think of all the things I could do."

"Are there things you want to do?" I asked, then bit my lip, realizing how callous that sounded. Of course there were things he wanted to do. It was all laid out on the table. I just wasn't aware of it until now.

"Of course there are things I want to do. I want . . . well, I want to have hobbies. Do you know that I don't have any hobbies?"

"Like scrapbooking?"

My husband wanted to be an artist. A starving artist who didn't actually create pictures, but just glued them into books with scraps of construction paper.

"Maybe. I don't know. But that's not all. I can cook and clean and do our laundry . . ."

Correction: My husband wanted to be a stay-at-home dad. Without the kids.

But we didn't need someone to cook—that was the joy of takeout. A ritual that was in danger of dying if he quit his job. And we had Tildy to do our cleaning. And the dry cleaners to do our laundry . . . It was just all so confusing.

I didn't know whether to be happy or worried. Because if he quit his job then he'd never see Sienna again, would he? Which meant he couldn't have suddenly remembered the affair. Because if he had—or if she'd told him—then surely he would've just kept his job so that he could continue to see her without me knowing. Having a job gave him all the work alibis in the world for missing dinners, working late, working weekends and getting phone calls from colleagues. It couldn't have been more perfect for having an affair.

So then why would he quit? Unless . . . what if the partners had confronted Parker about Sienna and told him that it was unprofessional and he'd have to voluntarily resign? Except, wouldn't they just make Sienna resign, since Parker was more senior? And was it even illegal to date a coworker? I knew that Uhma Rudimaker thought it improper, but really, her opinion was hardly scientific fact, was it? It was like trusting one of the doctors on *Grey's Anatomy* for medical advice.

Plus, if Parker didn't have a job, he'd have all the time in the world to cheat on me without meetings and files and spreadsheets to get in the way, and I'd have no way of knowing unless I, too, quit my job so I could stay home and spy on him. But then how would we pay the mortgage or have any money for food? We'd have to move out of our place and into some sort of subsidized housing project. This was a disaster.

I slumped down into one of the dining room chairs and stared at a picture of Parker and me on our wedding day. Everything had seemed so simple back then.

"Are you sure about this?" I asked Parker, feeling

drained. I was at a loss. He was my best friend. All I wanted to do was ask my best friend what the heck was going on, but of course, I couldn't.

He nodded. "I've never been more sure about anything. Except, of course, marrying you," he added. Which sounded positive, I supposed. In fact, it was exactly what I wanted to hear. I just wished I could believe him.

∿

There was just one problem with my theory that Parker quitting his job would ensure he never saw Sienna again. And that was that with hours of free time, he'd have nothing to stop him from seeing her whenever he wanted (especially if Sienna's work ethic was anything like her dating morals). I'd warned Sienna that dating a coworker wasn't ideal, but now that he was no longer a colleague, what was to stop Sienna from digging her fake nails into him, now that she had no reason not to?

Fake nails, I thought distractedly, looking at my own short nails, then added it—and a note to call Colin immediately to set up the date with Sienna—to my task list on my BlackBerry just as Parker rolled over and kissed me on the cheek the next morning.

Then he moved from my face down my neck and ran his hands over my butt and I squirmed away. I didn't want him to touch my butt without my secret padding, but obviously I couldn't wear my cycling shorts to bed.

"Are you okay?" he asked, pulling his hand away.

"Of course," I said, putting my BlackBerry on the nightstand. "Why?"

"It's just that ever since the accident . . . we haven't been very intimate."

Oh, that. It had only been five days. That wasn't unreasonable, even under normal circumstances.

And I just couldn't have sex. How could I bring myself to be intimate with him, knowing that the last person he'd had sex with was Sienna? I just couldn't get past that, not to mention the fear of being compared to her.

"I'm sorry," I said, leaning over to kiss his cheek. "I forgot to get my pill refilled and now Dr. Reidjik's on vacation. That's all."

"We could use a condom," he offered, and my mind instantly thought of the purple condom.

"Do we have to? You know I hate the feeling of latex. I thought you did too. Besides it'll just be a week or two until I can get my prescription refilled." A week or two would buy me some time to sort things out in my head. Although, if I was actually considering having sex with Parker, we were going to need a condom anyway. Because if he hadn't used a condom with Sienna . . .

My body felt numb.

Parker was silent for a moment, then turned over and propped himself up on his elbow and looked at me. "Actually, maybe it's a sign," he said and I turned to look at him, confused. Maybe *what* was a sign?

"You know what else I've been thinking?" he said, pulling me onto my side so he could spoon me. "We should have a baby." The alarm went off, but he reached back and shut it off, then nuzzled my neck, his unshaven chin scratching the back of my neck.

A *what?* I thought, as though the word were foreign.

"Wouldn't it be so great to have a little mini version of us?"

I couldn't breathe. I was glad I was facing the window and not him so that he couldn't see my face. It wasn't that I was opposed to babies. I liked them. I was godmother to Augusten, one of Elin and Terrence's triplets, and I liked buying him Thomas the Tank Engine and Diego toys, colouring books and stickers. But that was enough for me. It should've been enough for Parker, too, given he was the one who'd been so firm about *not* wanting to be a father for practically as long as I'd known him. Besides, a mini version of us would be . . . what? A cheater and a woman who was trying to turn herself into someone else?

"I just feel like our parents would be so happy. You know we're both their only chance to be grandparents."

Of course I knew that—we were both only children. But how was that *our* problem? If our parents wanted a better shot at being grandmas and grandpas they should've pumped out more kids themselves, I thought, pulling at a loose thread on the duvet cover.

"But you never wanted kids," I said, because unlike what I would think if I was watching a movie and this happened, we *did* talk about kids before marriage. Well before we were even seriously dating. Although I'd never really had an urge to be a mother, it was he who'd first broached the subject, on one of our first dates, saying that he wasn't looking to be a father. Ever. Sure, he was also a godparent to Augusten but it was by marriage default and he barely saw them since Elin was my friend and he never even wanted to come with me to Jackson's Point when I made the trek to visit her and the kids. Even during the holidays, he always made excuses not to attend friends' and coworkers' parties that he knew would involve dozens of kids running madly around the house. And he was always commenting how nice it was that we were both only children, so that whenever we went to visit his parents or mine, it was always quiet and peaceful.

You didn't say that if you secretly wished there were a gazillion kids running around screaming, did you?

"I never thought I'd have time for kids," he corrected me. "And I wouldn't want to bring a child into this world while working the kind of hours that I worked. But now that I'm staying home, it would be perfect. I would have time for them."

"I don't know what to say."

"Just say you won't get your pill refilled and we can just let things happen."

But I couldn't agree to that. Not yet. I turned over and pulled the covers closer to me.

I was sure that the baby talk was just a phase and that Parker would forget all about it, but just to be sure, before I left to see Ming about my nails later that morning, I flipped the TV on to *Jon & Kate Plus 8* in syndication. Look what happened to Jon and Kate—they used to be so happy. Is that what Parker wanted for his life? Although, to be fair I supposed their split had little to do with the kids. Still . . . maybe they would've been able to make their marriage work if they didn't have eight kids to take care of . . .

"I need fake nails," I said to Ming when I arrived at

Pretty Nail. I held out my hands. Ming looked up at me from the manicure station where she was sitting. She was wearing a camo T-shirt and cargo pants and had a green dust mask around her neck.

"Finally, you get pretty nails!" she said, her face lighting up. I thought she might start crying. Who knew that I hadn't been getting pretty nails from her all along? Still I wasn't convinced that long plastic nails were going to be prettier than my own natural ones. Especially when she got out the file to shave down my own nails so she could strap the acrylics on.

"What's wrong with your face?"

I looked in the mirror. I thought I'd done a fairly good job of covering up the remains of the redness with concealer, but I supposed I was still a bit flushed.

"Nothing," I said, mildly annoyed, then pulled out my BlackBerry. If Sienna wasn't going to agree to the date with Colin, I was going to have to figure out another way to entice her to meet him. I didn't know why, but I was clinging to the hope that he would distract her enough to make her forget all about attempting to continue what she and Parker had started.

But what? I thought as I scrolled through my emails. Then I stared at the screen. She'd replied.

Hi Uhma,

I'm not going to lie—I'm not really into setups and it seems weird coming from you. But your friend is super hot, and I Googled him and he seems normal enough (or at least well-connected enough that if he's crazy he'll have to pay). So sure, I'll meet him. Let me know what time and where.

Sienna

I couldn't believe it. I logged on to my Facebook account and sent her a message telling her to meet Colin at Roxy's in Kensington at 8:30. That would give me enough time to meet Colin first, make up an excuse to leave, yet ensure he stayed long enough to meet Sienna.

"Are you sure you can't just add gel to make them longer until I grow them?" I wasn't sure I wanted to ruin my own nails just to test a theory that Parker was attracted to fang-nails.

Ming looked at me as though I was crazy. "You could never grow your nails *that* long"—she pointed at a picture of a woman with nails so long they curled over the end of her fingers, and were spray-painted with a beach scene. She shook her head at me, as though I was a failure. Maybe I was, but there was no way I was getting nails that length—with any sort of a seaside scenario.

"Can you just make sure they're not that long?" I asked, as she affixed the first long nail to my finger.

Ming shook her head then leaned close to me. "Trust me, you're doing the right thing. When your husband sees your pretty nails, he'll forget all about skank he had boom-boom with." She nodded and pulled the mask up over her nose and mouth. So clearly she'd heard the whole conversation with Sienna's sister and her friend. Great, I thought, then chose a polish colour from the palette and slumped back in the chair to await my destiny: two-inch long, blood-red nails.

"You tell me if this works," Ming called after me as I left the salon. "If not, next time we do that." She pointed at the wall to a long nail with a butterfly decal.

I nodded. If this didn't work, though, I wasn't sure butterflies were going to save my marriage.

∿

Parker's cooking was *definitely* not going to save our marriage. He had gotten hold of one of those free calendars that come in the mail and was determined to "whip up each recipe in 20 minutes flat!" just like it promised. So while he channeled his inner Martha, I went into the bedroom to work on my outer Nigella. Although the cycling shorts were working out better than I ever could've hoped (my butt had gained at least a pound of curves), I'd had to try three different skirts this morning to find one long enough to cover the pink secret. Then I was off-balance, so I'd picked up a pair of bikini top inserts to stuff my bra (since obviously getting a boob job was slightly drastic, especially after Annabelle told me that I'd be laid up in bed for weeks while Parker would be forced to change the dressings on my oozing boobs, which didn't sound at all sexy).

After slipping the inserts into my bra, I went back to the kitchen. Parker told me to have a seat on one of the stools at the counter—and I did, realizing my hidden padding, though initially for cosmetic reasons, was functional, too—and I watched as he started to spoon out some sort of cream of mushroom soup–based creation from a pot onto one of our white-and-silver china plates. He looked down at it and frowned.

"Could you get me a couple of bowls instead?" he asked. I got up and went around to the other side of the counter and opened the cupboard. But as I went to lift up a bowl, I realized that my red claws were in the way. How on earth did people do anything with these things on?

"Do you have one?" Parker said a little impatiently as I dug all ten nails under the edges and came up with two bowls. I carried them over to him and set them on the counter in front of Parker, then peered at the runny mixture on the counter. "I guess it's more of a stew than a casserole," he said. "Can you hold one of the bowls up?" He dumped the contents from the plate into one of the bowls.

He eyed my hands. "Are you wearing fake nails?" As though it wasn't clear that my nails had not just grown two inches overnight.

"Mmm-hmm," I said, as sexily as I could. I set the second bowl on the counter and ran my nails down his back, something I never would've been able to do before, thinking maybe I could get used to having long nails, after all. Parker squirmed away.

"Could you not do that?" he said, sounding a bit put off.

"You don't like having your back scratched?"

I wondered if Sienna scratched his back, but the thought of her touching him—even if it was through his shirt, made me feel ill.

"They're kind of tacky." He turned to look at me. "I didn't think you were a fake nails kind of girl."

I'm not, I wanted to say. *But see what I'm doing for you?*

"I thought you'd like the look," I said instead and leaned over the pot to inspect our dinner.

"Hmmm," he said. I wasn't sure how to interpret that. "Well, I'm not really into them. One of the women in my office had them and I found them just so loud and clackety whenever she was typing and well, they just sort of freak me out."

I pulled my hands back and stuffed them in the pockets of my skirt, slightly annoyed. That was just great. I'd gone to all the trouble to get stupid fake nails that I didn't even like, and neither did Parker. I couldn't understand it—was he talking about Sienna? And if he was, why would he have sex with someone who did something that freaked him out? I assumed he'd liked everything about her: hair, face, clothes, shoes. Even nails. It was the whole package. Otherwise, you moved on. At least, that was the way I'd always looked at a relationship, and of course Parker was the same or we wouldn't be together. He'd never mentioned anything he didn't like about me, and vice versa. So if Sienna hadn't been perfect for him, why would he have cheated on me with her?

I wiped the thought from my mind. Obviously he hadn't been talking about Sienna. There were probably a dozen women in his office with fake nails. Besides, maybe *her* nails hadn't bothered him.

"So what did you do today?" I asked, changing the subject as he ladled the now-soup into his bowl.

"Sketching," he said, pointing at the dining room table. I walked over to look, worried that he was going to turn into one of those Parkdale artists who chose weird media, like crayons or soap. In which case he was going to run the risk of being a starving artist, and I was just going to be starving by association. I picked up a piece of eight by twelve paper with a drawing—in what appeared to be regular pencil lead—of the view from our apartment, overlooking the neighbourhood. It was actually quite good. I was surprised.

"This is really good," I said reluctantly, because as much as I thought he did have talent, I didn't really want to make a big deal about it. This *art* was the reason we were about to eat the March recipe of the month for dinner. "I didn't know you had such a talent."

Parker looked at me quizzically. "I used to draw you little pictures on coasters, remember?" he said, and I did remember. It just felt so long ago. "I know, but those were just little. I couldn't tell anything. And that was before."

"Before?"

"You know, before we had our real jobs."

He nodded, and for a moment he looked like he wanted to say something, but then changed his mind. We sat down at the counter with our bowls of mushroom soup. I took a sip, expecting the worst, but it wasn't actually that bad. It wasn't great, but it wasn't terrible.

"Do you like it?" he asked hopefully.

I nodded. "Of course."

He smiled and took a spoonful, then swore.

"What?"

"Ugh, there's something hard in here." He grimaced. I wanted to say that I found that surprising, since this was pretty much a puree, but I bit my lip as he pulled something red from his mouth.

I looked in horror and then down at my hands. I only had nine nails.

"Nice," Parker said, then threw the nail on the counter. "I guess that's the end of my dinner. Aren't those nails attached with toxic glue?" He took a sip of water then spit it out in the sink. "What a complete waste."

I felt terrible and mortified, but part of me wanted to say, *Don't blame me! I'm doing this for you!* But I didn't. Because it wasn't his fault my nail ended up in his soup.

"You can have mine," I said, pushing the bowl toward him.

"Forget it. I've lost my appetite."

"You know, you don't have to make dinner every night. If you want to spend more time drawing or painting or whatever, we can just order in," I said, looking down at my bowl as though I was the most selfless person in the world and was only thinking of him. Because with a choice between him doing something he loved or slaving over the stove to make Mushroom Mush, I supposed I could put up with our dining room table being turned into an art station.

"I thought you'd appreciate it."

I shook my head. There was no way I was winning this argument.

chapter seven

U nfortunately, sketching, cooking and cleaning—
another hobby Parker had taken up in the past few
days—had not taken his mind off his grandiose
plan to spread his seed because on Thursday morning as I
was getting out of the shower he handed me a pill.

"Folic acid. You'll need it if we're going to get pregnant," he said, as though he were handing me an ecstasy
pill and telling me I'd need it if I wanted to see everything
in magical multicolour.

I hid the pill under my tongue as though it were an
anti-psychotic drug that I'd later spit out, then realized
how ridiculous I was being and swallowed it dry. It wasn't
as though the folic acid would make me pregnant, but
as Parker edged closer to me, I realized that he, at any
minute, could. I tightened my towel around me and made
a dash into my walk-in closet.

When I emerged, fully dressed in record time, he was
in the living room, using the Swiffer to catch a cobweb in

the corner of the ceiling, and it suddenly dawned on me: he was nesting.

"I couldn't sleep last night," he said as I put on my shoes. "I kept thinking about being a dad."

I wanted to tell him I couldn't sleep either for the very same reason, except mine was dread, not happy excitement, but I didn't. How could I say that to him?

"I guess we'd have to get used to sleepless nights," I said logically, instead. "It might seem more like a nightmare than a lovely dream after the 356th sleepless night in a row." But inside I felt like a horrible human being. What kind of woman didn't want kids?

I didn't. And Parker knew that. So why was he bringing it up again?

"I meant it in a good way. A happy way," he said, shaking his head. I felt terrible. Suddenly I wanted to kiss him, and apologize, but he turned away and went back to cleaning.

I said goodbye but Parker just ignored me. I had an early appointment with Rennie Houpt, a homely girl whose mother had given her the gift of my services for her birthday (secretly hoping to get her married off before the age of thirty). While she led me to her bedroom in her tiny second-floor Queen West apartment, I asked her if she and her boyfriend had talked about kids.

"Oh yes," she said, her glum voice—which we were totally going to have to work on as it was depressing just to listen to her—raised half an octave. "We can't wait to have them. Lots of them."

See? This was what couples did. It was in all those relationship books. They confirmed the details of the contract while dating, and then neither of them broke the contracts. Only, Parker was breaking one of the sections of the contract. Which, come to think about it, made two sections that he was breaking: adultery *and* parenting.

I knew I should've been a lawyer.

"So are you supposed to be *doing* something?" Rennie asked, interrupting my thoughts as I stared into space while sitting on the edge of her bed. Oh, right.

I snapped to and stood up.

"Let's take a look at your closet, for starters."

She opened the door to a tiny closet.

"So, what are your goals?"

"Well, I guess my mother's goal is for me to look prettier. But honestly, I'm happy with the way I look. I guess I could get a haircut. Or, maybe a new twin set?"

A twin set was her goal? Oh no. I felt an intervention coming on.

"Well, your mother seems worried that your boyfriend's not going to ask you to marry him."

"We've only been dating for six months. I don't know what she's worried about."

Oh, I didn't know that. Six months wasn't very long at all. But I had to say something. That's what I was getting paid to do.

"Still, when you know you know . . ." I said in a warning tone.

Rennie looked uncertain.

"You want to secure him before a younger model comes along." *Or an older model.*

Rennie shook her head, her long brown ponytail swinging behind her. "Oh, Eddie's not into models."

I rolled my eyes. "I didn't mean an *actual* model. It was a figure of speech."

"Oh, good." Relief washed over Rennie's face. "Because once, we were in the mall, and there was one of those Glamour Shots booths, and he totally made fun of it."

This was going to be more difficult than I thought. Except, I always had a backup plan I saved for resistant clients like Rennie. It was really the only thing that worked. Because the problem with this type of client was that they were so sure of themselves and stuck in their ways that the only way to shake them loose was to show them that they were wrong. And to do that I used a little trick I called The Insecurity Check.

I shook my head and looked at her with shock, as though I was alarmed by what she'd just revealed. "Oh no," I said worriedly.

Rennie looked suitably alarmed. "What?"

I bit my lip. "It's classic contradiction. He's revealing something that he secretly likes by making fun of it."

Rennie looked doubtful. "I really don't think so."

I nodded. "Remember the fourth grade, when the boys used to pick on the girls they liked? Pull their hair? Call them names? Snap their bra straps?" Okay so maybe that last part didn't happen in the fourth grade, but whatever.

Rennie nodded slowly. The Insecurity Check was working like a charm, just like it always did.

I nodded too, and stared at her. The trick was to let her come to the realization herself. Then she'd be begging for me to help.

"So . . . you think that Eddie actually likes those made-up girls?"

I shrugged. "You tell me. You're the one who knows him so well that you think you're ready to marry him," I teased.

"But he's always saying how he loves how natural I am and how he never has to wait for me to get ready."

"So you're basically like his college roommate," I said, nodding. "Which is fine, if that's what you're happy with being for the rest of your life. But do you want to be a roommate or a wife?"

Rennie looked down at herself and back up at me. In baggy jean capris and a white T-shirt that was two sizes too big, her fine facial features untouched by makeup and her slightly wavy, slightly frizzy, long brown hair pulled back in a ponytail, she looked exactly how I imagined she looked in the eighth grade. She just hadn't progressed, and a part of me felt terrible for suggesting she needed to. I watched her as she pondered my question.

"A wife," she finally declared, though not convincingly, but I tried to get her excited. Maybe all she needed was some excitement in her life.

I clapped my hands together. "Excellent. Then here's what we have to do."

Two hours later, we'd cleaned house on Rennie's closet, keeping only her cutest (or in her words, most uncomfortable) items. I'd given her a list of tasks for the week, which included but was not limited to selecting three items from the most recent issue of *InStyle* that she wanted to add to her wardrobe, finding two new hairstyles in the hair magazine I'd left behind, deciding on one new form of exercise she wanted to add to her daily routine, eliminating phrases like "Sure" and "Whatever you want to do" and

"It doesn't matter to me" from her repertoire, coming up with a list of ten girlified reasons for not being able to watch any movie that had *Kung*, *Fight* or *Space* in the title and compiling a list of excuses, which she would use once a week to deny Eddie a date with her. Things like getting her hair straightened, going to Pilates class, or having a phone check-in with her image therapist (aka, me). "You need to make Eddie work for your attention," I explained to her. "Otherwise, he's just going to get comfortable. You need to make him realize how special you are, and how different you are from his guy friends. Otherwise, he'll just keep on making you watch sports and guy movies with him, thinking that's what you *want* to do. And then how are you different from his guy friends?" I folded my arms across my chest. "You're not. So why would he ask you to marry him?"

She didn't seem convinced, but I continued with my theory that if you limit a guy's guy-tendencies, he'll become sensitive to your girl-tendencies and wants, such as getting married. And he'll know that if he does something for you (aka propose) then you will do something for him (aka let them have guys' night in with beer and Fritos and other totally unclassy accoutrements).

Finally I mentioned a few key tricks when she *was* over at Eddie's, including spritzing his sheets with her perfume or leaving a piece of lingerie "by mistake."

"But I don't wear lingerie."

"You should start. Make him buy it for you."

"I would never make him do that," Rennie said. I actually agreed with her—I couldn't stand girls who made their boyfriends buy them things they could and *should* be buying themselves with their own money. But if Rennie's current behaviour wasn't getting her boyfriend to commit, then she needed to stop being the nice, cotton-underwear-wearing girl and start being a bit more of a princess.

"Well, you should start," I replied, then waved goodbye. She gave me a pained look as she stood in the doorway, wearing my floral Betsey Johnson wedges (as a trial run before she bought her own pair). I promised her that the pain was worth it. Because even if she didn't love the shoes this minute, they pulled her look together.

As I left her building, I looked down at my own Marc Jacobs ballet flats, which I always carried in my handbag in case of a blister or other emergency. Suddenly the flats seemed all wrong, though. Walking east on Queen, I stopped in front of Shoe Envy and eyed the purple pleather platform stilettos and red snakeskin shoes with metal spikes.

What I needed were Sienna shoes.

I stepped inside the store and asked a goth-like teen if he could bring me a pair of the purple pleather shoes.

"It's self serve," he grumbled, then twisted his lip ring.

I found a pair in my size and slipped them on, then walked over to a mirror. Maybe this was all I needed to transform my look.

Maybe not. My feet were sweating from the plastic insoles and the colour was highlighting the veins in my legs.

I sat down and pulled off one shoe, eyeing a slightly more subdued version of the shoe in black. Which still didn't solve the sweating issue.

"Just put baby powder in them," the sales guy said to me knowingly.

"I don't suppose you have anything with a leather lining, do you?"

He laughed. I didn't realize it was a joke.

I handed him the shoes and he took them to the counter. "Do you want the box?" he asked.

"Actually I'll just wear them home," I said, walking over to the register in my bare feet. I slipped my ballet flats back in my handbag while he rung up the black stilettos. I might as well break them in if I was going to start wearing these kind of shoes, I thought. I had a feeling, though, that this makeover was going to give me bunions before I knew it.

I shoved on my new shoes and left the store. I felt silly, but as I walked the few blocks to the nearest Starbucks, I passed a Sienna-lookalike wearing the exact same shoes in cranberry, and knew I was doing the right thing. Even if I looked like a prostitute.

Except I didn't really feel any better. The baby situation was still plaguing me. I knew I could call Elin, but she'd just tell me to get pregnant and move out to Jackson's Point. Instead, I decided to call my mom once I'd ordered my latte.

"Are you upset I haven't given you a grandchild yet?" I said when she answered. She hollered something at my father, then came back on the line.

"What are you talking about?" she said. "It's not too late."

I knew it wasn't too late. "I know. I was just wondering." I pulled out a stool at the bar by the window and sat down.

"I can't make that decision for you. It's a new era. And

if you don't want to have kids, that's your choice, honey-bunch. You know I'll love you no matter what. Besides, you have loads of time to have a baby. Geena Davis was forty-eight when she got pregnant."

My mother knew this because *Thelma and Louise* was her favourite movie. The year it came out, she made my father dress up as Louise for Halloween, just so she could dress up as Thelma.

"Don't feel you have to have one right away, like your father and I did."

Obviously I'd already passed the point of getting accidentally pregnant and having to get married, the way my mother had, so I wasn't worried about that. And I didn't really want to think about whether she was saying that she wouldn't have had me if she hadn't gotten knocked up. Besides, she was an amazing mom. She didn't work while I was growing up so that she could spend as much time with me as possible. She made me homemade lunches every day. She threw the best birthday parties—always a theme with coordinating prizes for every girl in my class: pink tutus at the Ballerina Ball, a Caboodles kit at my Sweet Valley Twins party, and instead of ever saying that she had only one child because she never even wanted one in the first place, she always said I was an only child because she didn't want to take any of the love she gave to me away to give to another. She even taught me (apparently) to make chicken noodle soup. She was the ideal mom. And maybe that was exactly the reason I didn't want to be one. I wouldn't live up.

It was like badminton in the seventh grade all over again. I was incredibly uncoordinated and didn't like sports anyway, but everyone knew that no one cool played badminton—not just at our school, but at any school. They had to recruit hard, getting girls who hadn't made the tennis or lacrosse teams to try out. And the year I entered junior high, the country-wide championship was being held in Orlando. Despite my loathing for getting sweaty in public, there was a high probability I'd be able to convince my parents to take me to Disney World afterward.

Only six people tried out for the team, including me. I knew I was terrible and it was confirmed when I missed nearly every birdie that came my way.

Swing. Miss. Pick up the birdie. Swing. Miss. Pick up the birdie.

Five girls were chosen for the team. I was the only one who wasn't, even though on the senior team, all seven girls who tried out made the club.

I was *that* terrible. It was mortifying. After that, I decided to never try anything that I knew I wasn't good at, or even suspected I *might* not be good at, ever again.

Now I was hardwired to that rule. And so, somewhere along the line, without me even noticing, motherhood had entered that category.

"So when are you coming to visit?" my mother said, as she always did whenever we spoke.

"Soon," I told her, as I always did, whether it was true or not. I loved going to my parents' cottage-turned-home, but I knew Parker didn't. He hated being out of the city, especially at my parents' place, where cellphone reception was spotty at best. I didn't blame him—his own parents' idea of getting out of the city was jetsetting to another one. From Beijing to London and Paris to Rome. He wasn't used to sitting on a dock, staring into space, listening to loons. And so I didn't push him to go, except for long weekends and holidays, because I didn't want to make him do something he didn't want to do.

After saying goodbye, I put my phone in my handbag and started walking again. I felt like a disappointment, not only to Parker but also to my parents, even if my mom *had* insisted she didn't care whether I had a baby or not.

A few blocks later, however, as I passed a woman pushing a Shih Tzu in a baby stroller, I got an idea. I would buy Parker a dog. I was always flipping past articles in magazines that advised getting a dog first before having a baby because even though it's not totally the same thing, it would show you just how much responsibility being a parent really was. Walking the dog a million times a day was just like changing the baby. And getting up in the middle of the night to let the dog out to pee was just like waking up every time the baby cried while you were trying to sleep. It was something you had to consider when you just wanted to go to a movie or meet friends for drinks after work.

It was perfect. Parker wanted a baby. I'd get him a dog. I practically skipped to the Humane Society. Except it was in the east end and I was still on Queen West in plastic shoes that were already pinching my feet, so instead, I hopped on the streetcar.

Inside the Humane Society, the woman behind the desk handed me a questionnaire.

I took it and sat down in the reception area. It was four pages long and filled with questions such as:

How long have you wanted a pet?

I could hardly write *Twenty minutes,* could I?

As long as I can remember, I wrote. Which was sort of

the truth, and besides, I thought it sounded particularly heartwarming.

Did you have any pets growing up?

Aha! I could write we had a dog. Which wasn't exactly true—my dad had just gotten Donner last Christmas, but he was always referring to him as my little brother, and if my parents had suddenly decided to have another child last year he'd be just as much my brother now as he would've been had they had him only a few years after I was born. So why couldn't the same theory apply to my brother, the dog? Besides, I still saw him all the time. When I was at my parents' place, anyway, which was all the time. Or like, every other month. Actually come to think of it, the last time I saw Donner he was just a puppy.

My parents got a puppy one Christmas.

Which was totally true, even if I wasn't saying which Christmas or that it wasn't really for me but for them to compensate for the lack of grandchildren, or whatever.

Finally, I finished the questionnaire and then the coordinator, Shelley, took me into the back to look at the dogs. To be honest, since I didn't actually want a dog, I hadn't really considered this aspect—the whole choosing the dog part—although I'm not sure what I expected: that they would just hand me a dog and a bag of kibble and I'd be on my way? (Actually, maybe that is what I expected.) Anyway, it didn't matter because I totally had a plan. After I took the dog home and Parker saw how much work it was, we'd have one of those movie-like scenes that went something like this:

Poppy (in a totally understanding and not at all condescending tone): Honey, if you think a dog is a lot of work,

*imagine what a baby would be like. And you said you wanted
to be the stay-at-home dad? Are you really sure? Because we
can give the dog back, but we can't give a baby back.*

*Parker (looking forlorn): Really? Do you think we could
give the dog back?*

*Poppy (nodding, eyes downcast at the dog, who would be
tearing up the area rug, which would be a totally crap carpet
that she'd have secretly swapped for their good rug, so that
Parker would feel bad but Poppy wouldn't lose her composure at the sight of her perfect rug being destroyed): I'll see
what I can do. But I think we've both learned a lesson here,
haven't we?*

(Cue anthemic music)

And then, of course, Parker would agree and thank me
for being such an understanding, caring wife, and never
bring up the baby thing again.

Which was why it totally didn't matter what the dog
looked like.

"Are you looking for a puppy or a full-size dog?" Shelley
asked, interrupting my movie-of-the-week moment.

"Which would you recommend?"

"Well a puppy is a lot of work—"

Perfect! "A lot of work" was exactly what I had to give
Parker to make him see how wrong he was to think having
a baby was a decision you made over orange juice.

"But the adult dogs we get here are often abused or
abandoned, so they can actually be a lot more work, and
harder to train. You know the saying—you can't teach an
old dog . . . And there are so many adult dogs, so it's actually easier to get one. Everyone wants puppies, of course,"
she said knowingly.

An old dog! That would be perfect! Especially if he was sort of dirty. That would be just like a baby!

"I'll take the oldest dog you have," I told her.

She looked at me in surprise.

"I have a soft spot for old fellas," I added. She smiled and led me over to a cage in the corner.

"This is Bartie."

I looked at Bartie. He was asleep. He didn't look like much trouble at all, to be honest. Maybe the oldest dog in the place wasn't the way to go. He'd probably just sleep all day and be pleasant and lovely and we'd get attached to him and what good would that be?

"Um . . ."

But Shelley was already unlocking his cage and before I knew it Bartie was bright eyed and drooling and walking along beside us as Shelley led me into another room.

"He's a Heinz 57—a mixed breed, but that's a good thing because he hasn't had any health problems," she said, patting Bartie on the head. "Now, we're just going to need to do a few reference checks. Namely, to your neighbours, who will be able to tell us how much time you spend at home, at work, travelling. Then to your parents, just to talk about your responsibilities with raising your childhood dog, and finally, we'll have to do a police check and then get a five-year commitment for the adoption of Bartie here."

What? They were going to call my parents and my neighbours? And not to be rude, but Bartie didn't look like he was going to live another five years. What happened if he died under our watch? Would I go to jail or be forced to take in another dog? And anyway, what happened to returning him in a week?

"Sorry, how long will all of that take? I mean, you brought Barney out here. I just assumed I would be taking him home today. I'm really excited," I added for good measure.

"Bartie," she corrected me. "I brought him out so that you could bond with him while we chatted. About the process."

Oh. Oops. I patted Bartie on the head, to show my ability to bond.

"So, right, how long will it take?" I asked again.

"A few weeks, maybe more, depending on how difficult it is to get through to all your references. We work with mostly volunteers here, you know," she said.

"Sorry, I thought these dogs were in need of homes, and this seems like an awfully long process. Why is it so difficult to rent a dog?"

"Rent?" she said, her eyebrows shooting up.

"I meant buy."

"Adopt," she clarified.

Oh, right.

"The process also allows time to ensure that you're positive about getting a dog. A pet is a big responsibility. You can't just give him back if you change your mind."

This was not going according to plan—the whole *point* was to give him back in a week. I sighed and sat down in a nearby chair. My feet were killing me from the ridiculous shoes.

Shelley noticed my distress. "If you're not sure, maybe you should consider volunteering. What some people do is come here twice a week and walk a couple of dogs. Get to know them. That way they're helping us, but they're also seeing which dog they best connect with. You might want to consider it. All we require is a commitment of six months, twice a week for two hours at a time."

Four hours a week? I didn't have four hours a week for six months. Besides, I didn't *want* a dog. I didn't even *like* dogs that much. Although, as I looked down at Bartie, he *was* pretty cute. But maybe I could sign Parker up to walk the dogs! That would keep him busy, *and* in the city. "Could I volunteer my husband instead?"

Shelley looked at me in alarm. "Does your husband *want* to volunteer?"

He will when I tell him, I thought.

"Why don't you go home and talk everything over with your husband?" she said.

I totally wasn't getting the dog, even if I wanted him.

"We just want to make sure that the owners have thought about this. That they love dogs. That they will love the dog forever and ever."

Okay, she didn't have to rub it in. I got it. It was sort of like a wedding vow. And how could I possibly vow to love the dog forever and ever, especially on Parker's behalf? He'd said our wedding vows and look what had happened with that. We didn't exactly have a stellar record on the whole vow front.

"I guess I better go." I stood up, patted Bartie one last time, and headed outside.

Now what? I thought as I walked back to the streetcar stop. I was back to square one.

And then I had an idea.

I quickly punched Colin's phone number into my BlackBerry.

"Pop Music!" he said, using the nickname he'd given me years before. "What's going on? You're not calling to cancel on me, are you? Because I'm really looking forward to our date."

"You are?" I said, suddenly flustered. I was sure my face was flushed (and not from the effects of the peel. The redness had subsided, but now, as Gretel had promised, the top layers of skin were peeling unattractively and exposing new skin, so my face still stung slightly) and I was glad he couldn't see me. Get down to business, I told myself. I always felt more in control of my emotions when I micromanaged a situation. "No, I'm not cancelling. But I remember you said you were heading out of town next week and were looking for a dog-sitter."

"That's right," he said with a half-laugh. "I leave Sunday morning for Whistler to shoot a segment for the show. I'm surprised you remembered. Why, you want to come with me?"

"Actually, I was thinking that I could take care of Ruff for you while you're gone," I told him and then launched into what I considered to be a very convincing soliloquy about my love for dogs and how in my spare time I like to dog-walk, dog-sit or even dog-visit the strays at the Humane Society.

"That's so selfless," he said with surprise—so much surprise, in fact, that I wondered if he knew me better than I thought.

"I know," I agreed. Obviously, I was clearly too selfish to volunteer my time to anything, I thought. But perhaps this good deed would help me make up for it. Although looking after Ruff was actually a self-serving venture to convince Parker he most certainly did not want a baby, which meant it wasn't selfless at all. God, I was infuriating. "So what do you say?"

"Well, if you're going to take care of him, you should probably call him Ralph not Ruff, since that's his name. Otherwise he might not listen to you," he corrected me with a laugh. "Though Ruff is more amusing."

"Oh. Oops." When you're trying to convince someone you love dogs, you should try to get their dog's name right. "So what do you think?"

"I think I don't know what I did to deserve this, but now I owe you dinner, too."

"Of course you don't. Like I said, I want to do this. You'd be helping me," I added, thinking of Sienna.

"Really? Well it would be amazing. So I'll just bring Ralph with me on Saturday to Roxy's and tie him up outside the patio while we catch up."

"Perfect."

∿

When I got home, Parker was already in bed. I decided to leave on my oh-so-sexy black shoes and head right to the bedroom. I knew I couldn't hold back from Parker forever. And the last thing I wanted to do was deprive him of sex until he got so horny he had a Sienna flashback and called her up, especially if he saw my plastic shoes in the closet. I climbed onto the bed beside him. He was reading *1000 Things to Do Before You Die*.

I looked over his shoulder to the page on Vietnam. I

nuzzled his ear and he looked at me and smiled. "I know we have a rule about taking our shoes off in the living room, but do we not have one about taking them off in bed?" he asked, bemused.

He was right—I was getting my pretty bedspread dirty. I sat up and pulled off one of my plastic shoes and stared in horror. My feet looked like I'd just taken a foot bath in charcoal.

I shoved them under the covers, then wriggled out of my clothes. Parker watched me with amused interest, as though I were a seal performing tricks at SeaWorld, then informed me he was heading to a baseball game the following afternoon and then out for drinks with the guys from work.

"But you hate sporting events," I said, as though it were written in the Parker Manual. I turned off the light on my night table. He shuffled over and slung an arm over me.

"You thought I bought season tickets to the Raptors for the past seven years because I hate sports?"

"That was different. I thought Ray pressured you into that."

"Ray didn't pressure me into anything. I *liked* going to the games with Ray."

I'd never really considered that Ray moving away might be a big deal for Parker. Sure, they'd been friends since high school, but they were complete opposites. Ray was a guy's guy, who worked in IT for one of the banks, effectively spending his days in front of a computer, and his nights playing online poker. They rarely saw each other except for the Raptors games. They'd shared season tickets for years, though I had no idea why. I just assumed it was one of those ruts people got into and didn't know how to get out of.

"So you remembered that he moved away?"

"You told me, remember? Besides, I called him the other day. I was thinking we should go visit him."

"We should?"

"Why not? We've never been to Vietnam. It would be fun."

"It would?"

I sounded like a parrot but I was flummoxed. Five years ago, I'd been the one who'd suggested it would be fun, and he'd shot it down.

"You didn't want to go with Elin and Geoff," I said, though it was petty.

"Elin and Geoff? That was ages ago. Besides, I'm saying I want to go now."

I wasn't sure why, but I felt betrayed and annoyed that when I'd suggested the idea, he didn't want to do it, so we didn't. But now that he did, I was suddenly supposed to find time to see a country I'd decided I didn't want to see either?

"I just don't think I have the time for that kind of trip. We'd need at least three weeks to do it properly."

"We should make the time." Parker's voice was a mix of angst and urgency.

"So what did you tell Ray?"

"Nothing. It was just a thought I had. Anyway, it was good to catch up with him. It brought everything back."

Everything? My heart fluttered. What had he remembered?

"So the game tomorrow. Do you want to come? It'll be fun."

I knew I should probably say yes. That somewhere in the Manual for What to Do When Your Husband Has Had an Affair and Been Struck by Lightning, it probably said you should throw him a bone and do things he wants to do every once in a while, but I seriously doubted my going to a baseball game was going to make him love me more. I was a terrible date at sporting events. I lacked a sports brain and the will to eat mystery-meat hot dogs and drink Miller Lites.

"I have a hair appointment." Which was the truth. And even if I thought the game would be fun—which I was certain it wouldn't be, since I didn't like sports—I didn't have time for fun. There were still so many things I needed to do if I was going to make myself into the woman he wanted me to be.

"All afternoon?"

To be honest, it likely would take all *day* if I was going to transform my own bird-like locks into Sienna's swishy raven-coloured waves. But I couldn't tell him that.

"I have to work, too, you know." Which was true. I really should have been working more than I was, but Sienna-fying myself was causing me to cancel appointments on a near-daily basis. "I'm not retired, like you."

"I'm not *retired*. I'm just taking some time off to enjoy life. You should do it too. Then we could enjoy each other . . ."

I couldn't help thinking, *Or what? Or you'll enjoy Sienna instead of me?* But I had to push that thought out of my mind. Parker wasn't going to see Sienna again unless Sienna contacted him, and as soon as she met Colin, who I was sure was going to be perfect for her, she would forget all about Parker. I was sure of it. Or at least hopeful.

"Come here," he said, sliding his hand around my waist and pulling me toward him, but I tensed up.

"I'm tired," I said, and for once it wasn't just an excuse. I was tired. I was exhausted from changing who I was in an attempt to be more like Parker's ideal. And I was barely halfway there.

"Big surprise," Parker grumbled and I wanted to point out that I was the one working full-time while he scrapbooked and became the next Rachael Ray, but I didn't.

"Don't move!" Parker said suddenly.

"What? What is it?" I flipped over to face him.

Parker rummaged his hand around between the sheets and then pulled his arm out from under the covers.

I screamed. "Oh my God. Is it a cockroach?" I grabbed the duvet cover tight to my chin and wiggled away from him.

He rolled over, flipped on the light and rolled back. We both stared at the long, smooth, red thing in his hand.

"What is it?" I said, aghast. It wasn't a cockroach, thank God.

"I believe this is yours?" he said, laughing.

It was another fake nail. I looked down at my hands and saw that not only was I missing the one in Parker's hand and the one that had landed in the Mushroom Mush, but somehow two more had gone missing.

He handed me the nail and chuckled. This was hardly

the sexy reaction I was aiming for. "It's like a scavenger hunt," he said. "You're like the Easter Bunny."

I groaned and rolled over. If I was going to be a bunny, I wanted to be a Playboy Bunny, not a furry white rodent with whiskers.

"Good night," I mumbled into the duvet cover and shut my eyes.

chapter eight

" Are you sure you don't want to come?" Parker asked on Saturday morning as I was getting ready to head out the door.

"I don't want to be the only girl with a bunch of guys," I said. I kissed him quickly on the cheek and picked up my handbag.

"It's not just going to be guys," Parker said, opening the door for me. I stopped and turned.

"It's not?" I asked, apprehensively.

He shrugged. "Anyone from the office can come."

Don't ask if Sienna's going to be there. Don't draw attention to her. Just smile, nod and walk out the door. You can pretend it's fine. You're an actor, remember, Uhma. Exit stage left. Exit. Now.

"Will S—" Oh God. What was I doing? "Steve Nash. Will he be playing?"

Parker looked at me like I'd just gotten hit in the head

with a baseball. "Probably not. Since Steve Nash plays basketball, not baseball." He gave me a smile.

"Right!" I snapped my fingers. "Well, have fun!" I gave a little wave with my raised hand and rushed out the door.

I had to find out. I dialed Sienna's number as soon as I was safely out on the street.

She answered on the first ring.

"Hi, Sienna. It's Uhma."

"Oh . . . hi there. What's up?" she said lightly.

"I was just wondering . . ." Oh God. What was I going to say? I couldn't very well just blurt out *Are you going to the baseball game with my husband?*, could I? Because of course, Uhma didn't have a husband. I needed to have a real invitation of my own so that I didn't sound like a crazy woman, and then, if she was going to the game, she could just say, "Sorry, I'm going to the baseball game with your husband and I'm going to swap spit with him, so there." Only, of course, she wouldn't call him my husband.

"I just wanted to check that you're still good for tonight?"

"Yep. Eight thirty, right?"

I confirmed the time but then went silent. I needed to invite her to something. Anything. But what? And it couldn't be anything good, because what if it sounded so good that she actually wanted to go? Then what? Perhaps I should've thought through my call before madly dialling her number.

"Sorry?" Sienna said. "I think you're cutting out. I can't hear anything."

That's because I'm crazy and I'm not talking. Say something. Say. Something.

"I'm . . . having a roundtable discussion this afternoon with a bunch of accident victims and I thought you might want to come."

Good one, Uhma. Who on earth would want to come to that on a sunny Saturday afternoon? Uhma really was a bore.

"Oh, that's so sweet of you to offer," Sienna said, and I could tell in her voice that even if she could not think of a single other thing to do this afternoon she was about to make up something, anything, just so she wouldn't have to hang out with me. And could I really blame her?

"But I actually have plans."

She had plans. I just had to ask. "So what are you up to?"

"Oh, just going to a baseball game."

She was going. She would be there, sitting in her too-tight top and too-tight jeans in a seat that was far too close to my husband. The only saving grace was that there was no way she'd have time for drinks and dinner and sex before meeting Colin. Was there?

Maybe I could go to the game. And make sure they got nowhere near each other. But of course I couldn't. Everyone at Feldman Davis knew me as Poppy and Sienna knew me as Uhma and how on earth would I explain that?

"Are you sure you'll have enough time to go to the game and then go home to get changed before your date?"

"I was just planning to stay in the same clothes. You know, tank top, jeans. Works for a ball game, works for a date."

"No!" I practically screamed. She couldn't wear one

of her tight "I've got perky C-cups" tops. But what was I going to tell her—that she had to show up in overalls?

"No?"

"You should definitely wear something sporty—for both. Guys love a girl in a jersey. Besides, it'll be a conversation starter since you just came from a game. And loose-fitting jeans. Baggy clothes leave something to the imagination. You know how a guy's favourite pastime is imagining a girl naked."

I couldn't help wondering if Parker had imagined her naked, but the thought made me sick. Besides, what was I saying? Sienna was a seasoned seductress. She wasn't going to take any what-to-wear-on-a-date tips from Uhma.

"Ooh good point. I think I have my brother's jersey from when he played hockey in high school. It's totally worn and authentic."

"Perfect." There's no way Parker would be attracted to her.

But a moment after Sienna hung up I realized there was a good chance Colin wouldn't be either.

∼

There was nothing I could do to stop Sienna and Parker from possibly sitting beside each other at the game, so I did the only thing I could. I went to my hair appointment and asked Christopher to turn on the game.

The TV in the corner was showing *Project Runway*. Christopher TiVo'd all the best shows so that there was always something good to watch when his clients were getting their hair done. That, and so that he could look smart when he shouted out the judges' comments before they did.

"Game? What game?"

"The Jays."

He gave me a look and grabbed the remote, then flipped the channels.

I squinted at the screen, realizing the pointlessness of this activity. There had to be hundreds of thousands of seats in the stands, and they weren't doing close-ups on anyone. Didn't they have multiple cameras? Why were they all pointed at the stupid field?

"Why don't they show the people in the stands?" I asked Christopher and he shrugged then passed me the remote. I turned up the volume.

"You're asking the wrong guy. I don't watch sports. You know that. And neither do you."

I sighed. It was true. What was I doing?

I slumped down in my chair. I'd thought I had the perfect plan. What I needed was a special TV station that spied only on people I wanted it to. Like the lobby security cam at the condo, only in colour.

"Can we change this yet?"

"No." I couldn't change the station. What if the one time they showed the stands, it was Parker and Sienna? I couldn't risk missing it.

"Why, is there someone famous at the game today?" Christopher asked, suddenly brightening.

"Yes!" I said, sitting up. I didn't have to tell him about Sienna. "Parker's at the game."

Christopher made a face. "Oh. Big deal. Don't you see him every day? Let's watch *Project Runway*," he whined.

I held the remote tight.

"Oh fine, then. Be that way." He ran his hands through my hair. "So what are we doing today—the usual?"

"I want to do something different," I said, still staring at the TV screen. Maybe if one of the players hit a ball into the stands, and someone at Parker's office caught it . . .

"Highlights?" he suggested. I always got lowlights. Highlights always felt a little too ostentatious.

I shook my head. "I want to go long. And dark. And can you ask one of the girls to give me lash extensions when we're done?"

He looked at me in alarm. "Absolutely not. Your face can't handle lashes. Besides which, what the hell's going on?" he said, pointing at my nails. "You come in here with falsies, ask to watch a *baseball* game and tell me you want me to dye your hair black and give you extensions? Do you want to tell me what's going on?"

What was I going to say? Ming understood the need for long nails because she knew my—or rather, Parker's— secret. That and the fact that she thought long nails *were* the way to a man's heart. But Christopher didn't know. Was I prepared to tell him that I was a jilted wife? It was just too mortifying. I had my perfect image to uphold. I had a perfect husband and a perfect job and a perfect life. I wasn't sure it was worth risking that image just to con- vince him I needed long hair. Besides, Christopher was one of my best referral methods for new clients. He was like my agent, and all I had to do was tip him well. He talked to new clients about me and what I could do for them if they just let me into their hearts, their homes, their closets . . . If he knew that my husband had slept with another woman, he might tell everyone. And what woman—especially a newly divorced one, which was the bulk of my clientele—would want an image makeover by someone who was so clearly a failure that her own husband wasn't attracted enough to her to be faithful?

"I just think I need a new look to attract new clients," I said. It was actually partly true. The "clients" just happened to include Parker.

"Are you sure?" Christopher asked, running his hands along the sides of my face. "I'm just not sure your skin tone can handle dark hair. And you've been short for so long. I think it really works. Remember your cowlicks . . ." he warned me.

He was right. I'd had short hair for the past four years. Sure, when I met Parker I had long hair but when I started my business I lopped it all off into a clean cut that accented my cheekbones and always looked perfectly in place. Actually, I'd done it after one disaster of a day where I'd gotten caught in the rain without an umbrella and so, to save my hair from frizz I'd slicked it (as much as possible) back into a ponytail and then ran to meet Parker for a client dinner, where everyone else had obviously taken cabs, because they were all perfectly coiffed. And dry. At which point the wife of one of his clients—whom I'd just met—told me about Christopher. Which was slightly mortifying. You don't suggest a great hairstylist to someone who has lovely hair, do you? Of course, it all worked out well because I *did* end up going to Christopher soon after and the rest was history. And Parker hadn't stopped me—so I'd just assumed he'd felt the same way, that I looked unprofessional with long hair, or at least long hair when I got caught in the rain. And the last thing I wanted to be was an embarrassment to my husband. Or myself.

But maybe Parker missed my long hair. Elin and I had an ongoing debate about short versus long hair. Her theory was that even the most beautiful women, who could totally pull off short hair, looked prettier with long hair. And, of course, I had to compete with Sienna's lustrous locks. "But I'm not *actually* going to grow my hair long, so I won't have to deal with the cowlicks."

"Maybe so, but you still know what you're in for, right? Extensions will take me four hours. That's not even including the colour."

Four hours was nothing. I once waited in line six hours just to get a limited edition Fendi bag. "Just do it."

So Christopher set to work and I set to studying the TV screen. Only, baseball was actually really boring. And clearly the two teams playing were terrible because none of the players ever hit the ball into the stands.

Twenty strands of someone else's hair attached to my head later, I realized I couldn't handle not knowing. I punched in Sienna's phone number.

"Hello?"

"Hi, Sienna!"

"Hi . . . who's this?"

"It's Uhma."

"Oh. Hi *again*." She didn't sound particularly pleased to hear from me for the second time in one day. "Is everything all right?"

"Fine! I just . . . wondered how the baseball game was going."

"Oh, um, good," she said, sounding confused. "Listen I can't really talk." Suddenly she lowered her voice. "Parker's here."

"Beside you?"

"What?"

"Is he beside you?"

I had to know.

"Um, not at this moment."

"Good. I mean, it's just—why waste your time when you're starting fresh with Colin tonight, right?" I gave a little laugh to hide the worry I was sure was evident in my voice.

"Sorry, I can't really hear you, and we're about to go get chili dogs so . . ."

And then she was gone. Damn.

Christopher tapped on my phone. "I need this side."

I hung up the phone. Chili dogs? I shook my head. Surely Parker wouldn't be eating a chili dog.

Five hours, a set of false lashes that were making my eyelids feel heavy, two lattes and six chocolate truffles later, I was ready to witness my new look. Long, flowing, raven locks . . .

I turned in my chair to face the mirror and opened my eyes.

I looked like Morticia. As in Addams.

"Why did you let me do this?" I cried.

"You wanted it!" Christopher threw up his hands.

"But you're supposed to stop me."

That's what hairstylists did. They stopped their clients from making big mistakes. Like black hair and extensions.

"But you always know what you want. You tell me. And I listen. You're a freaking image consultant. You're supposed to know what you want."

He was right. That was the way our relationship worked. I told him what I wanted and he gave it to me.

I just never expected that I'd make such a horrible, hideous mistake. Since I couldn't pull out the extensions, I yanked the ridiculous lashes off instead and tossed them on the counter.

"It's different. You wanted different," Christopher said unconvincingly, putting his hands on my shoulders. "But if you want me to undo it, I can," he added, though it was clearly the last thing he wanted to do. And who could blame him? He'd just spent an entire afternoon tying tiny strands of someone else's hair to my scalp.

I shook my head. No, this was what I had to do. Long black hair might not have been the old Poppy, but I no longer wanted to be the old Poppy. The old Poppy was a casualty, whose husband cheated on her. The new Poppy was sexy and dynamic and she needed sexy and dynamic hair. Like Angelina Jolie. This was part of the Transformation. It was fine. I just had to get used to it.

∼

Colin, on the other hand, adjusted incredibly well to my new look.

"Wow! You look hot," he said as I sat down across from

him at a corner table at Roxy's, an eclectic all-day restaurant that had mismatched, brightly painted chairs. Ralph was tied up on the other side of the fence. He wagged his tail as I leaned over to pet his head.

I do? I thought, self-consciously touching my hair as I sat down. I wasn't sure what to say to that. I didn't feel hot. I felt ridiculous, but knowing that Colin thought I looked good boosted my confidence and I tried to tell myself it wasn't that I cared what he thought as much as that if he thought I looked good, hopefully Parker would too.

A wave of guilt washed over me for letting Colin see my new look before my husband, but I pushed it away. It was research. I was just testing my look out on another member of the male species. Besides, the real reason I was here was to set up Sienna and to pick up Ralph—and that was for Parker the Baby Lover's sake, not my own. I wasn't sure what to say in response to Colin's compliment, so I said thanks, sure that my face was bright red, and focused my attention on Ralph, who was licking my toes through the peep in my shoes.

"I see you took my advice," he said, taking off his fedora and running a hand through his hair. Tonight he was wearing a T-shirt with a grey corduroy jacket, a chain around his neck, a leather band on his wrist, faded jeans and black Pumas. I didn't love the look, but he still looked suitably sexy for Sienna. I bet she was going to love the accessories.

"I did?" I said aloud this time, looking up at him.

"I told you I missed your long hair." He smiled and reached across the table for my hand.

Oh God. He thought I'd done this for him?

"Colin, I'm married."

He laughed. "I know. I'm just kidding with you. Can't an ex-boyfriend pay you a well-deserved compliment?"

He had a point. I tried to relax. What was wrong with me? I waved my hand in the air. "Of course. You look good too," I said, which was a mistake because I could feel my face getting hot all over again.

"So, speaking of long hair, I actually wanted to know if you'd do me a huge favour."

"Of course," he said, not missing a beat. "What is it?"

I explained the situation. That my friend Sienna was newly single and I wanted to set her up with Colin. Just a drink, I promised him.

"Oh. Uh . . ." He shrugged. "Why not?" His roguish smile returned.

I smiled back. "Good, she's on her way right now."

"What? Really? What would you have done if I said no?"

"I knew you wouldn't," I said with confidence.

He tilted his head and looked at me. "I've changed, Poppy. Sometimes I look back at the guy I was and I hate myself." He shook his head. "I can't imagine cheating on a girlfriend now. I can barely even go on two dates in one week. I'm a serial monogamist." He said it quite seriously, but I wanted to laugh. "And I know I was sort of joking before about paying for drinks to make it up to you, but I'm serious. I feel terribly about how I treated you."

Terrible, I thought, knowing that if Parker were here he'd immediately hate Colin based on grammar alone.

"It's okay," I said, and I meant it. Because if Colin hadn't cheated on me, I never would've sworn off guys like him and taken a chance on safe, reliable Parker. "You probably did me a favour," I added.

"So you're married and happy now," he confirmed. "I'm glad."

I nodded, but inside I felt torn. Colin was the exciting, risky guy who'd broken my heart. And Parker was the one who'd made me see what real love was. Only now, Parker was the one who'd cheated on me, even though we were married, and Colin was the one who'd turned out to be the serial monogamist—though I wasn't sure limiting yourself to a date a week was technically monogamy.

Still, where had I gone wrong?

One drink later, I checked my watch. It was almost eight thirty, so I gave Colin the new story I'd concocted, which I thought worked a bit better than the crazy one about Flanders Fields.

I explained that Sienna hadn't had very good experiences being set up by friends—particularly when they tend to know more about the guy than she does. "So she doesn't know that we actually know each other. I told her you were a friend of my friend Uhma, so it's probably better if you don't even bring up my name, since she doesn't think that you know me."

Colin looked at me, and shook his head as though trying to digest what I'd just said (I knew it was confusing, but it wasn't *that* confusing), then brushed a strand of my black hair out of my face. "You're crazy, you know that?" he said, handing me Ralph's leash, a container of food, a bag of treats and an envelope with instructions.

I was fairly certain he was right.

"What happened to your hair?" Parker said as soon as he saw me. It wasn't exactly the adoring reaction I was hoping for.

"I coloured it," I said with as much gusto as I could manage, and then tried flipping it over one shoulder. The thing was, if you hadn't had long hair in like a thousand days, you tended to forget what it was like to sexily flip it over your shoulder. I was definitely going to need some practice.

"It's really black," he said, staring at it.

"It's raven," I mumbled.

"Isn't a raven black?" he said, and laughed. I was fairly certain that I wasn't going to get a compliment out of him.

Who was I kidding? I didn't look a bit like Sienna.

"It's really long." He stared at it like he couldn't understand it. Or me. And then his expression turned to alarm as his eyes flicked down to Ralph, who had decided to join me after taking a tour of the hallway. He stood just outside the door.

"Come here, Lauren," I said and patted my leg. Then I turned back to Parker. "This is Lauren. He's ours."

"Ours?" he said, his brow wrinkling. I explained how Lauren had been abandoned and the Humane Society had rescued him and how all he needed was a good home. With two loving parents who weren't preoccupied with kids.

Parker continued to stare at me.

"What were you thinking?" Parker said then refocused

on Ralph, who was being pleasantly noncompliant about coming into the apartment and sitting pretty, likely because (a) he had no idea who I was and (b) I kept calling him Lauren. I felt a bit bad about that part, but Ralph and I had had a whole discussion about it on the walk home, and I explained to him it was really for the sake of my marriage that he be disobedient, and he seemed to understand. At least, he didn't seem upset about it and even nodded, though he may have just been begging for the doggie treats that Colin left with me, which I gave to him out of guilt for mashing dirt into his fur to make it filthy and matted before we got home so that he wouldn't look so darn cute.

I had to give him a new name, obviously, since he was playing the role of the Abandoned Dog. Since everyone knew the first rule of remembering a person's (or, in this instance, a dog's) name was word association, I was sure not to forget his new name. And I figured being called by a girl's name would make Ralph even more disobedient, and maybe he'd go to the bathroom on the floor or chew something, even though I didn't really want him to chew anything valuable. I would swap one of our area rugs for a crappy one so that I could pretend to be upset when he ruined it. Anyway, clearly Ralph was very well trained, because it took only a minute of coaxing to get him into the apartment. But I was confident that eventually he'd come around to being naughty. He just needed some temptations. And I'd work on that.

In the meantime, Parker's reaction was just what I had been hoping for, though I did feel sort of bad that it came at the expense of us fighting. But wasn't it better to disagree over an unwanted dog on our doorstep than an unwanted baby?

"I thought we should have a dog," I said sweetly. "I thought you'd be happy."

"But I never said I wanted a dog," Parker said, exasperated, adjusting the collar on his green polo shirt.

And I never wanted a baby, I wanted to say, but didn't.

"Are you upset?" I asked.

"I'm not upset. It's just that we always discuss these sorts of things before making any huge changes."

Exactly! I thought. You don't just blurt out that you want to have a baby. Although, to be fair, it wasn't as though he'd adopted a baby without asking me. But anyway. This was different.

"Sorry," I said, rather lamely.

"It's okay." He leaned over to pat Ralph on the head. "He is cute . . ."

No! He wasn't supposed to think he was cute! He was supposed to think he was dirty and an inconvenience. I sighed. Ralph/Lauren totally *was* cute, and I had this sudden wave of regret that I'd made the wrong decision in "borrowing" him from Colin, rather than just getting us our very own cute dog that we wouldn't have to return. But a dog was a lot of work. Which was what Parker was *supposed* to be thinking. Only he wasn't. And now, convincing him of that looked like it was going to be more work than the dog himself.

"He'll need to be taken for walks every day," I reminded him.

Parker looked at me thoughtfully. "Actually, that'll be great for getting me out of the house and getting some exercise now that I don't have a reason to leave every morning."

I inwardly groaned.

"Not just in the morning. He's going to have to go to the bathroom. All the time."

Parker nodded, clearly amused. "I'm familiar with dogs and how they work," he said with a smile.

"And he's really big. Gosh, he's probably too big for our place," I said, looking around as though noticing our square footage for the first time.

Parker nodded thoughtfully. "I know. I've been thinking about that a lot lately. All my stuff is taking over the dining room. And if we're going to add a dog and a baby to the mix . . ."

No! We weren't supposed to add a dog and *a baby.* The whole *point* of the dog was to make Parker realize he didn't *want* a baby after all. This was a disaster.

"Maybe we should consider moving out to the country. Closer to Elin or your parents?"

I stared at him, shocked. *Move to the country?* That's what I got for bringing home a dog? It wasn't enough that he wanted a baby, now he wanted Green Acres too?

If I didn't want a baby, I definitely didn't want a house in the country. Apparently my face had that written all over it.

Parker leaned over to scratch Ralph/Lauren behind the ears. He grabbed his camera off the dining room table and snapped a couple of shots of Ralph/Lauren, then one of me. "We can talk about it," he said.

But I didn't want to talk about it. I kicked off my stripper shoes. Parker winced. "Those shoes look incredibly uncomfortable," he said, pointing at my mangled feet, then putting his camera back down on the table. "Incredibly uncomfortable" was an understatement.

I sighed and shuffled into the kitchen, trying to stretch out my toes as I walked.

"You kind of look like Pippi Longstocking, but with black hair," Parker mused, following me. "Poppy Longstocking!"

I turned to face him. Poppy Longstocking? *Poppy Longstocking!* He thought I looked like some ten-year-old sailor girl? That wasn't sexy at all. I wanted to break down. To tell him everything. But I couldn't. I couldn't tell him that I was doing this for him. I couldn't tell him anything.

What I needed was confidence.

"I guess you'll just have to get used to it," I said, which sounded more like an empty threat than unbridled confidence.

Instead of asking why I'd done it or begging me to change it back, though, he just pulled me into him. "Of course I will. It's just . . . different. But I love you for you—whatever your hair looks like. And of course I'll get used to it."

He ran his hand over my hair. "It's very soft . . ." he said and then stopped as his hand got caught.

"Ow!" I tried to pull away but one of my locks of hair was caught between his fingers.

"What was that?"

What was I supposed to say? That he'd just caught his hand on the knot that tied a stranger's hair to mine?

I pulled away, but he pulled me in for an embrace. Once he'd untangled his fingers from my hair, he slowly ran them down my back toward my butt.

"Whoa, are you wearing padded underwear?" he asked, laughing.

"Of course not." Which was true. Technically. Besides, why didn't he just think it was voluptuous curves? Why did he have to be so critical?

I made a face and disentangled myself from him. Clearly being sexy required not being close to him. He was too judgmental.

"So how was the game?" I said, stepping back.

"Great," he said, walking into the kitchen, still laughing. At me. Even if he thought he was doing it in a loving way. I followed him, looking for any signs that he might have been unfaithful. He was home, so that was a good thing, I supposed. And he didn't *look* rumpled, though, actually, I had no idea what he had been wearing at the game, thanks to the stupid TV monitors that don't show the stands.

"I tried to look for you on TV."

"Oh?" He turned around. "I thought you didn't like baseball."

"Well I like *you*," I said, but it sounded more like an accusation than a nice statement.

"Well I like you *and* I love you. I wish you would've come."

I felt myself melting. This was the man I loved. For a split second I wished I'd never known anything about the affair. I wanted to just fold into him, to hug him and forget about Sienna, but I couldn't.

"So did you go out after the game?"

"Yep."

"Did everyone go?"

"Not everyone. But a bunch of the guys."

"Oh." I sighed. "Just the guys?" I added, hopefully.

"No, some girls too. Rebecca, Dyan, Sienna . . ."

I studied his face some more. He didn't look like he was hiding anything. Did that mean Sienna hadn't tried to remind him of their affair?

"Sienna?"

"Oh yeah . . . I asked her about that joke she played on me at the hospital and she acted really weird about it." But it was Parker who looked a bit weird, as though he were worried about something. My stomach tightened, but then he just shrugged and opened the fridge to pour himself a glass of orange juice.

Ralph/Lauren was far too well trained, even for our small space, which clearly meant Colin likely lived in an even smaller space or just had the World's Best Dog. Ralph/Lauren didn't pee on the rug and he didn't shed on the furniture. He didn't drool. He didn't bark. He didn't even look dirty—one of the first things Parker did was use my Frilly Lilly bubble bath to wash the dirt out of his fur and then gave him a blowout using my dryer, which actually made me a bit jealous. If I'd known it would be like having a Barbie doll, maybe I wouldn't have thought it would be such a pain to have a dog—or that it would make anyone *not* want to have a baby. Now he was fluffy and pretty and looked better than ever. He was a dog owner's dream, which made him my nightmare. Why couldn't he do one single thing wrong? The only thing he did wrong that he actually did right was that as we were getting into bed, he hopped up and nestled himself between us, effectively ensuring there would be no bedroom shenanigans between Parker and me. I wanted to high-five him, but refrained.

To make matters worse, I'd texted both Colin and Sienna to find out how the date had gone and neither had responded, and though I tried to convince myself that meant they were shacked up in some hotel remaking John and Yoko's famous love-in and so couldn't respond, I knew it likely wasn't true, since Colin had said he had to leave early Sunday morning to catch his flight out west.

What if they'd both found out the truth about every-thing—that I was Uhma and Colin was my ex-boyfriend and Sienna was my husband's ex-mistress? Then what?

chapter nine

'd been checking Sienna's status updates on Facebook incessantly all week but she had yet to update anything that could be related to her date with Colin, and by Friday I was starting to worry that she was secretly in contact with Parker, even though I had no proof. And Parker was being more attentive than usual. He'd bought a slow-cooker at Home Depot and made pulled pork sandwiches for dinner the night before, and this morning he was making muffins while I got ready for work.

Part of me wanted to stay home and hang out with him all day, but if I wanted to keep my clients, I knew I couldn't. Still, I felt sad that I'd so fully booked my schedule for the week, thinking it would give Parker much-needed alone time with Ralph/Lauren. And I hadn't completed a single item of self-improvement since Saturday, so when my last client of the day cancelled, I called Parker to see if he wanted to meet for a drink, but he didn't answer the phone, so instead, I decided to get a quick spray-tan before heading home. At the corner of Yonge and Eglinton there were not one, but two tanning options, so it felt like a sign. I chose Tan-o-matic, because they offered spray-tanning (obviously I wasn't about to start getting a *real* tan and the melanoma that came with it just to look like Sienna). I walked up three flights of stairs to the salon, where a college-aged receptionist with bleached blond hair—who clearly invested her paycheques back into the company—greeted me with a friendly smile and a view of the wad of pink gum in her mouth.

"What shade—light, medium, dark?"

Obviously I wasn't going to make the same mistake I had with the peel—the peeling had finally subsided. "I'll take light."

"Did you exfoliate?" she asked as she led me to the back, her yellow Old Navy flip-flops snapping against her heels as she walked.

"Was I supposed to? I've never done this before," I told her.

"Don't worry. Tony will lead you through the whole process."

Of exfoliating? I wondered, but instead, said, "Tony?"

"Tony the Trainer. He'll make you into a golden goddess in no time."

She opened the door to a room that had a booth. "There's a bit of a glitch in the system," she said, opening the door to a shower-type stall. "You've got to step inside the booth to get the directions. Don't worry, you can just take off your clothes when he tells you to."

I stepped into the booth and shut the door just as the receptionist left the room.

"Let's get ready to tan!" A voice boomed over the sound system as though I were preparing to be the next Ultimate Fighting Champion.

"First, take off your clothes!"

I did as I was told, afraid that if I didn't move quickly the spray tan might shoot out of the jets at any time, ruining my outfit.

"Including your undergarments," Tony reminded me. "You can hang everything on the hook on the other side of the door."

No way was I taking my underwear off. I had no proof that Tony the Trainer was just a voice. What if he emerged and saw me naked?

"To keep your hands and feet looking natural, apply cream to the tops of your hands and feet, including your nails."

Was I supposed to do that now? I looked around. Where was the cream?

"You can also wear protective footwear."

Protective footwear? What, like work boots?

"We strongly recommend you wear lip balm, eyewear and nose plugs."

Nose plugs? Was I supposed to have brought my own nose plugs? I had sunglasses in my handbag, but if I wore those, wouldn't it leave marks around my eyes? I had lip balm, too, but it was in my purse outside the booth. I eyed the jets. Could I get out and back in safely? Could Tony sense when I was in and out of the booth? Would he wait for me while I retrieved his list of requests? I grabbed the door handle and pushed it open.

"Stand on the magna-tan plate and place your eyewear

over your eyes!" Tony suddenly boomed. "Face forward, toward the jets!"

I quickly pulled the door closed and turned around just as the jets came to life and shot an orange-coloured juice in every direction.

"Push your elbows out with your forearms facing down, as though you're making the stop sign while riding a bike."

Hadn't Tony gotten the message that I had no need for spinning class after finding the perfect shorts? And given that I didn't own an actual bike, my third-grade memory of the hand signs while riding one were fuzzy. It made no difference though because, before I could figure it out, Tony moved on to the next position.

"Lift your arms toward the jets and make claws with your hands, as though you're a cheetah."

I channeled my inner cat.

"Now, make a quarter turn and walk like an Egyptian."

I turned to my right and tried to picture The Bangles video from my youth. Why didn't this booth have a TV screen to show me what to do?

"Now, make another quarter turn and make a Y."

I wondered if we'd make the M, C or A, then considered the marketing for spray-tanning karaoke.

"Now turn to your right and walk like an Egyptian again."

"All right, you've just completed Round 1," he boomed.

Round 1? I half expected a bell to ding and Tony to come out with a mini-stool and towel.

"Now, it's time to channel Sabrina, Kelly and Kris! That's right, strike your Charlie's Angels pose."

What? I stretched my arms out in front of me and

pointed my own finger gun at the spray guns, though I wasn't sure what to do with my legs. Spread them? One in front of the other?

"And turn!"

"And turn!"

"And turn!"

I barely got halfway around before Tony barked again, "And . . . you're done like dinner!"

Great, I thought. Just what I wanted—to look fried. I pushed open the door and collapsed on the bench. Then I stood up and walked over to the mirror and stared in horror. For one thing, my pretty Lejaby set was completely ruined, and everywhere else I was an orange, blotchy mess. I looked like a walking piece of orange finger-painting art.

"Hello?" I called out, hoping the receptionist would come back and tell me that it was fine, that it was temporary, that by the time I put on my clothes I'd have an even, all-over tan.

But she didn't come back to see me and when I finally put my clothes on—after wiping the excess orange juice off my skin—and made my way out to the front, she was less than reassuring.

"It's because you didn't exfoliate," she said simply.

"But I told you I didn't exfoliate."

She shrugged.

"Is there something I can do to fix it?"

She nodded.

"Exfoliate," we said in unison, just before she popped a fresh piece of pink Hubba Bubba in her mouth.

∿

"What happened to your skin?" Parker said as soon as I got through the door. I immediately felt annoyed. No matter what I did to try to look better for him, he just criticized me. I hit the dimmer switch on the wall beside me.

"Spray-tan incident."

"But you don't tan," he said, wrinkling his forehead. "And your pale skin is so pretty."

Suddenly, I had an overwhelming desire to crawl into bed and sleep for a month. I was tired of transforming myself without a positive reaction from him. But I still wasn't ready to give up. I loved him too much, which made me feel like a fool, but I had to follow my heart.

"I thought you'd like it. Everyone looks better with a tan." It *was* a general rule, but one that obviously did not apply to me.

"Not you," he said as though he could hear my thoughts.

"Thanks a lot. That's really nice of you to say." I felt hurt. I was doing this for him. Did he think I *wanted* blotchy orange skin?

He looked at me for a moment. Then he shook his head. "Poppy, I meant you look beautiful natural, that's all. Anyway, I'm glad you're home. I was worried about you. I called your phone to see when you'd be home, but you didn't answer."

"I called you. I wanted to see if you wanted to meet for a drink or dinner, but *you* didn't answer, so I got a tan," I said tersely.

"What's wrong with you?"

"Nothing!" *Aside from the fact that my skin is a mess and my head hurts because my hair is so heavy and I only have six nails and none of my pants fit thanks to my cycling shorts and my feet are in constant pain from wearing stripper shoes.* But I couldn't complain about any of that. Beauty wasn't like wearing sweatpants—it wasn't all fleece and terry cloth and coziness. "I'm sorry," I said, and I meant it. I leaned in for a hug.

"You just need a hug," he said, and he was right. Parker's arms around me felt good. As though we could reconnect and leave everything and everyone else behind. Except that we couldn't.

Parker broke away suddenly and looked at his watch, then announced that Terrence and Elin were coming over.

"Terrence and Elin?"

"I wanted to surprise you. I know you barely get to see Elin, so I thought if I initiated the date, Elin wouldn't feel guilty about having a night away from the babies. So they're going to drop the kids off with Terrence's parents and I'll watch the game with Terrence while you and Elin go do whatever you want to do—have drinks, go to a movie, get pedicures . . ."

"I wasn't expecting it."

"I thought you'd be happy," Parker said slightly defensively.

I looked at Parker, stunned. I wanted to cry, but I was afraid the salty tears might leave lines down my orange face, making it look even worse, if that was possible. Parker told me they'd be arriving in an hour, which gave me just enough time to have a bath and try to exfoliate my orange tan away.

After only ten minutes in the tub, I had already made good progress on project tan removal and so I leaned back and shut my eyes, thinking how sweet it was of Parker to arrange the double date. He really seemed to be a different person post-lightning. The old Parker just wouldn't have thought to do something as simple as arrange a surprise evening for me with my best friend. Especially not if it meant Parker had to hang out with Terrence. I wasn't even sure he *liked* Terrence. Which made it even more special. He really was changing.

I was changing too. We were both changing, and while his gesture was a nice one, it just reinforced how nothing was ever going to be the same again. I got out of the tub and dried myself off. I was less orange, but still slightly blotchy in spots. I rummaged around in my vanity until I found a bottle of tinted moisturizer and smoothed it on, unsure why I hadn't thought to do it myself in the first place. Maybe Parker would finally compliment me on my golden glow.

Parker knocked on the door then pushed it open and handed me my phone. "I think you've got a message. It keeps beeping. You might want to check in case Terrence or Elin called."

I looked at the screen. The missed call had been Colin. I looked at Parker to gauge his reaction in case he'd seen it too, then remembered that he had no idea who Colin was.

"Thanks," I said, and shut the bathroom door. I dialed Colin's number.

"Hey," Colin said. "The shoot went more quickly than we expected, so we caught a flight back this afternoon instead of tomorrow. I'm just in a cab heading home from the airport now. Do you want me to stop by and pick up Ralph?"

Of course I couldn't let him pick up Ralph, but what could I say to stop him?

"Tonight?" I stalled.

"Yeah. I can't wait to see the big guy. Besides, tomorrow I was hoping to head up north to a friend's cottage, so it's probably easier to meet up tonight. I hope he wasn't any trouble."

"Not at all," I said woefully. Which was precisely the problem.

"I'll bring him over to you," I said, and Colin gave me his address on Baldwin.

Now all I had to do was break the news to Parker. I slowly pulled on my new low-rise jeans and a tight black T-shirt, which looked nowhere as good on me with my own A-cups—even with the gel cookies I'd stuffed inside— as it did on Sienna with her Cs. Story of my life.

In the living room, Parker was sitting on the couch, Ralph curled up by his side. I explained to Parker that Ralph/Lauren had to go back.

"What?" Parker looked at me in alarm. "They can't do that!"

I was going to be in big trouble if Parker had solid proof that the Humane Society, in fact, couldn't take Ralph/ Lauren back.

"I thought you told me that the whole reason the Humane Society took Lauren away from his owner in the first place was because he was a deadbeat. So obviously they can't give him back. Are you sure it wasn't a prank call?"

"From who?"

"I don't know—what if his previous owner found out we had Lauren and it was him, trying to trick you."

"Parker, it was the Humane Society. I swear." My stomach dropped. I felt horrible lying to him. But this wasn't how things were supposed to work out. Ralph/Lauren was supposed to be a nightmare and Parker was supposed to be begging me to promise him we were never going to have babies, which I would, making Parker realize that I was the perfect wife and he only needed me to be happy and then we'd live happily ever after.

What had gone wrong?

"I'm supposed to take him back tonight."

"Don't be ridiculous. Elin and Terrence will be here any minute. And besides, it's almost seven. Is the Humane Society even open this late?"

Good point.

"This is ridiculous. He's not going back. I'll call them tomorrow myself and deal with this."

I could sense a sadness that was the reason behind his anger and I felt terrible. But I couldn't exactly tell Colin that I wasn't giving him his dog back.

"Parker . . ."

"I said no. We're not giving him back. Marriage is supposed to be a partnership, a compromise, and I'm willing to compromise on a lot, but not this. I've sat at home alone while you're off working and dying your hair and basically becoming the most superficial person I've ever met. You're obsessed with your looks. You come and go without even asking me how my day was, or how I'm doing. I asked you to have a baby with me and you won't even have sex even when I offered to use a condom. You even bought a dog without consulting me. But Lauren is the one thing that's worked out. I like him. We're not giving him back."

The doorbell rang and Ralph/Lauren perked up, then jumped off the couch and followed me toward the door. "Well I'm not willing to get arrested for breaking some animal rights law. He's going back. Say goodbye."

"Poppy, *don't*."

I'd never heard Parker so serious. But there was nothing else I could do. I had to get out of the house. I wished I could tell him I was doing all this for him. Maybe one day I'd be able to. But at that moment, I simply had to return that dog. And Parker . . . I stared at him, and felt a wave of anger. Well, *he* was just going to have to deal with it. I hadn't wanted to borrow a dog and lie about it and then have to take him back—when I wanted to keep Ralph as much as he did. And I knew I was never home, but that was only because we were now a one-income family. And I was obsessed with my looks? Did he think I liked looking like a tramp rather than a lady? I opened my mouth, and closed it again. I couldn't tell him any of this. I couldn't tell my husband—my best friend—anything. He had betrayed me. This was his fault.

Tears welled up in my eyes, but I brushed them away with my sleeve and grabbed my coat and Ralph/Lauren's leash off the hook by the door and attached it to his collar, then pulled the bag of doggie treats from the shelf and shoved them in my pocket. I opened the door to find Elin and Terrence standing, pale-faced outside. Elin had Augusten in her arms.

"Hi, guys!" Elin said brightly.

"Hi," I said, forcing a smile. "Good to see you, Terrence. Come on in. Elin, we have to go," I mumbled.

"Do you want me to keep Augusten?" Terrence said

to Elin. He turned to me. "My parents can only handle one each so we had to bring one of the kids with us. We brought your godson. I hope you don't mind. We can keep him here while you girls go out."

"No, no," I insisted. "We can take him with us."

I wanted to have some time with my godson, but, more than that, I was secretly worried that Augusten—who was the most sweet-natured of the three babies—would only spur Parker's desire to have a baby of his own. Especially now that I was taking his pseudo-baby Ralph/Lauren away.

I pulled Ralph/Lauren out the door and shut it behind me.

Elin was looking at the dog, an alarmed expression on her face. "Who's this?"

"Never mind. You have to come with me." I handed Ralph/Lauren a doggie treat as we walked toward the elevator.

As soon as we were inside the elevator she turned to me. "What happened to you?"

I looked at my reflection in the mirrored walls.

"It was all part of the plan," I said to her.

"*What* plan?"

I just shook my head.

"Do you want me to carry Augusten?" I offered, looking at him asleep on Elin's chest. We'd reached the street and were headed west to Colin's. "You can hold the dog."

"It's fine. But are you going to tell me what's going on?"

"See? You don't want to let me carry him because you think I'd make a bad mother. That's what I've been trying to tell Parker all this time."

Only, I really hadn't been trying to tell him that at

all, I supposed. I'd just been acting like a crazy woman. A self-absorbed crazy woman. Ralph stopped to drink from a dog bowl outside Starbucks and we paused to wait until he was finished.

"You've been trying to tell Parker you'd make a bad mother? What? Are you guys trying to have kids?"

"He is. I'm not."

Elin shook her head. "Stop. Start at the top. With your hair. What is this?" She touched my hair. "Extensions? A wig?"

Don't ask her what she thinks. Don't ask her. It doesn't matter. But of course it mattered. Elin was my best friend. "What do you think?" I said, flipping my hair over my shoulder.

"I like your hair short. It suits your features."

"But I was doing what you told me to do. Besides, you always said women look prettier with long hair. You had a list." It was true. She *did* have a list. She'd made it when I'd first mentioned cutting my hair, years ago. She'd used it as an argument to stop me. It hadn't worked. "You know, Gwyneth Paltrow, Natalie Portman, Claire Danes, Jon Bon Jovi . . ."

"That was years ago, Poppy. And you never listened to me anyway. But black?"

"You don't like it?"

"It's just . . ."

"What?"

"You look like Cher."

I sighed. "You should've seen me before I got the tan, after the chemical peel. My face was whiter than white. I looked like Cher on heroin."

"You got a peel and a fake tan? And what's with the nails? And . . . are you stuffing your butt?

I felt a little pleased that at least she had noticed my new bottom.

"Come on, Poppy, this is me. Your best friend. What is going on?"

I told her how I had met Sienna in the hospital and how, ever since, I'd been trying to make myself look more like her.

"What?" Elin said in disbelief. "You met her? What did you say?"

"I pretended I was a sociologist. She didn't know that it was *me*."

"So this"—Elin waved a hand around me—"is what Sienna looks like?" Elin asked doubtfully.

I nodded. "I almost got fake teeth, too, but apparently I didn't need veneers. But I did get my teeth whitened," I said proudly, smiling.

"What? Poppy—"

"The only problem was that I couldn't eat for a few days. And even now, my teeth are still really sensitive so I can't really drink coffee. But it's fine, because I was trying to cut back anyway. And my face still stings from the peel because so many layers of skin flaked off. So basically I haven't really let Parker kiss me much, but I haven't really wanted him to anyway, because I haven't really wrapped my head around being intimate with him yet. I mean, he had *sex* with another woman."

"Poppy, stop." Elin put her hands on my shoulders. "Are you listening to yourself? And why would you do all of this? You looked amazing before."

"Well obviously I wasn't perfect or Parker wouldn't have cheated."

"Poppy, did you ever think that maybe it wasn't about her looks? That it's not about you being perfect? Anyway, you saw her, what, once? Maybe you're misremembering what she looks like," Elin said.

I shook my head. "I've seen her twice. And I have a picture of her on my BlackBerry. Plus, I'm her Facebook friend so I have access to her profile picture."

"You're her *Facebook* friend?"

I pulled out my BlackBerry and logged on to Facebook under Uhma's name while Elin looked on.

"You have a fake name?" She grabbed the BlackBerry and studied it.

"Of course. How else did you think I could get her to be my friend?"

"Oh . . . I don't know. Admit you're the wife of the man she was having an affair with, and tell her straight up that you know about it?"

I turned to keep walking toward Colin's. "I couldn't do that. She's the kind of woman who would've just seen it as a challenge. She didn't care that Parker was married when she decided to go after him. Why would she care once I told her I knew?"

"So have they seen each other, then?"

I told her I didn't think so, except for the baseball game.

"Why didn't you go to the game if you knew she'd be there?"

"Because Sienna knew me as Uhma," I said, as though it were obvious. "Besides I hate baseball, you know that."

"But you love Parker."

I nodded and tugged on my hair. "Of course. That's why I'm doing all this. Obviously."

Elin shook her head, but didn't say anything.

"It's what you told me to do."

Elin stared at me, aghast. "I told you to do this?"

"On the phone. When I wasn't sure what to do." We turned the corner onto Baldwin.

Elin grabbed my arm. "I most certainly did *not* tell you to do this."

Just then I heard my name and looked across the street to see Colin waving at us from the front steps of his building.

Elin followed my gaze. "What the. . . ? Oh my God. Is that Diesel Cartwright?"

I nodded. "I probably should've told you about that part."

Colin jogged across the street. He was wearing frayed jeans, a retro tee and flip-flops. When he reached us, he immediately bent down to give Ralph a hug. When he stood up, he pulled me in for a hug, then eyed Elin.

"Colin, this is my friend Elin. I'm not sure if you remember her?"

He nodded slowly. "Nice to see you." He stuck out his hand but Elin pretended hers were encumbered by Augusten and her diaper bag.

"Hmmm," she said coldly, then turned away and started bouncing Augusten in the BabyBjörn on her chest.

"So did everything go well with Ralph?"

"Too well," I said.

"Good to hear. And thanks again. I can't really believe

you just volunteered to take care of him," he said. "You're some girl," he added with a knowing smile.

"She sure is," Elin said sarcastically, turning around and raising her eyebrows at me. I gave her a dirty look before she turned her back on us again.

"So you didn't tell me," I said, knowing what I was about to say was only going to get me into more trouble with Elin than I was already in. "How did it go with Sienna?" I mentally crossed my fingers, willing him to say they'd hit it off so well he'd taken Sienna with him to Whistler.

"It was . . . *interesting,*" he said slowly, then looked to Elin and back at me with wide eyes, as though he wanted to say something but wasn't sure he should.

"Interesting?" I prodded. There was nothing he couldn't say, at this point, in front of Elin.

"Not really my type. Nice girl, but not who I'm looking for."

"Really . . ." I said, deflated. "Did you notice any similarities between us?" I said, as Elin pointedly jabbed me as if to say, *Seriously?*

Colin considered my question for a moment then shook his head. "Not really. Actually, not at all."

Not at all?

"But I certainly learned a few things that I think you'd be interested in knowing . . . We should talk. Do you have time for a drink or do you two have plans together?" Colin asked. I started to answer no, but as though she didn't trust me to make the right decision, Elin cut in.

"No. I've got a baby on my boob that needs to be breastfed, like, *now,* and I came into the city especially to see Poppy. We have plans." The breastfeeding part was a total lie. Elin had stopped breastfeeding when the triplets were three months old, once she realized she was essentially a trough on two feet. And I totally owed her more than a drink.

Colin looked taken aback. "Okay, sure. Well maybe another time, Poppy? I actually have something I wanted to talk to you about."

He did? I wondered. "Sure."

Colin handed me the bag in his right hand. "I brought you a little something from Whistler. We were filming a little chocolate shop that makes chocolates to look like celebrities. I got one made to look like you."

I pulled the box out of the bag and looked at the chocolate through the clear plastic top. "Wow. Thanks." The chocolate was impressive, but it didn't look a thing like me. And then I realized, it really did look like the new me.

Elin stared at us, agape. "We have to go."

"This is so nice of you," I said, genuinely shocked, as Elin grabbed my arm and began pulling me across the street. I called out an apology to Colin, who looked confused but gave me a smile and a half wave.

"That was so rude," I hissed to Elin once we'd crossed the street.

"Are you freaking kidding me?" she said. "Are you *seeing* him?"

"No!" I said, shocked. "Of course not. I just . . . ran into him. And he had a dog and I needed a dog—"

"You needed a dog?"

"Because Parker wants to have a baby."

"Just stop right there. This is too much." She pulled me

into a sidewalk patio of a café on College, sat me down at a table, then pulled a bottle out of her bag and gave it to Augusten. A waiter, about twenty, with shoulder-length hair pulled back in a ponytail, shuffled over, slapped two menus on the table and stuck his hands in the front of his half apron.

"We'll have two glasses of your most inexpensive red. Actually, we'll take a bottle." The waiter snapped his fingers, gave us two thumbs up and shuffled away.

Elin turned to me. "Do you want to save your marriage?" she asked me, quite seriously.

I looked at her, wide-eyed, then gestured to myself. "Would I have turned into some sort of Vegas drag queen Cher if I didn't?"

"I just want to be sure this is what you want to do."

"I'm sure."

"And you don't want to just kick him out of the house for good?"

I shrugged. "Not yet. I don't want to fail. I don't . . . I don't want to lose him."

"Then changing yourself into someone you're not is not the way to get him back."

"It's not?" I was doubtful, and frankly skeptical of Elin's motives.

Elin shook her head firmly. "No. Besides, no offence, but you don't look anything like her," Elin said, turning her attention back to the thumbnail of Sienna on my BlackBerry, which she was still holding. Even in two-inch diameter, she was gorgeous. And I just looked like a mess.

"But I can try harder. Surely there are other things I can do. I've only just hit the tip of the makeover iceberg, or however the saying goes. I could still get my lips plumped or get breast implants . . ." I made a face and shook my head. "But I really don't want to do either of those things. I still haven't perfected my wardrobe, but I'm sort of losing steam. I think the real problem is I don't really *want* to look like Sienna. I think she looks like a slut. I want to look like me. But I guess Parker doesn't want that." I shrugged. "Anyway, marriage is all about compromises, right?"

Elin nodded slowly. "It is, but you're being crazy. Even in a best case of worst-case scenarios, all you'll end up doing is reminding Parker of her. Is that what you want?"

"Of course it isn't what I want! I just . . . Oh my God. You're right. You're totally right. But if I don't transform myself to look like her, then what do I do?"

"Come up with a new plan."

"But what?"

"What you need to do is eliminate her."

I looked at her, eyes wide. "Like, *kill* her? Oh no. I'm not about to re-enact an Amy Fisher TV movie-of-the-week and go to jail to save my marriage. I already ruled that out weeks ago. I mean, what would become of me? Cafeteria dinners with mashed potatoes from a box? Conjugal visits? A jail birth like Leighton Meester from *Gossip Girl*? Sure, she turned out to be all famous and fabulous, but what if my own child didn't fare so well? Which is totally irrelevant anyway because I am never having kids. And anyway, isn't the statistic that something like two-thirds of couples stop having sex after becoming parents because they have no time? Not that we're having sex right now anyway, but that's different because (a) I'm punishing Parker for having sex with Sienna and (b) I just . . . well, I just can't."

"Poppy, you're babbling. And being ridiculous. No one is killing anyone."

"Oh, well okay." I should've known I would never have a best friend who would convince me to commit a felony. "Don't you see though—that's why I set Sienna up with Colin. To preoccupy her and get her out of the picture."

Elin made a face. "Really? That was your plan?"

I shrugged. "Okay, so what's *your* plan?"

"You're going to focus on you and Parker. Do things together. Rebuild your marriage."

I had to admit, it sounded like a good idea. And it would be fairly easy—at least, much easier than getting claw-like nails and hair extensions and an orange tan.

"But where does Operation Eliminate Sienna come into it then?"

"You're going to eliminate her from your *mind.*"

"Really? That's the plan? It sounds like something Dr. Phil would spout."

"It's time to get real," Elin said, and I *knew* that was something Dr. Phil would say.

The waiter returned with our bottle of wine and two glasses.

"What happened has nothing to do with Sienna," she said to me while tasting the wine, then nodding at the waiter.

"It has everything to do with Sienna. If there were no Sienna there would've been no affair."

"If there was no Sienna, there would've been an Ashley or a Jessica or a Melody . . ."

"Are you naming Pussycat Dolls?"

"I'm making a point."

I took a sip of my wine and thought about what Elin was saying. Was she right? Did this really have nothing to do with Sienna at all? I wasn't willing to go that far—I didn't doubt Sienna's powers of persuasion—but I was willing to agree that this whole debacle had more to do with Parker and me than I was admitting.

"I wish we'd had this conversation weeks ago."

Elin tapped at one of my two remaining red nails. "Me too. I'm sorry I haven't been there for you."

I shook my head. "Don't be silly. I did this to myself. I could've told you I was doing this. But maybe subconsciously I knew you'd tell me I was being crazy."

"Well, it's not too late now. It's just time to get real."

"Okay, but can we not quote Dr. Phil?"

I told Elin all about my makeover disasters and the dog fiasco while we ordered a round of appetizers to share, and then we spent the rest of the evening talking about Terrence and the triplets while I held Augusten, who'd finally woken up. Or maybe he'd just been faking it to miss out on all the girl drama.

"You're good with him," Elin said.

I made a face. "He's so easy. And holding him doesn't mean I'd make a good mom."

"Maybe not. But you're not a monster. Otherwise I wouldn't have asked you to be his godmother."

I stared at Augusten, wondering whether I really could be a mom. But I decided not to get ahead of myself. One step at a time.

∿

When Elin and I got home, Parker and Terrence were on the couch, watching Hugh Jackman as Wolverine on the TV. Parker turned it off when Elin pointedly announced to Terrence that she was ready to go home. "Apparently, I'm driving," she said, eying the lineup of beer cans on the coffee table. Parker rarely drank beer—and certainly not from a can. She grabbed the bag that held Chocolate Poppy from my hand and shoved it into her diaper bag.

Parker didn't make eye contact with me, but said goodnight to our friends and then went to the bedroom. I briefly considered getting a blanket from the cupboard and sleeping on the couch but remembered Elin's advice. I had to make this work. And neither Parker nor I had ever slept on the couch. It wouldn't be a good idea to start now.

Parker was already asleep—or pretending to be—by the time I brushed my teeth and got into bed. I faced the opposite wall, and tried to fall asleep. But all I could think of was what a mess I'd made of everything. I knew I had to change things, but I wasn't sure where to start.

I couldn't sleep.

"I'm sorry about Lauren," I said finally.

Parker sighed. Clearly he couldn't sleep either. "Me too. It didn't seem like you really wanted to fight for him."

"I just—maybe you were right. Maybe we needed to talk about these sorts of decisions before actually making a move. I should've asked you about getting a dog first. Maybe it just wasn't meant to be."

Parker sighed. "Maybe we can get a dog once we move to the country. Have a fresh start. Get a puppy that's all ours."

"What?" I flipped over to face him, but he was still facing the other wall.

"I thought you agreed that we should move. And why put it off any longer?"

"But Toronto is convenient. You love living in the city," I said. I knew I was being argumentative, but when I made a pact with Elin to try harder, I didn't expect that it would start with a conversation about relocation that very evening. "Besides, you've never wanted to go visit Terrence and Elin before and you complain every time I drag you to visit my parents."

He turned to face me. "I only complained about going to your parents because they still have dialup—and it barely works. I couldn't get any work done. But now that I'm not tied to my job, I'd be happy to go there. And I never said I only loved the city. I liked being close to work, but now that I'm home, that's not an issue. And you could find clients anywhere—they don't have to be downtown. You probably wouldn't even have any competition. There's money in the country, you know."

There are mice in the country, I thought.

"And we could have a house with several rooms and you could have a real office and an actual walk-in closet."

He was officially playing dirty.

"And if we wanted to come in to the city, it would be special. Like a date to a concert or out for dinner."

Special? I didn't want special. I didn't want to be a tourist in my own city. And I didn't want to live in the country, even if a walk-in closet and my own office sounded incredibly tempting. I wanted to live right here, in our condo. And I didn't want to talk about it anymore.

I kissed him on the cheek, said goodnight and flipped over onto my side. I was hoping that it was the beer talking.

∿

Clearly it wasn't the beer talking because on Saturday morning Parker was still thinking about the country. And even though I wanted to give him a list of reasons why we couldn't move to the country, I knew I couldn't. Because I'd made a promise to Elin that I would try. And even if she wasn't checking in (which she already was), I would stick to my promise. Besides, Parker kept mentioning all these incredibly tempting aspects of living in the country, like having an indoor and an outdoor hot tub. A fireplace. A spare bedroom so that Elin could spend the night if she wanted to (though I couldn't imagine that actually happening before the triplets were old enough to stay home alone). Still, it was a nice thought.

I also realized that if we *did* move to the country we'd be even farther away from Sienna, which meant I'd really never have to worry about Parker bumping into her ever again. And that would definitely help in Operation Elimination.

"And I guess it wouldn't be as though he'd find anyone at the grocery store attractive, right?" I whispered to Elin when she called to find out how things were going with the new plan. I'd already scrubbed off most of the fake tan, given the cycling shorts to Goodwill and given myself a manicure—on my own nails. "Don't all the women wear their robes and rollers while pushing multi-seat strollers filled with screaming kids?"

"I don't live in an episode of *Green Acres*," Elin said. "Women wear their Tiffany pearls to do the grocery shopping."

"Oh." That didn't sound good at all. Maybe I'd have to do the grocery shopping then, just to be safe. But how was I going to do the grocery shopping when I would have to commute for hours into downtown Toronto every day? And why was I even trying to figure out the logistics? I wasn't moving to the country.

"Elin says that all the women wear Tiffany pearls to do their grocery shopping," I told Parker once he was back in bed, resuming our Saturday morning ritual. It was actually becoming something I looked forward to, and would've been relaxing if I wasn't so stressed out about the idea that we were suddenly going to be moving to the country.

"Tiffany pearls?" He eyed me doubtfully.

"It's true." There was no way he was going to buy me Tiffany *anything* on his fixed income, let alone just so that I could pick up some cans of vegetables and OJ from concentrate. Which meant one thing: we'd have to stay in the city.

"That's ridiculous," he said, folding the newspaper and picking up a book on his nightstand. I glanced at the cover: *Save Your Money: How to Live for Free.*

I wondered if it explained how to get Tiffany pearls for free.

"Well, you wouldn't want us to be social outcasts in the country, would you?" I continued.

He turned to look at me, studying my face. "No, Poppy. I wouldn't want us to be social outcasts. I'd do the grocery shopping then. I wouldn't mind." He turned back to his book.

But he was *supposed* to mind. I sighed dramatically, flopped back on my pillow and banged my head on the wrought iron headboard.

This wasn't going very well.

I was supposed to be trying, but I wasn't trying very hard at all. I just didn't think this was fair. Sure, I was supposed to be trying to be more loving, more attentive, but did I have to move to the country to do so when I really, *really* didn't want to?

Maybe there was something else I could do.

"My mom was asking when we were going to come visit. Maybe we should plan to go up for a few days."

Parker clapped his hands together like I'd just solved world hunger. "That'd be awesome." He leaned over and kissed me on the lips. "You're the best, Poppy. I think this is exactly what we need."

I felt a warm feeling wash over me. It was the first time I'd felt Parker was truly happy with anything I'd done since his accident. And it was as simple as suggesting a mini getaway.

And so it was decided. We were going to the country.

chapter ten

My mother couldn't have been more thrilled when I called to ask her if we could come up for a week—a compromise between my few days and Parker's two-week suggestion.

"You never need to ask!" she said almost reprovingly, then told me Mitzi Bosworth wanted to know when I'd be visiting because her granddaughter's christening was approaching and she wanted my advice on what to wear.

"She's going through menopause so she sweats like Niagara Falls and needs a fabric that won't show that. And she has a tummy tire so it needs to be loose around the midsection. And between you and me she's really self-conscious about her cankles, so you might want to go long. Or a pantsuit. Maybe you can pop over while you're here and give her some suggestions?"

I told her I would, although it sounded like my mom had things pretty well in hand.

"Oh, but you should probably act like I didn't just tell

you all that. Our little secret." My mother was constantly saying things she shouldn't and then asking people to forget.

"Someone already wants your fashion advice?" Parker said when I hung up.

"Mrs. Bosworth."

"See? We're not even there and you've already got a burgeoning business."

~

I'd convinced Christopher to come into the salon on Sunday morning, and Parker picked me up at my hair appointment so we could get out of the city before noon. When I opened the passenger side door, there was a cooler bag on my seat.

"What's this?" I asked, picking up the foreign-looking pack.

"I made sandwiches for the road."

We never made sandwiches—we usually just stopped along the highway. "And I made a road-trip mix on my iPod," he said, leaning over to kiss me on the cheek.

"Your hair looks great. All natural again. Just the way I like it," Parker said, pulling away from the curb.

I didn't have the heart to tell him that the return to my "natural" look cost more than $300 and another several hundred dollars in salon maintenance products to keep it that way. Christopher had to use some sort of industrial-type bleach to get the black out and then conditioned it for nearly an hour just to prep my hair so it wouldn't fall out when he coloured it.

I eyed Parker's outfit: faded jeans and a hooded khaki sweatshirt that said TGIF: Thank God I Fish.

He caught me staring at his chest and glanced down before focusing his attention back on the road. "I thought I'd wear one of the Christmas gifts from your dad." He smiled proudly. I wasn't sure what surprised me most: that he was actually wearing it, or that he'd kept one of the many unwanted gifts he'd never worn. I supposed the gesture *was* pretty cute. I looked into the cooler bag. And the sandwiches looked pretty tasty. Plus, I was hungry.

"With that shirt on you might get roped into actually catching our dinner," I warned.

"Yeah," Parker said happily, as though I'd just suggested my dad might leave him a huge inheritance, not hand him bait and tackle. "It'd be great to spend some time on the water."

"It *would?*" Usually, Parker used a trip to my parents' as a way to spend some time on his BlackBerry, catching up on emails. I'd given up trying to get him to do anything with my parents.

"Sure."

Three hours, four bathroom stops and a yummy ham-and-cheese sandwich later, we arrived at the cottage. My father emerged through the screen door wearing his summer cottage uniform: swim trunks and a grubby sweat-shirt—this time it was a Ryerson sweatshirt I'd given him for Father's Day my first year of university. His grey hair was wild (he never took time to get it cut in the summer) and it fluttered in the wind as he hurried over in his black Crocs to meet us. He pulled me in for a huge hug and kissed me on the cheek, then took a look at Parker, clapped his hands when he saw his shirt and immediately went into the house to change into his blue version of the same sweatshirt. He also brought out matching hats and fishing gear, and suggested they hit the water. "We'll catch dinner!" he announced as he passed my mom in the doorway.

I managed a smile. "Awesome!" I was deathly afraid of lake fish (ever since a three-eyed trout sighting) and of having the kind of husband who liked to fish. But Parker had never been that kind of guy. I knew I should be happy that he actually wanted to make an effort, but I was worried that his newfound love of the outdoors would mean we'd have to move. And I didn't want to move.

"I was just making lemonade!" my mom announced from the porch, wiping her hands on a dish towel and smiling broadly at us. I carried my red weekender bag up to the porch and dropped it by my feet as my mom gave me a hug.

Parker came up behind me and handed my mom the wildflowers he'd picked on the side of the road when we'd pulled off for gas on the way up.

"These are beautiful," she gushed as my father came back out of the house.

"Let's go!" He practically raced down to the dock and Parker gave me a kiss on the cheek then followed him down the hill.

"Don't go spending the whole afternoon out on the water," my mother hollered after them. "You'll get hemorrhoids from sitting on the metal."

"Inside voice, Mom," I hissed.

"Inside voice?" My mother looked at me in surprise. "But we're outside! We can be as loud as we like!" She laughed and put an arm around me and gave me a squeeze. "Go on, give a holler!"

I rolled my eyes. I was not going to give a holler.

I watched as Parker buckled up his life jacket then helped my father push the tin boat away from the dock. My mom put an arm around me and led me toward the house. "You sit down and I'll go get the lemonade." She picked up my bag and took it into the house.

Just then, my BlackBerry buzzed. It was Elin.

"What are you doing?"

"Elin, I just got here. Relax."

"Then I called at just the right time. So what exactly are you doing?"

"Waving goodbye to my husband. He's going fishing with my father."

"So why aren't you out there with him?" Elin demanded.

"I don't fish."

"Poppy . . . I thought we agreed."

"We didn't agree that I had to fish. Besides, I'm bonding with my mom. We're going to have lemonade."

"You're supposed to be bonding with Parker. That was the assignment. You just got your one and only get-out-of-jail-free card. I hope you enjoy the lemonade. Because from this point on, you must do everything with Parker. Whether you want to or not."

"How is that realistic? No couple does everything together. I don't make him see girly movies with me or go for pedicures."

"Poppy, we talked about this. It's an experiment. It's

not forever, but for one week you have to put your pre-judgments aside and *try*. And see what happens."

"I know. I was just kidding." *Sort of,* I added to myself. I hung up the phone.

"So Parker seems so much more relaxed than usual," my mom commented a few minutes later as she played with a leaf on the bouquet of flowers between us, while watching our husbands out on the water. I nodded, shifting around uncomfortably in the rocker, which was missing several slats.

"I know," I said with a small sigh. It was true. He was so different. He was caring and loving. It's not that he wasn't before, but suddenly he had *time* to be the guy I'd fallen in love with. "Parker wants us to live in the country. Though I'm a bit concerned it might be out of necessity now that he doesn't have a job." Which wasn't actually the truth. Parker had never said we couldn't afford our place, and with the kind of house he was envisioning, with guest rooms and mud rooms and who knew what else, it probably wouldn't be cheaper than our place.

"The country!" my mother said excitedly. "Near us?"

To be honest, I wasn't quite sure where he wanted to live. I felt guilty for not giving him more attention.

"Don't get your hopes up, Mom. How on earth am I going to work if we live way out here? I mean, I love coming here, but we can't live out here."

"Oh, but you could! Everyone needs help with their image." While I didn't doubt that might be true, I wasn't sure how much I could do when the only clothing store within a five-mile radius was a second-hand shop. "And I told you Mitzi is always asking me to ask you for advice."

"She is? You only told me she wanted help with an outfit for the christening. When did she want my advice before that?"

"Oh all the time. You know she keeps applying for part-time positions at the bank, but she never gets them. I thought maybe she needs a refresher on her interviewing skills or the way she's presenting herself. But I know how busy you are, and also that you aren't about to dole out free advice, so mostly I just tell her what I think and pretend it's from you. No black-on-black, firm handshake, eye contact, thank-you cards within two weeks . . . all that," she said with a wink, but suddenly I felt terrible. I mean, my own mother shouldn't feel like she couldn't call me, should she?

Oh, what did it matter? We couldn't live out in the country because even if somehow I wrapped my head around it, we didn't know *how* to live in the country and I didn't *want* to learn how. I just needed Parker to see that it wasn't as easy as spending three hours catching one fish for one night's dinner.

I knew it was against my promise to Elin, but if I was going to play Yes-Man to everything Parker wanted to do, I had to make sure he got a fair taste of what living in the country was really all about.

"Do you think maybe you could get Dad to get Parker to help out with some chores while we're here? You know, any projects he's working on? Just so Parker gets an idea of all the upkeep?"

My mom looked at me and for a moment I thought she was going to say no. But then she smiled and patted me on the knee. "If it will make you happy, Poppy, then you know I'll do anything to help. Our little secret. You just leave it to me." She shrugged. "Besides, it's not as though your father doesn't have an endless list of projects on the go. You know he'd love the help, and to spend time with his only son-in-law."

I smiled at my mom. But I couldn't help getting stuck on her words. *If it'll make you happy, Poppy.*

Would it make me happy to see Parker hammering nails, fixing windows and weeding the garden? Would it make me happy to know I was having him do it only so he'd be miserable?

My dad took the Chore Challenge to heart when my mother gave him and Parker a To-Do list. The next day Parker willingly helped my dad fix a clogged toilet, de-squeak an old door, clean the eavestroughs and re-stain the patio furniture.

But Parker didn't seem to mind at all. And after he finished all his chores he came to find me inside, where I was washing all the windows, a terrible task, but one I was enduring after I realized I couldn't be even more of a bitch by making Parker do chores while I sat around and sunned myself. Especially since I didn't tan.

"Some vacation, hmm?" I joked, pushing my bangs out of my eyes.

"It's okay. Many hands make quick work. And your dad and I are really churning through his list, and it's only been two days, so I'm sure we're going to be done pretty soon and then we'll have the rest of the week to do whatever we like. Not that I mind chores. I haven't had many real tasks lately, so it feels good to have something to do."

I wanted to say that if he missed having something to

do he could go back to work, but I stopped myself. I would have said it a few days ago, but I knew it wasn't a very nice thing to say. In fact, it was sort of sad, to feel like to have anything to do you had to have a job, making money that you had no time to spend. Instead, I thanked Parker for being so helpful.

"I like to play too, though," he said coyly and grabbed me around the waist. "Let's take a break and go for a swim."

"In the lake?" I said, as though there was any other option. "But it's freezing!"

"How do you know if you haven't been in?"

"Because it's always freezing!" I said, then stopped myself from saying anything else. I had to agree to anything Parker wanted to do, and that meant swimming whether I wanted to or not. And it wasn't that I didn't want to take a break, but Christopher had explicitly instructed me not to wash my hair for at least three days to make sure the blond covered the black.

"I'm not supposed to get my hair wet."

Parker looked at me, crestfallen.

I felt terrible.

And as Elin had said, I'd had my one get-out-of-jail-free card when Parker went fishing. Even at the expense of my overpriced hair colouring session. "Let's do it!"

Parker grinned like a little kid. "Race ya."

～

Parker and I spent the next two days helping my parents make their house more pristine than it had ever been while my own appearance deteriorated. I had dirt under my nails from gardening, scrapes on my legs from picking raspberries and my freshly bleached blond hair had a green tinge to it thanks to our dip in the lake, but I was trying not to think about my appearance. And although I didn't consider the cottage a vacation given all the chores we were doing, I couldn't help but be put in a good mood by Parker, who was able to find the joy in even the crappiest jobs.

"Your dad taught me a great new way to compost," Parker had declared joyfully on Thursday afternoon when he came in to get a couple of beers from the fridge—my dad was going to be overjoyed that his only son-in-law was finally a beer drinker.

I abandoned my egg noodle dough, which I was rolling out as part of the chicken noodle soup lesson my mom was giving me, and turned to face Parker, the skirt of the retro-style floral apron I'd given my mother for Mother's Day fanning out around me.

"A new way to compost?" I didn't know Parker knew an old way. *I* certainly didn't.

"We can even do it in our place."

"We can?" I said skeptically, then remembered my pact. "Sounds great!" I said with all the enthusiasm I could muster for a plan that was potentially going to turn our condo into a stinky garbage dump. I'd be sure to invite Elin over often to enjoy the fruits of her plan. "So where will we put the compost?" I asked with actual interest. We already had a recycling bin under the kitchen sink that took up all the available space.

"The guest bathroom," he announced.

"But where are our guests going to go to the bathroom?"

Parker explained that the compost was movable, and that he would be completely in charge of it. "Don't worry."

But I *was* worried.

Especially when I realized that composting was just another change that was moving us closer to the country. The next morning, Parker showed me the picture of a cottage in the real estate pages of the *Lakeview Times*. I could barely see the house through all the trees. It looked like something straight out of *Little Red Riding Hood*. A fairy tale. Not reality.

"What do you think? It's a rental on Lake Simcoe— we could give it a try this summer. See what we think of country living."

I nodded, unconvinced. "Looks good."

"Really?" he asked with surprise, which made me feel like the Big Bad Wolf.

"Really," I said, and when I saw how big Parker's smile got I tried to make myself believe it would be okay. It was just a picture, and, more importantly, it was just a rental. I wasn't committing to a new life. Yet.

And so we spent our days embracing the country and manual labour, and our evenings playing games: euchre (my mother's choice), snooker (my dad's), Pay Day (Parker's, a choice I found ironic) and dominoes (my own choice, which wasn't ironic at all—I loved the organizational factor).

"I love this," Parker told me on Friday night after

dinner. We were sitting on the dock while my parents were next door playing bridge with their neighbours. He was taking pictures of our feet dangling over the side of the dock, his feet submerged in the water and my toes just barely grazing the surface.

We'd polished off a bottle of wine at dinner and now we were eating ice cream sundaes—Parker's idea (which, to be honest, wasn't exactly hard to agree to) and drinking sweet dessert wine. He put down his camera and picked up his bowl, then dipped his spoon into mine and took a spoonful. "Mmm . . ." he said, then kissed me on the lips. Then he put his bowl down and took my face in his. "I love getting to be with you like this, Poppy," he said.

"Me too," I said, and I meant it. For the first time since the accident, I was truly, honestly happy to be with Parker.

I hadn't forgotten about Sienna, but she wasn't a constant thought anymore either.

"I love you so much," he said earnestly, then kissed me more passionately than he had in months. I felt breathless and aflutter and I knew it wasn't just the wine going to my head. And when Parker took my hands in his and lifted me to my feet, I stood and followed him back to our room in my parents' cottage, and, after shutting and locking the door, let him undress me and then make love to me.

∿

On Saturday afternoon, when Parker was out channelling Paul Bunyan, chopping some low branches off an oak tree for my dad, and I was in the bedroom looking for my lip balm before heading back outside to finish weeding the front garden with my mom, Parker's BlackBerry buzzed. I was going to ignore it, obviously, but, well, it was lying right in front of me. Or at least, it was right in front of me when I went over to his bedside night table and opened the drawer and looked at the call display. It was Sienna. I knew it.

Calling him. Wanting something. And why was her name showing up on the call display when I'd removed her from his contacts? Did that mean she'd called before, or did anyone's name appear if they were listed with directory assistance? I wasn't sure. I got dozens of calls every day. How did I not know this?

I thought about answering the phone and telling Sienna that she had the wrong number, or that she had the right number but that this was Parker's wife and she should stop calling or I'd call the police. Only, of course, that would've been an empty threat, because you can't exactly call the police because a former co-worker is calling your husband, and if I told the police it was his former mistress, well, then they'd probably want to talk to Parker to confirm the accusation, and then he'd *know* that Sienna was his former mistress. And what if I answered the phone and Sienna recognized my voice and wondered what Uhma was doing answering Parker's phone . . . and then before I could decide to do anything at all the phone stopped buzzing and so the decision was made for me. All I could do was stare at the phone and wait to see if the tiny tape icon appeared, indicating that Sienna had left a message.

But she didn't leave a message, which was so aggravating. At least if she'd left a message I'd know what she wanted. Maybe she hit his name by mistake and called the wrong number! *Parker* when she'd meant to call Patrick or Patricia. But I'd never know. All I could do was speculate, I thought, sitting down on the bed. But before I could even do that, my own BlackBerry rang.

I froze. Was Sienna calling me?

Had she figured everything out? But how?

I grabbed my BlackBerry off the dresser and looked at the call display and let out the breath I'd been holding in. It wasn't Sienna at all. It was Colin.

"Hey," I said, slightly confused as to why Colin would be calling me and still feeling shaken about Sienna's call. Unless—unless Colin was telling me that he *did* like Sienna and wanted to make sure it was okay with me, and maybe Sienna had been calling at the exact same moment to tell Parker that she was totally over him and was going to marry Colin and live happily ever after. Except, that would make no sense to Parker, since he didn't know Sienna and he had ever had sex. He just thought she was some crazy woman he worked with. "What's up?" I sat down on the bed.

"I have a job opportunity I think you'll be interested in."

"What is it?"

Colin wouldn't say. "You've got to come meet me in person tomorrow," he said coyly. Was he flirting with me? I felt instantly guilty, but then considered Sienna's call.

"So?" he prodded when I didn't say anything.

"Well, I'm curious, but I'm up north at my parents' place for the week."

Colin didn't seem to think that was a problem.

But it wasn't just that I was out of town. I was here with Parker. And we were making some real headway in our relationship. And even though I knew that Colin's proposal was work related, it still felt wrong to put him first. "I'm sorry, I really can't," I said.

"Okay, well, I wanted to tell you in person, but if you're going to be difficult . . ." he said.

"Colin . . ."

"Okay, okay. I wanted to offer you a guest spot on *This Morning* this Friday," he said.

"What?" I said in disbelief.

"I *thought* you'd be excited."

Excited wasn't a big enough word to describe how I felt. Being a guest on *This Morning*? It was a huge career opportunity. They had more than a million viewers. The exposure for my business would be incredible.

But I couldn't accept the offer. How could I explain it to Parker? That my ex-boyfriend Diesel had just called me out of the blue? He'd wonder how he got my number, and then I'd have to explain everything, and I couldn't. Not when, after two months, we'd finally reconnected. We'd had sex for the first time since the accident, and I truly felt like we were on the track to mending our relationship.

Just then, Parker poked his head into the bedroom and waved his hands—which were filthy—in the air, then motioned that he was going to wash them and then he'd be ready to watch a movie with me—we'd rented *When Harry Met Sally* in town.

"Can you tell my mom I'll finish weeding tomorrow?" I whispered, and he gave me the thumbs-up, then disappeared.

I turned my attention back to Colin. "I can't," I told him.

"Are you kidding me?"

"It's an incredible opportunity, and I really appreciate that you thought of me, but I just can't."

"Is this because of your husband?"

I wanted to say yes, but I didn't want to blame Parker, who had nothing to do with this. "No, this is my choice."

"Consider it a thank-you for taking care of Ralph. Nothing more," he said, but just the fact that he was saying "nothing more" made me wonder if he really meant it.

"I just can't. You should call Libby Lewis. She's my biggest competition. She'll do it in an instant. Sorry," I said again and hung up, then slipped my phone into my overnight bag and fixed my hair in front of the mirror.

"Are you ready to watch the movie?" I called to Parker.

He came out of the bathroom, holding a small blue packet in his hand, a look of genuine confusion and hurt on his face.

"What's this?"

I stared at his hand and felt a chill run through my body.

"I thought you said you ran out of pills," he said, a tinge of anger in his voice.

I nodded.

"I did, but . . ." I didn't know what to say. I felt so terrible lying to him.

"But what? You said you were waiting until your doctor got back from vacation to refill this. But more than half this pack is empty. Besides which, I thought you said we could just let things happen."

"We didn't agree on that," I said.

"We didn't? Then why didn't you say something? I thought you were on board. Not that we were having sex until last night anyway . . . but I just thought . . ."

"What? You thought you were going to get me knocked up last night?" I said angrily. Suddenly I felt used. "Is that why you got me drunk?" I added, though he really hadn't gotten me drunk. I'd done a very good job of refilling my own wine glass, but still. I truly thought that we were making love to show our *love*. Not to procreate. That he wanted to be with *me*, because he still loved me. Not because he was trying to make this work so that he could be a father.

"What's wrong with you? You act like it would be such a terrible thing."

"Yes! Exactly. That's exactly what I've been trying to tell you. I don't want a baby. I don't get why you don't get that. It's not news. It's exactly what I told you before we got married. It's the same thing you told me. But clearly you forgot that when you got struck by lightning. So I'll say it once more: I. Don't. Want. Kids."

Parker stared at me, his brow furrowed, as though he couldn't figure me out.

"I just don't think I'd make a good mom," I added, trying to soften my voice a bit. I looked down at the carpet and then back up at him.

But instead of agreeing that he was wrong to pressure me, Parker nodded. "Maybe you're right," he said bitterly. "Maybe you wouldn't be a good mother. You're so wrapped up in yourself and your appearance lately, how would you find time to take care of anyone but yourself?" He looked at me long and hard, as though testing me.

I stared at him, disbelieving.

"Is that how you really feel?" My voice was barely above a whisper.

"Maybe it is." He walked out of the room.

I stood unmoving for what seemed like forever. And then I grabbed my overnight bag and threw in my clothes, which were strewn across the floor, grabbed the car keys from Parker's side of the bed and left.

～

I called my parents as soon as I was out onto the main highway to tell them that Parker and I had gotten in a fight and I was driving home.

"I figured as much," my mother said, her voice filled with worry. "I can see Parker down at the water throwing fistfuls of rocks at the lake. Why don't you turn around and come back. I'll make you a cup of tea and you can get a good night's sleep and then in the morning everything won't seem so bad."

"I can't." I sighed. "I'm sorry for ruining the week. Do you—do you think you could drive Parker to the bus station when he wants to leave?"

"Oh, Poppy. Of course, but I just don't like you driving home alone at night."

It was still hours before dusk, but I told her I'd be careful, and not to worry, then clicked off my phone and turned onto the two-lane highway.

The drive home was exhausting. On the way up it had been fun, but now it seemed to go on forever, with nothing but my own conscience to keep me company. I passed one of the pull-offs where we always stopped when Parker needed a bathroom break. Usually I felt annoyed for the delay (I never had to go to the bathroom on the trip—and I hated public bathrooms to begin with, never mind ones on the side of the highway), but now I felt sad not to have a reason to stop.

A Nirvana song came on the radio and I instinctively turned up the volume. Parker loved Nirvana, but could never remember the lyrics, so he made them up. I found myself singing Parker's lyrics—"here we are now, with potatoes" instead of the real ones, and then caught myself and stopped, annoyed that I couldn't push Parker out of my mind. When the song ended the DJ came on and asked if anyone else was constantly wondering what the correct lyrics to the song were, and if so, to turn up your dials because he'd Googled them and was about to share them with everyone out there while he replayed the song.

I wanted to call Parker and tell him to turn on the radio so we could listen together. If my life were a movie, I'd pull over to the side of the road just as it started to rain, and we'd listen to the song together. Or I'd turn around and drive back to my parents' cottage and tell him that the song was a sign. That no one else would ever understand him the way I did. That we were meant to be together. And he'd tell me the same, only in more romantic words. And the song on the radio would become our wedding song when we renewed our vows while the closing credits rolled. But this wasn't a movie. This was my life. And I was far from a cheer-worthy heroine.

chapter eleven

I almost cancelled on Colin.

I'd texted him on the drive home to tell him I'd changed my mind and would love to do the show, but then was immediately plagued by second thoughts.

I couldn't help wondering if Parker was right—that maybe all I did care about was my job. But after a good night's sleep I realized I'd simply been tired and delusional. And I was pissed off at Parker. So what if I prioritized my job? How was that a fault—especially when he'd been the one to convince me to make it a priority right from the start of our relationship?

And I was good at my job. Otherwise Colin wouldn't have asked me to be on *This Morning*.

Colin had texted me back to tell me to meet him at a little Italian patio near the studio for lunch—he had to work on Sunday—and was already waiting with two glasses of champagne when I arrived.

"We're celebrating?"

"Hopefully," he said.

He explained that the show involved an image makeover segment with tips on how to revamp your life after having kids. By the time he was finished pitching it to me I'd forgotten all about Parker and how awful he'd been. Almost.

I couldn't wait to tell my mom—she absolutely *loved* watching *This Morning*. She had a total married crush on the male host, a Richard Gere lookalike. Maybe I could get her an autograph, or get him to call her! And my dad—he'd be so proud. Maybe this would make up for not being a very good grandchild-making machine. I couldn't wait.

"Poppy?" Colin was looking at me over the top of his glass. "You're smiling and have a sort of dazed look in your eye. Is that a yes?"

My heart was palpitating. Of course it was a yes.

"Yes!"

"Excellent. So it's tomorrow," he said. I was surprised it was so soon, and wondered if Christopher would be able to fit me into his schedule in time to fix my streaky hair. I realized that if I hadn't come back from the cottage when I had, I wouldn't have gotten this chance.

"What would you have done if I'd said no?"

"I knew you wouldn't," he said, not missing a beat. I wasn't quite sure how to respond.

"So I think this is cause for celebration," Colin said and motioned the waitress over, then ordered two more glasses of champagne before I could stop him. I was already feeling slightly tipsy after one, without any food. I didn't know anyone did liquid lunches anymore.

When the second glasses of champagne arrived he raised his glass to mine. "We make a good team."

I wanted to tell him that we weren't exactly a team, but I didn't want to be rude. "Colin . . ."

"What?" he said innocently, then smiled.

I took a sip and shook my head, then listened as Colin went over the details for the show. When we finished our lunch I told Colin I'd better get going. I punched in Parker's number as soon as I was out on the street and listened as it rang. I was almost going to hang up and try my parents' line instead when he answered.

"Hi. It's me," I said, even though I knew he had call display.

"Yep."

He wasn't going to make this easy, but I was determined not to let him take away my excitement.

"I'm sorry for taking off and leaving you alone with my parents."

Silence.

"Hello?"

"Will you come back and get me?" Parker said finally. "So we can talk things out?"

My first instinct was to say yes, but I'd just had two glasses of champagne, so driving to get him was out of the question for at least a few hours, and if I was going to be on TV tomorrow morning I really needed the rest of the day to prep for the show. I only had one chance to make my first on-TV impression.

I had to tell him the truth. I took a deep breath and told him all about the show.

"Hmm . . ." Parker mused when I finished.

Sure, he got excited about a sump pump, but couldn't show an ounce of merriment at the thought of me getting to sit in front of a live audience and being watched by thousands, maybe millions, of people at home and maybe even getting to read from a teleprompter?

"You don't sound excited. What if this is just the start? What if Oprah sees me and asks me to be on her show?"

"Maybe . . ." he said doubtfully.

"Can't you at least be excited for me that I'll get my hair and makeup and nails done and get a free mini-wardrobe?"

"Don't you get that practically on a weekly basis? Anyway, it's not that I'm not happy for you. Of course I am. It's just that I don't quite get how this actually happened. Who is this guy and how come I've never heard of him before?"

I'd already glossed over the fact that it had been set up by Colin, but, of course, Parker knew Colin only as Diesel. I'd felt terrible about misrepresenting the situation, but I didn't see the need to highlight the fact that he was my ex-boyfriend. But now I wasn't sure what to say. I didn't want to lie, but I knew he wasn't going to be happy when he heard the truth.

I really wished that Colin from the show was a different Colin from the one I'd dated, but I didn't want to get caught in any more double personality lies. I still had Uhma to deal with and I'd just gotten rid of Ralph/Lauren. I did not need to add two different Colins to the mix.

"Colin is actually Diesel. Diesel Cartwright. He changed his name." I paused, waiting for Parker's reaction.

"Diesel Cartwright?" Parker said slowly. "I don't get it—your ex-boyfriend Diesel set this up for you?" Parker asked, the shock evident in his voice. I wanted to point out that he wasn't really my boyfriend—at least, not for any substantial amount of time, but I supposed now wasn't the time to get into technicalities.

Anyway, Parker was totally focusing on the wrong aspect. The point was that this was my television debut! He was supposed to be focusing on how good this would be for my career, *not* on the fact that Colin had set this up for me. I tried to put myself in Parker's position—that his wife was talking to her ex-boyfriend—to see how it felt, but in comparison to finding out your husband was having an affair, it wasn't a big deal at all.

Besides which, I didn't even like Colin as anything more than a friend who was doing something nice for me.

"So now you're talking to your ex-boyfriends?" he accused me.

Which wasn't at all fair. For one thing, it was one boyfriend, not several, and for another, it wasn't as though I'd sought Colin out. I'd randomly run into him. That wasn't my fault.

And Colin had said this was a thank-you for taking care of Ralph. Nothing more. Of course, I couldn't very well tell Parker that, could I? He didn't know that Lauren was really Ralph and that we'd just been dog-sitting my ex-boyfriend's dog—the dog he'd so lovingly washed and blow-dried to perfection. No, I couldn't tell him that.

"I just ran into him," I explained. "By accident. And he asked what I was doing and I told him I was an image consultant. That's it. Can't you just be happy for me?"

"Of course I'm happy for you," he said. "I just find Diesel's motives suspicious."

"How can you find his motives suspicious? You barely know him!"

"But he's your *ex-boyfriend*. So I know that at one point in his life he felt the way I feel about you. And so I know how I would act if I ran into you after not seeing you for some time."

I didn't want Parker to keep talking, because I knew he was right. But he wouldn't stop.

"I'd want to do anything I could to get you back. Don't you see? He's doing this because he wants something in return."

"But I'm married," I said.

"So?"

I didn't know what to say. What could I say? That married people were off-limits? That married people didn't cheat? Because that wasn't always true, apparently. And it wasn't just a statistic. It was a proven fact, right in our very own marriage. Parker just didn't remember.

"I mean," Parker said suddenly, as if he could read my thoughts, "I wouldn't do anything and I know you wouldn't, but lots of people don't care that someone's married."

And he was proof.

My body started to shake and my eyes filled with tears. My body felt cold and my stomach felt empty. Tears welled up in my eyes. But that wasn't the only thing causing me to break down and cry. What Parker was really saying was that he didn't think I was talented enough to warrant being asked to be a guest on a show. That it had to be about sex. Which hurt my feelings.

"He asked me because I'm good at my job, and he thought I'd be *good* on the show." I could've said no to Colin, and he would've had to find another image consultant, which might not have been the easiest thing in the world, even if we *were,* according to Parker, a dime a dozen. But I had said yes and I knew that Colin didn't want to sleep with me. And even if he did, I didn't want to sleep with him.

"You're not being very supportive," I told Parker angrily.

"All I'm saying is that you should call the producers yourself. If they really want you to do it, then do it."

"But that isn't the way it works," I told him, annoyed. "He's reaching out to me. If I go behind his back and talk to the producers myself they might just blow me off because they don't know me. Besides, there's no time for that. The show is tomorrow. And I *want* to do it. Plus, if I don't do it, I'll be letting Colin down."

"Why do you care? You said you just ran into him. That you haven't seen him in practically a decade. Unless you're lying to me . . ."

Lying? Did he really want to talk about lying?

"Of course not!" I was shouting. I didn't care.

"I just don't think you should do it," he said. He waited for me to say that I wouldn't.

But I didn't.

As long as Parker didn't suddenly start watching *This Morning* (which I was fairly certain he wouldn't), he'd never know whether I did the show or not. And that was a slight problem, because it meant that I was having a problem thinking of a reason *not* to do the show. I'd spent the last few weeks doing everything for Parker, and now I wanted to do something for me. I knew it was wrong to deceive him, but I was so angry—this was *my* life and *my* career. Still, I felt guilty. And so after hanging up with Parker I called my mom to ask her advice. Even though I knew exactly what she'd say.

"You have to do the show," she practically screamed with excitement. I was glad I'd told her to hide in the bathroom with the water running in the tub before I told her the news.

"Parker's upset that I can't drive up and get him today. And what if he watches the show tomorrow to see if I actually do it?"

"You don't worry about that. I'll disconnect the satellite feed so the TV doesn't work. And I'll pop over to Mitzi's to watch it. I'll even see if Mitzi wants to drive into the city with me tomorrow and we'll take Parker home. It doesn't make sense for you to drive up here and back when you have a show to get ready for. Besides, Parker can wait an extra day or two—it's not like he has a job to get back to, now does he?"

"Thanks, Mom."

"You know I'd do anything for you. Now promise me you'll email all your clients and let them know! This is *so* exciting. I'm so proud of you!" my mother squealed. Even though I knew this might have to be a secret I kept from Parker for life, it felt good that my mom could share my excitement.

∿

On Monday morning I arrived at the TV station at exactly eight o'clock as planned. Although I'd initially felt it was too self-promoting to email all my clients as my mother suggested, I changed my mind once I approached the studio and sent a quick email from my BlackBerry to let my clients and closest friends, including Elin, of course, know. It *was* exciting, after all.

Colin told me to bypass all the people standing on the street waiting to get in, and come to the front doors, where the security guard would let me in. I tried to act nonchalant, like it was totally no big deal that I was just breezing into the station because I was going to be *on the show* (!), and not an audience member like everyone else on the sidewalk, but on the inside I could hardly contain myself. I had to slow myself down just so that I wasn't skipping past everyone to the doors. And then at the door I tried to make my voice as blasé as possible when I told the security guard that I was a guest.

He didn't look as impressed as I'd hoped he would, but he did scan his clipboard and mumble "Name?" When I told him, he checked me off and let me inside. Colin was standing right inside the entrance to the street-level studio, and he waved me over. Within minutes he'd introduced me to a gaggle of interns (everyone else was preparing for the show, but I didn't care) and then he took me to get my hair and makeup done.

And, sure, they didn't show me to a clothes closet for myself but that was fine because I'd picked out my outfit at home—cream pencil skirt, short-sleeve cream and black polka-dot blouse with a bow at the neck. Conservative, but my gold metallic sandals and bangles made the outfit fabulous without trying too hard. "You look fantastic," Colin said. He put a hand on my shoulder as he led me through the studio, sending chills everywhere. I told myself I was just nervous about being on the show, and not about seeing him. Obviously. Still, there was something about spending the morning with my ex-boyfriend when my husband didn't know. It felt . . . wrong. And maybe a bit exciting, even if I was totally, completely not attracted to Colin whatsoever. And even if I knew nothing was going to happen because I would never do that to Parker. "I actually have to head into a meeting for another show I work on, so I'm going to miss your segment," Colin said.

I was surprised. I felt a little like he was my guardian here at the studio, though I had to remind myself that it wasn't just because of Colin that I'd gotten the spot, no matter what Parker had said. Actually, Colin leaving in the middle of the show confirmed it. After all, if he was doing this just to get me to repay the favour, he'd be savouring every minute of my being at the station, making sure that I realized it was all his doing.

"But give me a call to let me know how it goes," he said and leaned over to give me a hug.

"Definitely. And thanks again," I said sincerely. Because whatever his motives, I was grateful. I was going to be on TV in mere minutes!

One of the other assistant producers came over and explained how the segment was going to work and it seemed fairly straightforward. They were going to bring out a whole rack of clothes and then I had to choose items for a variety of events: children's birthday party, spouse's holiday party, job interview, sporting event. Then I'd give tips on how to match your hair and accessories to an outfit, and suggest one signature question or statement to use in each scenario when there was a lull in the conversation. It was going to be a breeze.

The show started. The hosts—Kendra, a cute twenty-something redhead who was wearing a gold silk V-neck shirt dress and taupe ankle-wrap sandals and Alex (aka Richard Gere)—did a segment with a party planner about hosting dinner parties for multi-generations and then it was my turn! Alex moved off stage and I took his seat with Kendra. One of the interns brought out the rack of shirts, skirts, tunics, dresses, accessories and shoes, and I went to work, suggesting total image makeovers for every event. And the audience clapped enthusiastically throughout, so I thought it went quite well. Except, perhaps, for the part where I was supposed to recommend an outfit for a sporting event and I said that unless it was figure skating or a synchronized swimming competition, I strongly suggested that any woman avoid such an event at all costs, unless she wanted to be bound to a life of sports airing on TV at all hours of the day, constantly picking up errant baseball caps around the house and finding sunflower seed shells between the cushions of the couch. Kendra sort of laughed a little too loudly at this, and then said what an odd sense of humour I had and that we should move on to the next event—the afternoon tea with friends. Which was a breeze. Obviously. Because everyone knows you should wear your cutest silk cap-sleeve blouse to afternoon tea, and gloves, if you have them. And then, before I knew it, I was done and Kendra announced that since we had some time left, we'd take calls from our viewers at home who had questions about their own images and I'd answer them for the rest of the show. I couldn't believe it! I must be doing a good job if they wanted me to stay on the air. Although maybe we'd just finished too quickly because of the skipped-over sporting event segment. But frankly, it would've been silly to humour such a request. I mean, really.

"Let's take the first caller," Kendra said into the camera. "Who's this?"

"Hi," said a woman, her voice a bit shaky. I could understand being nervous on national television. Except, I totally wasn't nervous at all! It was like I was *made* to be on TV. For a split second I felt sad that I would never be able to share this with Parker. But then I snapped back into the moment and focused on the camera, my eyes a bit squinty, my head nodding, the way I always saw TV hosts doing when they were listening to a caller that they couldn't see. "My name is Etta. I just started dating again and my boyfriend wants me to meet his kids. I'm worried that this will be a deciding factor on whether we take things to a more serious level, because his kids' opinions are really important to him. I was wondering what you think I should wear and if there's somewhere I should suggest that we meet or if I should just go over to his house?"

"How old are the kids?" I asked, already working out the answers in my mind.

"Seventeen and fifteen. Both girls."

I nodded thoughtfully, giving my best *I'm taking this quite seriously* look to the camera. "You should definitely dress young, for starters. Your boyfriend's probably seen his daughters' friends and you don't want to look frumpy in front of them. You should definitely swap your handbag for a graffiti satchel."

"A graffiti satchel?" she said skeptically.

"Yes," I said, nodding and holding a cream-and-golf Coach version up for the camera so that the audience and viewers at home could see what I meant. "Fill it with fun items—lip glosses, nail polishes, a pretty notebook and pen. As for your outfit . . ." I snapped my fingers. "A cute tunic with bright leggings."

"Leggings? It's the end of June. Are you sure that's the best outfit? It doesn't seem age-appropriate."

"It's perfect," I told her. "You're probably just nervous because you're meeting the kids for the first time. And it's okay if you're self-conscious. Tunics and leggings are so flattering and even if you're carrying a bit of extra weight you'll look amazing because you'll be showcasing your best asset—your legs." Kendra looked at me, and I could tell she was impressed. I mean, giving advice without even seeing what this woman looked like! But I had a theory: nine out of ten times, an older woman's best asset *was* her legs.

"Actually, I'm not overweight at all," the woman corrected me. She sounded slightly pissed off, actually.

A few members of the audience gasped.

I bit my lip. How was I supposed to know? I was just taking a guess. She *sounded* like she could've been overweight. And she was totally hesitating about wearing leggings—a sure sign of someone who has body image problems. Otherwise, who wouldn't want to wear leggings? They were so cute! Besides, we were having a chilly summer.

"Oh, sorry!" I said, and laughed nervously. "So, then, what's the problem? You'll look fantastic! I bet you and his daughters will hit it off! Maybe you could go over for dinner and then, if it goes well, you could even suggest a sleepover with caramel corn and ice cream and then a shopping date together the next day!" I could totally see it. Of course, that probably wasn't something I'd suggest an actual mother-daughter do on a regular basis, since a mother should be a parent, not a best friend, which was something I'd definitely follow if I was going to be a mom. Only . . . I wasn't going to be a mom. Why was I even thinking like that?

"It's just that I don't want to show up in the same outfit as his daughters. I don't want them to feel like I'm trying too hard. Or to feel threatened by me, like I'm trying to be one of their friends."

Oh, that was a good point, actually, but the woman behind one of the camera guys was rolling her hands in a way that seemed like I was supposed to be wrapping things up, so I couldn't really suggest a new outfit. I put on my most dazzling smile.

"I wouldn't worry. And it's just one dinner!" I said brightly. "Anyway, it's what your boyfriend thinks, not what his kids think. Who cares what they think?" I said a bit too boisterously. "Do you want to get the guy or not?"

"Yes . . ."

"Then take my advice. Ooh! And another thing—"

"Great!" Kendra cut me off, and although she was smiling pleasantly, her eyes were sort of buggy and she looked as though she really wanted the call to be over. Who wouldn't? That was definitely a woman stuck in a rut. Did she want my help or not?

"Let's take the next caller," Kendra said, her face strained. "Hi there—what's your name?"

"Rennie."

Oh my God! It was Rennie Houpt—I'd recognize her

glum-bum voice anywhere! This was fantastic! I'd hoped my clients would watch me, but having them call in—this was going to be a cinch!

"I wanted to tell you that your advice was horrible and I'm going to make sure that nobody I know ever pays for your services. Eddie broke up with me."

"What?" I said, slightly confused. This wasn't going as planned. I was about to ask her if she'd remembered to leave a set of lingerie "by accident" at Eddie's house or spritz his sheets with perfume so he'd think of her even when she wasn't there, but Kendra spoke up first.

"Sorry, do you already know this caller?" Kendra asked, her eyes wide and her voice conspiratorial, as though she was Jerry Springer. She sat up straight, adjusting her dress. "Let's start from the beginning and get all the juicy details. Rennie, why don't you tell us what happened?"

"Well, I went to Poppy because, well, actually I didn't even *want* to go to her for help but my mother wanted me to get a makeover because she thought it was what I needed so that my boyfriend would ask me to marry him."

"Why?" Kendra whispered. "Had you been dating for years and years without commitment?"

"Not even a year! And I knew Eddie wanted to marry me—we were already talking about it, and about having kids and everything. So really I didn't even need Poppy's advice, but I agreed to meet with her anyway."

"And what did Poppy tell you to do?" Kendra asked.

I listened on in horror. I was starting to sweat.

"Essentially, she told me to act like a princess. Because if he thought I was too good for him and didn't want to spend all my time with him then he'd *definitely* propose."

Her voice was thick with sarcasm, and for my own safety I was sort of glad she was on the other end of the phone line and not in the studio.

The audience gasped. I wanted to throw something at them. Or hide. Or something.

"And?"

"He broke up with me! He told me I was fake and flighty and how could he possibly marry a woman who was so superficial and stuck-up? He wanted to be with someone who was kind and caring and could be the mother of his children and the way I was acting he thought that I would be a terrible mother! And all I've ever wanted is to be married and have kids and now I've lost the chance at both." Rennie wailed and Kendra looked alarmed.

"Maybe you misunderstood Poppy. Surely she wouldn't have told you to act in a way that made you uncomfortable . . ."

But I did. That was exactly what I had done. I felt terrible. I had said all those things. I was a horrible person.

Kendra stared at me, waiting for me to say something, to fix the situation, but I couldn't.

"I'm sorry," I whispered in total humiliation, but Kendra just glared at me, then started waving her arms at one of the cameramen, who turned and started filming the audience.

"Rennie? Rennie?" Kendra said dramatically. One of the cameras turned back to her. "Oops! We seem to have lost connection with Rennie," she said into the lens. "But we'll get her back and get to the bottom of this. I'm sure you have a solution for this problem, don't you, Poppy? You must deal with this all the time." She practically glared at me and I realized that they didn't "accidentally" hang up on Rennie, they were trying to save the show from disaster. I wished I could just disappear, too, but I couldn't. There was nowhere for me to go. All eyes, and all cameras, were on me.

But I didn't have a solution. I didn't know what to say.

"Let's take one more caller, shall we?" Kendra said, then took a deep breath. "Poppy, let's give this woman some good advice, okay?" She practically spat the words at me.

I nodded, then tried to sit up straight. I could redeem myself. I could. I just needed one nice, normal caller. And I would give her considerate, useful advice. And then everything would be fine and the show would be over and I could escape, leaving everyone in the audience and at home with a good impression. They'd forget all about Etta and Rennie. Hopefully.

"Hi there, what's your name?" Kendra said to the air.

"Sienna."

I froze. It couldn't be. Surely it wasn't—I mean, there had to be a million Siennas out there.

"Hi, Uhma," Sienna said sarcastically, in her unmistakable British accent.

Oh God. And I didn't think it could get any worse. I was as wrong as a mock turtleneck.

"Hi, Sienna," said Kendra, totally oblivious to my stunned expression. "What's your question?"

"It's not so much a question as a statement. The woman you're talking to is a total imposter."

"I'm sorry?" Kendra said with a gritted smile, then glared at one of the producers, obviously indicating that we should be cutting to commercial. Except the producers were all watching the events unfold as though it really were a *Jerry Springer* episode.

"Her real name isn't Poppy. It's Uhma Rudimaker and she's not an image consultant, she's a sociologist. She's clearly doing some sort of experiment on your audience at the expense of your poor callers. Just ask her."

Kendra looked at me and then back to the camera. "Perhaps you're just mistaken. Maybe your reception is a bit fuzzy and you can't see Poppy properly," Kendra suggested, looking from producer to cameraman to me.

"My cable is not fuzzy. That woman came to see me in the hospital after I got struck by lightning. She looked exactly like the woman sitting right beside you. She talked the same. She's my Facebook friend. Type in Uhma Rudimaker. You'll see."

Obviously they were not going to type "Uhma Rudimaker" into Facebook. I mean, we were *live on the air*. Surely—

And then one of the producers held up his laptop. They had found me on Facebook. Correction: They had found Uhma Rudimaker.

Kendra turned to stare at me. My career was over. What on earth was I going to do? Kendra forced a smile into the camera. "Thanks for calling, but I'm afraid we're all out of time . . ."

And then music came up out of nowhere. I looked around. I was going to be escorted off the set. Humiliated in front of the entire audience. But the worst part was that I'd told all my clients to watch me on TV. I was so, so stupid.

My life was officially over.

~

I'd tried calling Sienna nearly a dozen times on my way home from the disaster scene but it kept going straight through to her voice mail.

There was no way she was *that* stupid that she believed that I was actually Uhma. Surely the name Poppy was rare enough that she put it together. But she wouldn't answer her phone.

Just as she'd promised, my mom saw the whole thing and called me before I'd even gotten home from the show.

"I don't understand what happened. The first part of the show was so good and then those funny callers, they just didn't make any sense!" my mother said, her voice an octave higher than normal. "Did you really know the girl whose boyfriend dumped her? And what about that last caller—what was she talking about? Why was she saying you were somebody you're not? Poppy, do you think you have a doppelgänger?"

I had two choices. I could lie to my mother or I could come clean. I told her everything. It all just came spilling out. About the affair and Sienna and Uhma and my black hair and my padded shorts and Ralph/Lauren and Colin . . . everything.

For a moment, when I'd finished blabbing, there was silence and I wondered if my mother had just hung up on me. That I'd failed her as a daughter for not keeping my husband happy enough that he wouldn't stray. But then she spoke.

"Oh, sweetie. I wish I could give you a hug."

I sniffed. I wished she would give me a hug too. What was wrong with me? How had I suddenly become this insufferable bitch, who cared more about appearances than character?

"And then I'd shake some sense into you."

It was probably just what I needed.

"What I don't understand is why you did all this."

"Don't you see?" I said, exasperated. "I wanted to win him back. I just wanted him to forget all about Sienna and for everything to go back to normal."

"Normal? It doesn't sound like normal was that great," she said after a pause.

"What do you mean?"

"Well, if Parker did have an affair, maybe you should think about why. Or talk to him about it."

"But I didn't want to tell him, don't you see? I just wanted our perfect life back."

My mother chuckled. "Your perfect life?"

"Why are you laughing?"

"No one has a perfect life. Not even you. I don't know where you came up with this idea that everything had to be perfect." She paused and when I didn't say anything, asked, "Was your relationship really that perfect?"

Of course it was perfect, I thought. "We liked all the same things. We never fought. We were like the same person. Just like you're supposed to be when you're married."

My mother sighed. "Who says you have to be the same person? Your father and I certainly aren't two peas in a pod. But we're in the same garden. And that's all that matters. That we're both vegetables." She thought about that for a moment, then reconsidered. "That sounds very lazy. It's not like we're potatoes. I'm an ear of corn and your father, well, your father's a carrot. A real stick in the mud. But I love him."

"But you're always squabbling about something."

"But that's just us. We've always been that way. Our bickering doesn't mean we're not in love . . . Is this what this is all about? Is this my fault?"

I felt totally guilty. "No, it's not your fault. That's not what I meant. I just—I guess I just figured you two stayed together because of me. I mean, you don't like to do anything together."

"What? Just because I don't like to go fishing and your dad doesn't like to bake cakes? That doesn't mean anything. There's lots of things we do together, when it's just the two of us. And you and Parker like to do things together, too, don't you?"

But that was just the problem. "Not anymore. Parker and I *used* to like to do all the same things."

"Like what?"

I was about to answer, but caught myself. When I thought back to before the accident, I actually couldn't think of what we did together. We *liked* the same things—working and eating in nice restaurants and having a tidy apartment thanks to our cleaning lady—but what did we actually *do* together? I wasn't sure. We actually didn't have *time* to do anything together.

In fact, the most time we'd spent together in months were those few days at the cottage. And I'd abandoned him there.

I didn't leave my bed for weeks I was so depressed.

Okay, so it wasn't really weeks, but it felt like it. In reality, according to the alarm clock on my nightstand (though I was sure there was something wrong with it) it was six a.m., which meant not even twenty-four hours had passed since the fateful show. Still, those hours would soon turn into days and those days into months because my life was over. I was sure of it. I couldn't even sleep it off. I'd tried since the previous afternoon, positive that when I finally woke up I'd feel better about the previous day's events, but now, as the sun peeked through the blinds, which should've at least raised my spirits a bit, I didn't feel any better at all.

I felt terrible about Rennie, but when I tried calling her after the show she wouldn't answer her phone. And two of my other clients who saw me on TV had already called to cancel their appointments with me.

And Parker hadn't called either. When I'd called my parents' cottage to see if my mom was driving him home, there was no answer.

All I wanted was for him to come home so that I could fix things. I'd tell him everything—that I'd done the show, that I knew about Sienna—even if he didn't. No more lies. And I'd be the best wife ever. I would love and support him and we'd put everything behind us and start fresh.

I was finally ready to make a change.

I was in the kitchen on Wednesday afternoon, making myself a cup of tea, when I heard someone unlock the door to our place. I unplugged the kettle and walked tentatively over to the front alcove. He was unshaven and unwashed. He dropped his leather bag, which was covered in dust, on the floor.

"Did you . . . *hitchhike?*" I asked, taken aback.

He wrinkled his brow. "No. I took the bus."

"My mom would've driven you."

He shook his head. "I wanted to be alone. Besides, your mother didn't leave me three hours north of the city."

"I know. I'm sorry. But we have to talk." I was going to tell him everything. Whether he liked it or not.

"I know," he said, and then reached down and unzipped his bag, and pulled out a bouquet of daisies—my favourite—and handed them to me.

"You bought me flowers?" He wasn't supposed to be doing anything nice for me. I was the jerk.

"Yeah. I had a lot of time to think. And I felt really bad about the way I reacted when you told me about the show," he said. "I know your career is important—and I guess maybe I was a bit jealous because you still have a career, and I gave mine up. And I really just didn't like the idea of you seeing your ex-boyfriend again." He pulled me close to him and wrapped his bare arms around me. I took a deep breath. His T-shirt smelled like fresh-cut grass. "But I got to thinking about it and I realized I was just overreacting and being jealous. And I'm sorry."

I felt terrible. He was apologizing to me? How could I tell him everything now?

"Why don't you call Colin and say that you can do it after all? That your stupid husband was just being jealous but that he totally trusts you."

It was official. I was the Worst Wife Ever. I took a deep breath and was about to tell him that I *had* done the show two days earlier, even though I knew he'd be furious. Just then, though, Bartie barked from the bathroom, where I'd hid him after bringing him home from the Humane Society. Because they were overfull at the moment, the Humane Society had given Bartie to me after an hour of begging and pleading, although they'd reminded me again and again it was only temporary until they cleared all the reference checks.

"What was that?" Parker asked, and walked past me. I followed him to the bathroom and opened the door. Bartie came out and looked at the two of us, then sniffed Parker's bare toes through his sandals.

"I know how much you fell in love with Lauren, and I felt terrible that we had to give him back. I know I didn't ask you first, but . . ."

Parker ruffed up Bartie's fur then looked at me, and I was certain he was going to say that I'd made a mistake. That he really *didn't* want a dog.

"I can't believe you did this," he said incredulously.

"In a good way?"

"In a good way." He put his hands on my cheeks and pulled me into him, then kissed me on the lips. "I love you." He stared deep into my eyes and I felt a tiny glimmer of hope for our relationship. I had done something good. And it felt good.

"This is exactly what we need. Something—someone—to love. Together. What's his name?"

"Bartie."

"Bartie," he said, nodding.

"You probably think we don't have enough space for him here, so I guess what I'm also saying is that I'm willing to talk about a place in the country—for the summer, anyway."

"Really? But you were so against it."

I nodded. "I tried to figure out why, and I realized that it's partly because you haven't been thinking about how we can afford it. You don't have a job and I won't be able to keep all my clients if I'm not here for an entire summer. But if it really means that much to you . . ."

I was about to add, *And I'm about to lose half my clients thanks to my appalling performance on* This Morning, when Parker grabbed my hands in his and led me over to the couch. Bartie followed us and lay down on top of my feet.

"Poppy, there's something I need to tell you."

I squirmed uncomfortably. This was it.

"I didn't quit my job."

What? I wasn't sure what he meant—that he'd been going to work all this time? That he'd been seeing Sienna? That the affair had continued? It didn't explain why he was often at home though. "You didn't?"

"I was let go."

"What? Why?"

"Remember the big deal I'd been working on?"

I nodded, though to be honest I wasn't really sure what deal he was talking about. He seemed to sense my confusion, and continued.

"The one that I lost the day of the accident. The reason I called you to come with me to the client dinner. I could barely focus on entertaining other clients knowing I'd just screwed up big time. I needed you there for support. But you didn't come meet me."

I stared at him. I had to wonder if I'd just cancelled my plans with Elin I'd have been able to stop him from having sex with Sienna. But that was ridiculous. And I had no idea if they'd had sex before that fateful night. So all I'd have done was stopped him from getting struck by lightning. Lightning that effectively put the brakes on his affair. In fact, saying no to him that night might have been the best thing I could've done.

"You didn't tell me you'd lost a deal."

"I didn't?" he said, raising his eyebrows.

I shook my head.

"Oh." He shrugged helplessly. "I can't remember. I'm only piecing together what everyone told me happened that day. I totally forget. But Ian didn't. When I went back to work, I thought I was still working on that deal. I didn't remember I'd lost it. And that's when they gave me the package. They said I was too much of a liability to keep on, especially after the accident."

I stared at him, taking it all in. "Why didn't you tell me this?"

"I was afraid to tell you. I was worried that you'd be disappointed in me. That you'd think I was a failure for getting fired."

So you lied? I thought. I didn't say it, though—after all, who was I to judge?

"So if you didn't quit, then were you lying about not wanting to work?" I asked, realizing how much his one lie had changed our lives. What did this mean? That he was pretending to like scrapbooking? That he didn't really want to be Betty Crocker?

"At first I wasn't sure. But then I realized how nice it was to take a break. To be around you. And the severance package enabled me to do it. That's why I thought it would be nice to get a place outside the city. So we could both take a break. I just want to be with you. I borrowed your mom's car yesterday and stopped by the place that I showed you in the paper. It was really great. I think you'd like it."

How could I say no to that?

But I still had to tell him that I knew about Sienna. "Parker, now there's something I need to tell you."

Parker put his hands on my face and kissed me. "Later," he murmured, nuzzling my neck.

chapter twelve

"I planned a surprise for your birthday," Parker announced on Friday morning when he came in from taking Bartie for a walk along the Rosedale Ravine Trail. Bartie pounded across the floor to greet me, and I leaned down so that he could give me slobbering kisses, though I couldn't help but cringe at the wet-factor.

My birthday? With everything going on, I'd actually forgotten that my birthday was only a week away. That had never happened to me before in my entire life.

"Really?" I felt a bit giddy at the prospect of a surprise.

He nodded. "I'm going all out. A real party. I'm taking care of all the details—your only job is to find yourself a pretty dress." After everything we'd been through, a night out to just forget about everything was exactly what I needed. The past few days had been near perfect (even if we weren't *supposed* to be perfect). Parker loved Bartie, and loved me for the gesture, which made me happy—and made me feel guilty, since it was supposed to be a selfless deed. I also never got around to telling Parker about Sienna. I was a total coward. I'd wanted to change, and I knew that I *should* tell him that I knew about the affair, but everything had been going so well these past few days that I couldn't bring myself to.

There just didn't seem to be a point anymore.

I really did feel like we had gotten over the hump. It wasn't just about having my blond hair, flat butt, short nails and fair skin back; I had my sense of self back. And my self-confidence, and I felt a renewed sense of hope for Parker and my relationship. We seemed to be back on the path to normalcy. And so instead I focused on the upcoming evening of friends and fabulous shoes. "Can you at least give me a hint where we're going?"

"Nope. It's a total surprise. But I know you're going to love it," he said with a wink.

For once, I didn't mind.

~

Having the party to look forward to was the best thing Parker could've done to take my mind off the fact that I'd lost three clients thanks to the Uhma-outing, and humiliated myself on national television. After a few days of shopping (partly with clients, partly without), I finally decided on a shirred silk Nicole Miller cocktail dress in plum with black patent leather peep-toe stilettos.

When I came out of the bedroom on Friday night, the evening of my surprise dinner, Parker gave a low whistle.

He was wearing a dark grey suit with a French cuff white shirt that had a fine purple line that matched his tie. His hair was lightly gelled, and as he stepped closer I caught a faint whiff of cologne—Bvlgari Aqva, a scent Parker used to wear when we were first dating.

"You're wearing cologne."

"I know you like it," he said, then kissed me.

It was like the old Parker was back. Suddenly I was overwhelmed by a sense of love for him, for what we had. Maybe we could erase the past. At that moment I was beginning to see that the accident and the makeover and the last month had all been worth it.

I pulled him close. "Let's be fashionably late."

He growled and nuzzled my ear. "But you hate to be late."

"Just this once."

"What about your hair?"

"You won't mess it," I said, almost as a warning, though for the first time I didn't even care about my appearance.

I pulled him into the bedroom.

Frites? He was taking me to Frites?

All the love in the world I had for him an hour earlier vanished as quickly as the sun had on our ride over. How could he do this to me? I felt like I'd just been punched in the face.

He, on the other hand, was pleased as punch, thanks to the action he'd just gotten in the bedroom. "I hope it lives up to our expectations. I know how much you've been wanting to go," he said as the cab pulled up in front of the restaurant.

Yes. I did. Before I found out that you went with Sienna. Before I found out that you were cheating on me. I don't want to go to Frites now! I wanted to scream. *I wanted to go to Frites two months ago when everything between us was perfect.*

The thing was, I supposed my mom was right. Maybe our marriage hadn't been perfect. Or he wouldn't have cheated on me.

"I'm sorry we never got around to going. Anyway, at least now it will be special."

I nodded. I wasn't sure what to think about how he'd changed our lifestyle just to hide his secret that he'd lost his job, so I pushed it to the back of my mind and focused on his other comment—that going out now *was* special. And he was being incredibly sweet to me, especially after how crazy I'd been for the last few months. And it was my birthday. A fresh start. Maybe this was all we'd need to go back to normal. Even if it was at Frites.

"It'll be perfect," I said, but I knew I was lying. How could everything be perfect and normal when we were going back to the scene of the crime—even if he didn't know he'd already been?

I took a deep breath and got out of the cab while Parker paid the driver. A moment later Parker grabbed my hand, a huge smile on his face. "Happy birthday," he said and kissed me on the cheek. Then we walked inside.

Elin rushed over to me immediately. She was carrying two glasses of champagne and handed me one. "You look amazing!" she said, then leaned over to whisper in my ear. "Are you okay?" I knew her question was two-fold: the fact that I was more than a half hour late for my own party, and the fact that I was here, at Frites. She was the only one who knew the secret.

I nodded and she gave a sympathetic smile and pulled me in for a hug. "I really wanted to tell you when I got the evite from Parker but I was worried that if I did you wouldn't come, and then you'd *have* to explain to Parker why you were boycotting your own birthday. And the thing is, we're the only ones who know what happened. I think you should just push it out of your mind and consider this a do-over. So that every time you think about this restaurant you'll think of your fabulous twenty-eighth birthday party that you celebrated with everyone who loves you."

I bit my lip and then gave Elin another hug. "You're such a good friend," I whispered, then blinked back tears. Elin was right. That was exactly what I would do. I had to.

I took a sip from the flute and forced a smile for any of my guests who were looking over at me. I wasn't going to think about what table Sienna and Parker had sat at, or anything else that happened that night. This was my night.

Parker had planned that the first hour would just be cocktails and appetizers, which were my favourite, although we'd missed a good part of the hour by arriving so late. Still, I made the rounds to greet our friends. I was just getting caught up with a couple of girls I used to work with at Holts when Elin grabbed my elbow, practically hyperventilating. I turned to look at her.

"Did you invite *Colin?*" she said, stunned. I turned around. There, standing about ten feet away on the other side of the glass that separated our private dining room from the rest of the restaurant, was Colin. What was he doing here?

I watched as he made his way over to the takeout counter. *Why on earth did nice restaurants allow takeout?* I thought angrily, as though that were the biggest problem here. I turned around to see where Parker was, but he was on the other side of the room, engrossed in a conversation with one of his friends. He hadn't noticed a thing. And Colin hadn't seen me. Yet. Maybe he would just get his food and go.

And then, all of a sudden, he looked up, spotted me, and raised a hand to wave.

"Oh my God, he saw you," Elin whispered. I thought about turning away, but what good would that do? No, the key here was to get Colin out of here as soon as possible. I quickly made my way toward him.

"Hi," I said tersely, my eyes wide and questioning, as if to say *what the hell are you doing here?*

"Hey, what's the big event?" he said, looking past me into the glass room. Then he snapped his fingers. "Your birthday?"

I felt a flutter in my stomach that he remembered when my birthday was. But I had to get him out of here.

I nodded. "My birthday. But don't let me keep you. Is your takeout ready?"

He waved a hand over at the counter. "I just placed my order. It'll be a few minutes. Have you tried the grilled sandwiches? They're almost twenty bucks a pop, but like crack."

And then, before I could shoo Colin away, Parker appeared at my side and put a hand on the small of my back, kissing me on the cheek. "Hi, sweetie, who's this?"

Colin looked from me back to Parker. "Oh, hey—Parker,

right?" He stuck out his hand. "Colin. I didn't mean to interrupt the party, I just wanted to wish Poppy a happy birthday."

"That's very kind," Parker said politely. "Are you one of her clients?"

Colin chuckled. I wanted to die. *Please don't say you're my ex-boyfriend, please don't say you're my ex-boyfriend . . .*

"I guess you could say I was Poppy's boss, for a day. I'm a producer with *This Morning*," he said.

Assistant producer, I seethed silently. But what did it matter? I looked at Parker to see his reaction. Suddenly he was putting two and two together. Colin, *This Morning*, my ex-boyfriend.

"Well, thanks, Colin!" I said brightly. *Leave. Leave now.* I tried to command him, using my powers of persuasion.

"Diesel?" Parker asked, wrinkling his forehead and frowning.

Colin laughed. "Yeah, man. It's Colin now. I thought maybe you didn't remember me." He slapped Parker on the shoulder and Parker winced, as though he'd been stung.

Then he nodded slowly. Of course he remembered Colin. They'd worked together at Cleats.

"You must be very proud of Poppy," Colin said. *Oh no. Please don't say any more.* "So what did you think of her big debut?" he asked, gesturing to me.

No. No, he did not just say that.

"Debut?" Parker asked and looked at me. I watched as the realization washed over him.

I wanted to say something, to explain it all, but it was too late. I'd had days to explain everything to Parker, and now I was going to pay for it. Parker had put it all together.

I could tell by his eyes and his body language as his arm stiffened around me. But of course Parker would never make a scene, so he simply offered a closed-mouth smile.

"I was out of town for a few days, and Poppy's so modest she didn't even tell me how the show went. So it was a success?"

Colin nodded. "There were a few glitches," he said with a laugh. "But overall she was great."

Yeah. So great that I'd lost three clients and outed myself as an imposter in sociologist's clothing. Why was he praising me?

"I can't believe she didn't tell you all about it. Especially . . ." Then he snapped his fingers and nodded, as though figuring something out for himself, though I wasn't sure what. "Oh . . ." he said knowingly and nodded.

Would he never stop talking?

"Oh, I'm not surprised," Parker said with a frozen smile, not looking at me.

What did he mean—that he expected me to lie to him?

Colin looked from Parker to me, then shrugged and laughed again. "Anyway, I really didn't mean to interrupt your party. I was just grabbing a bite, but I should get going—Ralph's waiting outside for me." He pointed to the window and Ralph's ears perked up and then he stood up and started wagging his tail. *Oh no.*

Parker followed Colin's gaze and focused on the adorable dog on the sidewalk, who was now licking the air excitedly.

I wanted to die.

"Ralph?" Parker said, studying the dog, then shaking his head. "That dog . . . doesn't he look just like Lauren?" Parker said to me.

"Oh yeah, and thanks again for looking after him when I was away." Colin patted Parker on the shoulder. "Good to see you again, Parker. Poppy, happy birthday." And then he leaned over and, right in front of Parker, kissed me so close to my mouth that I was afraid to move for fear he'd actually touch my lips.

And then, a second later, he was gone.

I couldn't look at Parker, but I could feel the tension brewing between us. The door to the restaurant closed and Colin untied Ralph, gave a little wave and continued down the sidewalk. I wanted to throw my stiletto at him, right through the floor-to-ceiling window.

It was over. I had to tell Parker everything. Right now. I had to explain why I'd done the show and borrowed the dog. I had to.

"Would you like another glass of champagne?" one of the waiters said, coming between Parker and me. Parker grabbed two from the tray.

I would just have a little sip of champagne and then ask Parker to go outside and I'd tell him everything. So what if my birthday was ruined? I had to be honest. I turned to Parker to accept one of the glasses, but instead of handing me one he gulped the first down, slammed it on a table beside us then started in on the second. Then he turned around and glided back into the private dining room. I chased after him.

"To Poppy!" Parker said, smiling tersely at the crowd as soon as he entered the room. Everyone raised their glasses.

"To Poppy!"

I wanted to crawl under the table and disappear. As

my friends all took a drink from their glasses, I grabbed Parker's arm.

"I can explain . . ."

"Not now," he said. "I don't think we have enough hours to even get started on what the hell just happened." He was still smiling, the same awful fake smile that had been plastered to his face for the past five minutes. "Enjoy your birthday."

Ordinarily, I would not condone public displays of dispute between couples, and I'd always thought Parker was so smooth for never making a scene. But now I just wanted him to talk to me, to yell, scream, anything. I didn't care who heard.

"How can I enjoy my birthday? Please talk to me. Let's just go outside. I know what you're thinking, but it's really not what you think. I can explain everything."

But Parker refused to even look at me, and instead took another gulp of champagne and then walked over to the bar.

For some reason, I didn't follow. And then I realized why: I wanted him to be jealous. I wanted him to know what it felt like to think that your spouse had betrayed you, but to not know any real details. To feel what it felt like to be me.

A moment later, Parker clinked a fork against his champagne glass and asked everyone to take their seats. I half expected him to take a seat at the other end of the table, as far away from me as possible, but he didn't. He sat down in the chair to my left. Elin sat down at my right and looked at me as if to say, *What happened?* but I just shook my head and opened my menu.

No one else seemed to have any idea what was going on, and they continued to talk as they all took their seats around the square table. Parker turned to talk to Aiko, one of my friends from university. She had her own maternity clothing line and was wearing one of her jersey dresses over her pregnant belly. He sounded almost jovial as he asked her about baby names, though I could tell from his voice that he was drunk. Still, I felt my heartbeat slow a bit. Maybe everything would be okay by the end of the night. I turned to Elin, about to compliment her on her new haircut, when Terrence leaned forward.

"So who's been here before? What's good on the menu?"

I looked around the table, but most people were shaking their heads. "Parker, haven't you been here before?" Clint, one of Parker's friends from work that we'd known forever, and whose wife was now a friend, too, asked from across the table. Parker turned his attention away from Aiko and nodded. "Try the osso bucco. I had it the last time."

It was such a simple statement that at first I thought I heard him wrong.

Last time?

As far as I knew, he didn't even know that he'd been to Frites—Sienna hadn't told him at the hospital and I certainly hadn't brought it up.

He'd returned to work for only one day. If someone at the office had told him he'd been to Frites the night of the accident, there'd have been no reason to hide it from me. After all, according to Parker it had been a client dinner. There was no reason to hide that fact. Unless he'd remembered that night all on his own, and knew it hadn't just been a business dinner.

Unless he'd remembered everything.

My menu slipped from my hands and I turned to look at Parker, but he was already looking at me, almost as though he realized he'd made a mistake and didn't know what to do about it.

I stared at him.

"You've eaten here before?"

He looked around the table and then back at me. His face drained of all colour.

"Well, just once. I just—I didn't want to spoil the surprise because I knew you wanted to come here."

Which was total bullshit. Sure, maybe I'd wanted to come here when it had opened two months ago, but there were a million new restaurants. We hadn't been out to eat since the accident. He could've taken me to any one of the new spots in town. He didn't have to take me here—unless he was trying to erase the past.

I grabbed the napkin on my lap and placed it on the table.

"Get up. I need to talk to you." I stood up but he grabbed my hand. I shook it free.

"Poppy." His tone was warning me not to make a scene.

I knew everyone was looking at us, but I didn't care. Elin already knew about the affair, and she was my only true friend. I'd already been embarrassed enough.

"Parker, *now*." I couldn't contain my anger. Two months of holding in the secret of his affair was finally too much. I pushed back my chair.

He stood up. "If you'll just excuse us a moment. Go ahead and order, though," he said to everyone else. The private room was dead silent. Every one of my friends was staring as I turned and walked over to the corner of the restaurant, near the staircase down to the basement. I waited for him to reach me. My palms were sweating and my heart was pounding through my dress so hard I thought it might shake it free and leave me standing in my bra and panties in front of all my friends. But I had to say it. No more secrets.

"Parker . . ."

"Just calm down. Let me explain this all to you when we go home."

"There's nothing to explain, and nothing that can't be said right now. You've been here before. You were here with Sienna. You didn't forget who she was. And I'm willing to bet you didn't forget what you'd done with her. So my only question is if you were trying to keep it a secret from me, why on earth would you bring me back to the last restaurant you were in with her?"

Tears streamed down my cheeks, collecting in miniature pools at the corners of my mouth. I wanted to stop them, to show Parker that I didn't care. That he meant nothing to me anymore. I wiped at them furiously.

"Obviously you think I'm a fool." I knew I was speaking far more loudly than necessary and I wanted to blame it on the champagne, but I wasn't sure it was just the alcohol. I couldn't control myself.

He reached out to touch my arm but I yanked it away. "Don't. Don't touch me. You already embarrassed me once and I lived with it for the past two months, and now you're embarrassing me again, in front of *my* friends. On *my* birthday. You—"

"Poppy, if you'd just let me explain to you why . . ." he said, his voice low and calm.

"There's nothing to explain. Don't you see? You hurt me and then you lied to me, all this time. You thought I wouldn't find out, but I did. I did and I had to *live with it* while you flitted around being a carefree househusband. Not a care in the world. Snapping pictures, making recipes," I spat at him, my voice shrill and my tone sarcastic.

Tears were streaming down my face, and my nose. I could barely even see him. He put his hands on my shoulders but I shrugged them free.

"I want you to leave."

"Poppy, don't be ridiculous. This is something we need to talk about. Later. I'm not the only one who's been lying."

"How dare you turn this around on me! What I did was *nothing* compared to what you did. I hate you. I hate you and I want you to leave right now and get your stuff from the apartment. I don't want to see you ever again."

"Poppy, you *hate* me?" he said in disbelief, and for a moment I felt terrible. But at least I was being honest. Because at that point, I really did hate him. Or at least, I hated what he'd done to me.

"Just—just leave." I was practically begging him, between hysterical sobs. I felt hot and cold at the same time, and my whole body was shaking.

"I promised everyone I'd pay for their dinner. I can't very well leave. Everyone has just ordered."

"Fine," I said. "Then I'll leave. Don't come home."

I turned and pushed through the front door out onto the street.

In hindsight, that wasn't the best idea. For one, it was *my* birthday party and they were *my* friends. And for another thing, once I was outside I realized that I didn't have my clutch, or, more importantly, my house keys. Luckily, Elin came out after me, my purse in her hand, and carted me off to the nearest pub and proceeded to get me drunk on cheap wine.

chapter thirteen

was barely into my twenty-eighth year and I was already a divorcee. Well, not technically of course, but I was en route and what was the name for a woman who was separated from her cheating, lying, pretend-amnesia-having husband? I was jilted. A jilted divorcee in the making. My life was over.

I knew I should've been furious with Parker for not only cheating on me, but once he remembered, keeping it a secret, but I could only think of one thing. I missed him already. I wondered where he'd spent the night and when he was going to come home (even though I'd told him not to).

I was pathetic.

Why wasn't I angry? Maybe it was because I'd already had so much time to get used to the idea that he'd cheated. But I'd still thought we had a chance, and now that we didn't, I was just sad.

But also, I couldn't help thinking about what my mother had said. That maybe, if Parker had cheated, our marriage wasn't as perfect as I'd thought it was. I'd been so focused on Sienna and becoming her that I hadn't dealt with the real issue: *why* he had cheated.

Because there really, truly, was something wrong with me. Not my appearance, but *me*.

"There's nothing wrong with you," Elin said when she called on Sunday morning to make sure I wasn't drowning my sorrows in ice cream.

"I don't eat ice cream," I told her, then ate another spoonful of Triple Caramel Chunk. Bartie was beside me in the bed, curled up on Parker's pillow, and he licked the air, trying for a taste of the ice cream, but I moved the container and my spoon away from him and handed him a dog treat instead.

"You're lying! You're only going to feel worse when you crash from the sugar rush."

"I don't think that's possible."

"Nonsense. You just have a hangover."

"No . . . I'm jilted. Abandoned. It's too late. It's over."

"Don't be ridiculous. So he lied. You lied too. You're upset with each other. Married couples have fights. It happens."

"But we don't fight." At least, we hadn't fought until recently.

"Well then it's time to start."

"I don't think fighting with me is a top priority for Parker. He's probably already with Sienna. Right now. He probably went to her place last night after he finished paying for everyone's meals, like nothing had even happened."

"You can't think that way. And so what if he did? It wouldn't have been the first time."

"How can you be so insensitive?"

"I'm telling it like it is. It's time to face reality."

"Reality? I've been living the reality of this for the past two months. And look what good it did me."

Elin groaned. "Reality TV show, maybe," she said sarcastically. "Now's the time to decide what you really want," she added, a bit more gently.

"I want to go to sleep and wake up and find out that this was all a dream. That Parker never got hit on the head with a lightning bolt."

"I thought it struck his hand."

"Whatever." A lightning bolt to the head was much more dramatic, and this was my sob story, darn it.

"Again, not reality," Elin reminded me.

I sighed. "I know. And that's just the problem."

"Do you want to end your marriage, or fix it?"

"I want to fix it."

"Then it's time to do it the real way. By talking to Parker. Really talking. Do you guys even do that?"

"Yes," I said, but inside, I wasn't so sure. I used to think we talked about stuff, that we were close, but maybe we hadn't been close in quite a while. "Even if I do talk to him, I'm not sure what good it's going to do. We used to be so alike, and we're so different now. We barely have anything in common."

"So? You and I are nothing alike," Elin said, exasperated. "In fact, we couldn't be more different. I love the country and big family gatherings and being a stay-at-home mom and cooking and Rachael Ray and Dr. Phil and you . . ."

I mustered a laugh. "I hate all those things."

"And we're best friends."

"But that's different. We've known each other forever. And we're friends—we're not married."

"Okay, then look at me and Terrence. We're different, but the bottom line is that I love Terrence and so we make it work. I do things with him that make him happy. And he does the same for me. And then it's worthwhile."

I believed Elin—it was the same thing my mother had been trying to tell me only days earlier. I just wasn't sure I believed it was the same for Parker and me. I wasn't sure we could really change to accommodate each other's wants and needs. I still wasn't sure I fully understood why Parker had changed in the first place.

"I just don't know if I can do it."

"You can if you *want* to. I'm not saying you have to do everything Parker wants—he has to compromise for you, too. But you have to talk to him. And you can do that. Besides, when was the last time you didn't get something you put your mind to?"

"Lots of times. I didn't get beautiful sexy brown hair like I wanted."

"And you got your pretty blond hair back in the end because of it."

"I failed my lifeguarding exam."

"Now you're just being ridiculous. That was eons ago. And if you'd passed it you never would've met Parker."

She had a point. I tried to remember my life before Parker. It was so different. I was such . . . I was such a screw up. I dated losers who treated me like crap. I settled for mediocre. Parker changed all that in me. He was part of the reason I was who I was. But now I had to wonder, was that really who he'd wanted me to be? And more importantly, was that who I wanted to be? Look at what I'd done to Rennie, and how superficial I'd become.

Maybe it wasn't just Parker who had a choice whether to decide to make our marriage work. We both had a choice.

I told her I'd be fine, and then I hung up the phone and hunkered into the covers to take a hard look at myself. Figuratively speaking, of course, because I hadn't yet showered and I was sure my face was still streaked with makeup from the previous night. I did not want to see my reflection.

And then, suddenly—well, actually, like three hours later (I knew because Bartie's bladder seemed to have a three-hour limit)—I realized what I needed to do.

I had to figure out exactly what I wanted. I'd spent so much time trying to do the things I thought would make Parker forget all about Sienna and win him back, but I hadn't thought at all about the consequences of all my actions. What did I actually want? Did I want Parker back?

As if on cue, my phone rang. I looked at the call display. It was Parker.

I desperately wanted to answer it, to hear his voice. To hear what he had to say. But I couldn't answer it. If I did, all I'd be doing is reacting to whatever he said, and I knew that the possibilities were endless. Or at least included four:

1. That he was sorry.
2. That he wasn't sorry and that he wanted a divorce.
3. That he was going back to Sienna.
4. That I was getting Punk'd.

Option #4 aside, these were all very real scenarios. The worst thing I could do was hear what he had to say before knowing in my mind what I wanted to hear. What I *wanted*.

Did I want to make things work? Or did I want our marriage to be over, so I could just put it behind me and move on?

I had no idea. I'd spent so many weeks making myself over for Parker, wishing everything could just go back to the way it was, without really understanding that the way it was wasn't even ideal. My entire focus had been on making sure he forgot about Sienna, and that had failed miserably. Now I had to figure out what I wanted.

And so, I stared at my BlackBerry as the little tape icon popped up on the screen indicating I had a new message. I would wait to listen to the message until I really knew the answer.

The problem was, the answer didn't just come to me while I was sleeping, as I'd hoped, and so I had two options: stay in bed, or get up. And since the ice cream had run out, on Monday afternoon I decided on the latter, and then realized that if I was going to get dressed to go to the store (rather than slipping out the back entrance of our building in my bra-less T-shirt and leggings to let Bartie pee), I should probably try to be productive and undo some of the damage I'd done in the past few weeks. So once I'd gone downstairs to take Bartie for a proper walk, stopping off at Whole Foods on the way home to get a container of vanilla ice cream, I sat down at my laptop and got to work. First, I tried to find Rennie's boyfriend's phone number, but I didn't know his last name, so instead I tracked him down on Facebook through Rennie's profile and sent him a message, explaining that Rennie's odd behaviour was all my doing. I gave specific examples, just to be sure he believed me, and then begged him to forgive her. Finally, I attached an electronic gift card for a weekend away at a little inn in Prince Edward County to the message and clicked Send. Next I called all my other clients and personally apologized if they had seen me on TV and wondered what kind of sub-par operation I was running, and then offered each of them a free session with me, where I'd help them become exactly the person *they* wanted to be—not who I thought they should be.

I'd always prided myself on being an image consultant, but somehow I'd lost focus on why I'd become an image consultant in the first place, which was to assess the best qualities in each of my clients and find a way to highlight those qualities. Somehow, somewhere along the way I'd become a glorified personal shopper, focusing solely on my clients' outer appearances, and the only bit of internal advice I'd been giving was to turn them into superficial princesses, just like Rennie had said.

I was going to change that. As long as at least some of my clients gave me the chance. What I needed was a clean slate, I told myself, and then went to the kitchen to get out the Windex and a roll of paper towels from under the sink. Bartie followed me, and then sat at my feet and wagged his tail, watching my every move. I would *actually, physically,* make a clean start. It would be totally therapeutic.

Five minutes later I reconsidered. Who was I kidding? I hated cleaning. I didn't actually need a tidy apartment to symbolize my metaphorical clean slate. I set the cleaning supplies down on the dining room table beside a pile of papers. I picked up the section of newspaper on top and saw it was the real estate section of the *Lakeview Times,* with the cottage Parker had shown me circled in blue ink. I dialed the number on the ad, and when I got the voice mail I left a message.

Beside the papers was a box of Parker's scrapbooking supplies: coloured sheets of paper, cutting tools, various types of glue and those impossible corners you're sup-posed to slip the photos into.

I went to the front hall closet, taking a dining room chair with me, and reached up to the top shelf for the blue tin that was hidden away in the corner. I pulled it down and went back into the living room.

I lifted the lid and looked inside. The box was filled with every photo we'd ever taken since we'd started dating. Our honeymoon, our wedding, even the European holiday he'd taken me on, where he'd proposed. So what if he'd been working some of the time? When he hadn't been working we'd had a great time.

I didn't have an empty album, so instead I borrowed a selection of the coloured paper in Parker's supplies and began arranging photos, a few on each page. I attempted to use the photo corners but gave up after the second photo and retrieved my glue gun instead. One by one, I affixed photos of Parker and me to the pages. At some point I ran out of glue but I wasn't finished. I had to keep going. Finally, I ran out of paper, and so I gathered the stack, hole-punched each page along one side and then tied a piece of ribbon through each hole to hold the album together.

I had just finished when Colin called. I debated not answering his call either, but I had to know why he was calling.

"It was great to see you the other night," Colin said as soon as I answered. "You looked amazing. Did you have a good birthday?"

"Hardly," I said miserably. "And you showing up didn't help and neither did kissing me."

"What do you mean?" he asked, mock-innocently. "What happened?"

"I don't want to get into it." Which was the truth. Colin and I weren't friends, and although Parker may have betrayed me I wasn't about to start spilling the details about my messy marriage to my ex-boyfriend. And as much as I thought Colin had acted like a jerk, he really hadn't done anything wrong. I was the one who'd caused all the drama by keeping so many secrets. "What do you want?"

"I wondered if I could coerce you into taking Ralph for a couple of days?" he asked.

"No. Sorry. Besides, I've got my own dog now." I patted Bartie, who was curled up beside me, on the head.

"Ah, that was just an excuse anyway. I wanted to see if you're free for dinner tomorrow night. I still owe you a thank-you meal for taking care of Ralph last time, and I'd like to buy you a belated birthday drink. If your husband will let you go out with me," he added quickly.

"He won't care what I do," I said miserably.

"Uh oh. Then it sounds like you could really use a friend. I'm shooting in your area tomorrow afternoon.

Want to meet at the Hazelton, say, five o'clock? Come on, just one drink."

And because I felt alone and unwanted, I agreed.

~

"I ordered you a martini," Colin said as soon as I sat down beside him in the dimly lit lounge on Tuesday afternoon. The table was set with only two chairs, kitty corner rather than facing, so that we were intimately close. As though it were a date.

"Thanks," I said, smoothing my navy jersey dress. I'd had my first shower in two days and put on some lip gloss and a pair of heels in an attempt to make myself feel better, but it didn't really work. I took a sip of my martini, even though I usually never drank hard alcohol, especially not so early in the evening. It always went straight to my head, but that was exactly what I needed tonight.

"You look great," Colin said and I touched my hair self-consciously. "So tell me what's going on."

I took another gulp and paused. "So, uh, how's Ralph?"

"Come on, Poppy," Colin said, pushing up the sleeves of his long-sleeve cotton tee. "Just tell me what's going on."

And maybe it was the martini, or maybe I really just needed someone to talk to, but I told him everything.

"Whoa," he said, two martinis later, when I'd recounted the last of the sordid details.

"I know. Good story, right?" I said and slung back the rest of my third drink.

"Really good. Way better than the version Sienna told me."

I caught my breath and stared at him. "What?"

"Yeah. Sienna told me she tried to jump your husband's bones in some alley, but that she barely got anything more than a slip of the tongue. So you're saying he actually slept with her?"

Colin pushed his drink toward me but I shook my head. "What are you *talking* about? Why were you and Sienna talking about Parker?"

"Oh yeah . . . I think I totally blew your undercover name that night that I went out with Sienna. We got pretty wasted and I guess I started talking about you and she figured it all out."

"What?" My head felt fuzzy and I couldn't focus on what he was really saying.

"I tried to tell you when you were with Elin the night you brought Ralph home, but you didn't want to listen."

"You tried to tell me?" I didn't remember him trying to tell me anything.

"Yeah . . ." Colin ran a hand through his hair then took a final sip of his drink as the waiter put two more glasses in front of us. "I totally didn't get what you were up to. Until Sienna called into the show and blew your cover. That was pretty wild. Everyone's still talking about it at the studio. Although I have to say, you sort of burned me. No one trusts me to choose guests anymore." He grinned conspiratorially.

My throat was tight and my cheeks were hot and it felt like I was sinking through my chair. I took a gulp of my fresh drink and shook my head, trying to clear it.

"But you can make it up to me," he said, putting his hand on top of mine. I looked at him. I didn't know whether it was the martinis suggesting it or Colin himself, but I knew what he meant. We were in a dark bar. We were both drunk. Parker and I were unofficially separated and he may or may not have actually had sex with Sienna. For all I knew his voice mail said that he didn't love me anymore. Maybe he hadn't gone back to Sienna—maybe he'd just decided he didn't want to be with me at all. That he'd rather be alone than with me.

Colin gazed at me with his deep brown eyes and his eyebrows raised. "I always felt like we never really got closure on our relationship," he said, sliding his fingers between mine. I stared at him and blinked, trying to focus. My heart was pounding. "I still have feelings for you, Poppy."

I looked down at our hands, and then back up at his face.

"You do?" I wanted to add, *Since when?* but didn't.

He nodded. "I was young and stupid, Poppy. But I've changed."

"You have?"

"I think you still have feelings for me, too," he continued, not even listening to me.

I wasn't sure what to say. I realized I was staring at his mouth. Was he right? Did I still have feelings for him? And then, before I had a chance to say anything, he leaned over and I knew he was going to kiss me. He looked into my eyes as though looking for confirmation. His lips were inches from mine, but suddenly I pulled away and shook my head.

I couldn't. As much as I knew that it would put Parker and I on an even playing field, I couldn't do it. I couldn't cheat on my husband, no matter how many times he had or hadn't cheated on me.

I shook my head more forcefully. "I can't."

It was more than that. I didn't *want* to. I'd made a vow to Parker and I wanted to keep it.

"I have to go." I stood up suddenly.

"Poppy, I just thought . . ."

"I'm sorry."

"You don't have to go." But I was already halfway across the bar.

It was only when I'd reached the street and my heart rate had slowed that I realized I'd done it again.

What was wrong with me? Why couldn't I ever seem to remember to leave with my purse in hand? I contemplated going back in to get it, but I didn't want to be anywhere near Colin. My head was spinning. I just wanted to go home.

And so I started walking.

Thankfully, when I got there Amir opened the door and led me to my apartment, unlocking the door for me. "You're sure you're going to be okay, Mrs. Ross?"

I nodded, hanging on to the door handle for support. Bartie wiggled over to the door and licked my bare legs. I groaned. I couldn't make it back downstairs but I knew Bartie couldn't hold it much longer.

"I'll take him," Amir said, and picked up his leash off the table beside the door. I was still leaning against the door when Amir knocked on it what seemed like only a minute later. I pulled open the door and Bartie trotted in.

"Thanks, Amir," I mumbled.

Amir gave a half smile, nodded and backed away from the door. I closed it and looked at the clock in the kitchen. It was only seven o'clock and I was completely plastered. I stumbled over to the dining room table where I'd left the scrapbook I'd made. Then I picked up the home phone and punched in Parker's cellphone number, but my call went straight through to his voice mail. I stared at the phone. Was he purposely not answering my call? I could hardly blame him. I hadn't even listened to his message yet. Was he doing the same to me? I hung up without saying anything, then picked up the scrapbook. I took it into the bedroom and pulled out Parker's brown leather overnight bag from under the bed. I put the scrapbook inside then opened his armoire and pulled out a handful of clothes and shoved them into the bag.

If he came back to get some of his stuff when I wasn't home, hopefully he'd take the bag with him. I wondered where he was right then.

I slipped my dress over my head and collapsed in my underwear on the bed just as the awful buzzing in my head suddenly got louder. God, why did I have to drink so much? I buried my head under the pillow, but when the buzzing turned to banging I realized that it was someone at the door. I dragged myself off the bed and shuffled over to the door and looked through the hole. It was Colin. Remembering I was only wearing my bra and panties, I went back to my room and got my champagne-coloured silk robe and pulled it on, then fumbled with the tie in the front as I made my way back to the door. For some reason I still had my black platform heels on, but my feet were so hot and swollen that I couldn't seem to shake them off. As I passed the hallway mirror I realized I looked like a hooker in this getup. A hooker who didn't have sex. I peered through the peephole at Colin on the other side.

"What do you want?" If I wouldn't have sex with him

when I was drunk, did he really think I was going to when I was already halfway to a hangover? "Go away."

He held his hands up in defence. "I just thought you might want your stuff. But if you don't need your wallet or your phone or . . ."

I opened the door a crack.

"You went through my stuff?"

"Yes," he said matter-of-factly. "Because when I called you to tell you you'd left your purse, it rang. And so I looked inside to see if you had a business card so I could find out your address and bring your stuff back. But if you don't want it . . ."

I grabbed my purse without opening the door any wider. "I do. Thanks."

"Listen, Poppy, please let me apologize. I promise not to touch you." He put his hands behind his back. "I swear."

I looked at him skeptically, then opened the door wider. "Go on."

"I don't know what I was thinking. Well, I do know. I saw you again and you were so perfect and I started thinking about what a mistake I made letting you get away all those years ago. And then you told me how things were on the rocks with your husband, and instead of being a good friend, I tried to take advantage of the situation. Which wasn't fair. Obviously even if you did want to start something with me, you need to figure out what's going on with your marriage first."

"I don't want to start anything with you," I said as clearly as I could manage.

"Got it. Anyway, I wasn't being a very good friend. And I'm sure right now, that's all you really need."

He was right. I did need a friend, but Colin wasn't it. "I want to fix things with my husband, and I don't think that's going to happen if you're in the picture."

He nodded. "So then . . ."

"So then *goodbye*," I said pointedly.

He nodded. "Then a hug goodbye?" he said, and before I could react, he pulled me halfway through the door frame into him. I didn't want a hug. I really just wanted him to leave.

But I let him give me a quick hug until, out of the corner of my eye, something caught my attention. I turned my head to look down the hall and if Colin hadn't been holding me up I think I might have fallen over.

It was Parker. He was standing in front of the open elevator, staring at me in disbelief.

I thought for a moment he was going to step right back onto the elevator, but then it closed and he took a step forward. I detangled myself from Colin and straightened my robe.

"Parker."

His eyes narrowed. "It looks like I'm interrupting something."

I looked at Colin. It didn't look very good. I was wearing my robe and heels, hugging my ex-boyfriend on the door-step. Our doorstep.

"It's not what it looks like," I said, shaking my head. "Colin was just dropping off my handbag."

Which didn't sound very good, either. "I mean, I just forgot it." I wanted to tell him that I'd just called him. That I wanted to make everything up to him. That I was so incredibly sorry for everything that had happened. That I didn't care that he'd slept with Sienna. That if he wanted to fix our marriage, I did too. But in my drunken state I couldn't find the right words and he interrupted before I could say anything.

"I don't need to hear the details," Parker said roughly. "I just came to drop off the money for the mortgage payment. It's due tomorrow." He thrust an envelope at me.

"I didn't know you were coming."

"And if you had . . . what? You would've kicked Diesel—Colin, whatever your name is—out sooner?"

"Maybe I should go," Colin said, backing up, and I wanted to say, *Yes, like five minutes ago,* though it was my fault he was here at all. If I hadn't forgotten my handbag . . . actually none of this would've happened if I'd never agreed to have drinks with Colin in the first place. He started walking to the elevator.

"Don't bother. I'm not staying." Parker gave me a hard look and then brushed past me into our place.

"Wait," I said, grabbing his arm, but he shook it loose.

"I might as well get some stuff while I'm here." He went into the bedroom and emerged a moment later. "How thoughtful that you already packed my bag." He glared at me. "I guess you weren't hoping I'd move back in after all," he said spitefully, then stormed past me and into the hall. He turned the opposite way from the elevators, where Colin was standing, and pushed open the door to the stairwell.

"Parker, wait!" I yanked off my shoes and raced barefoot down the hall to the stairwell. "Parker!" I ran down the stairs and pushed open the door to the lobby, but he was gone. I looked helplessly at Amir.

"He just left."

I pushed open the door onto the street and looked both ways. A couple walking a dog stopped and stared at me. I didn't blame them.

Parker was nowhere to be seen.

I turned and went back inside, pressed the button to the elevator and leaned against the wall. Colin was nowhere in sight, thank God—though I could've used a shoulder to lean on, if nothing else.

The door to our apartment was still open and my handbag was sitting inside the door, beside the envelope I'd thrown on the floor. I picked up the handbag and threw it against the wall. It hit the vase of daisies Parker had given me after returning from the cottage. They both tumbled to the ground, the vase spilling over onto my handbag, ruining it. I was glad. That handbag was the devil in leather.

Then I remembered my BlackBerry was inside and I pulled it out and hit the message button.

"Poppy, it's me. I'm so sorry for everything. For ruining your birthday and for keeping everything a secret. I'm sorry I didn't tell you that my memory came back or what happened, which I'm assuming you already know. But you have to know that I only kept it a secret because what happened was a mistake. I know it sounds like a cliché, but I really mean it. It was nothing. We were drunk and she told me she had a crush on me, and I was feeling lonely and I let her kiss me. I know I should've stopped her, but I just wasn't thinking. But I promise it was just that one time. And it was just a kiss. I don't want to see her again. I know I should've told you as soon as I remembered, but I was afraid. And I know I should've talked to you and told you how I was feeling before the accident, but I didn't, because I was an idiot. And then I got hit by lightning and I forgot everything. I truly did. When I finally remembered, I couldn't tell you because I didn't want to hurt you. And I was so worried that if I told you I'd lose you forever. Poppy, I love you. I just want to be with you. Please. Call me."

Had Colin been telling the truth about what Sienna said? More importantly, had Sienna told the truth to Colin? It didn't matter. I could tell by Parker's voice, *he* was telling me the truth.

And I'd ruined everything. If only I'd listened to the message days ago. Now it was too late.

I slumped down in the hallway and cried like I'd never cried before.

∿

I woke up with the worst hangover ever, a kink in my neck from falling asleep on the floor and a hazy memory. I looked around, then noticed my BlackBerry. It all came flooding back to me.

I punched in Parker's number. I had to talk to him. His voice mail clicked on.

"Parker, I'm so sorry. For everything. I'm sorry that I'm just calling you now, but I only just listened to your message last night. I didn't know you still loved me. I was so worried you were calling to say it was over, and I just couldn't bring myself to listen to you say that. I don't care about Sienna. If you're willing to put it behind you, so am I."

I hung up and my phone rang immediately and I pressed the Talk button without even looking at the display. "Parker?"

"Is this Poppy Ross?" said a lovely female voice.

"Yes," I said, deflated.

"This is Bella Birks. I'm the co-producer of a new show called *Teen Talk*."

"Uh . . ." I said, confused.

"It's a brand new show that's going to air on community access television. Do you have a moment?"

"Um, sure."

"Excellent. So the show is a talk-show format, aimed at teens, and will air in one of the afternoon slots once a week. It's going to be all about self-esteem, self-image, self-respect, but we want to make it really fun, with dating tips, and fashion and beauty segments, all tied into the theme," she said, her voice full of energy. "Anyway, I'll be the moderator of the show, but we're looking for a host—someone engaging and fun, to answer the kids' questions and lead the conversation. I saw you on *This Morning* a while back and I thought, now there's a gal that'd be perfect for our show."

"You *saw* me on *This Morning*?" I wasn't sure what sort of standards this Bella Birks had if she thought I'd be good at *anything* on TV.

Bella laughed. "Okay, I'm going to be honest with you. You were pretty much a disaster. But you *did* have grace under fire."

"I did?"

"Well, yes. Sort of. Anyway the show is a not-for-profit project so all the revenue will go to Teens in Need, a charity that helps keep kids off the street and out of unhealthy homes. And we have very little funding. Which means, well, we wouldn't actually be able to pay you. I'll be frank: you're not the first person I'm calling about the show. I've tried dozens of other hosts that I think would be excellent, but no one's willing to donate a day a week to the show. Then someone mentioned you and showed me a tape of *This Morning*. I figured after what happened, well, the other networks probably weren't beating down your door to invite you to be a guest on their shows . . ."

Free. I was getting an offer to work for free.

"If you need a few days to think about it . . . but the show debuts in a week, so, actually . . ."

"I'll do it."

Parker didn't call for the rest of the week, and as much as I tried to immerse myself in preparing for the debut of the show, I couldn't stop thinking about him. I tried to tell myself that maybe he'd lost his phone or didn't notice there was a message or, like me, just needed a few days to figure out what *he* wanted, but another part of me worried we really were done for good. And as much as I wanted to stay in bed and shut myself off from the world, I couldn't. For once, this wasn't about me. Bella Birks was giving me a second chance, and I had to take it.

Bella hadn't just handed me the job, even though

it was unpaid and she was desperate. After I'd agreed, I threw myself into preparing with her and her co-producer, Kat, an excitable, full-of-life woman in her mid-forties with wild grey hair she wore in a bun on top of her head. We went over a whole range of topics and scenarios, so that both Bella and Kat could be certain I wasn't going to provide bad advice to the teens who would be on the show. Thankfully, Bella had confirmed that we wouldn't be taking any calls from viewers.

But I didn't mind. I *did* screw up the first time around and I *did* have to prove myself. And I wanted to.

This time, I wasn't going to tell anyone they had to act like superficial princesses to get ahead in life, and especially not to get a job or a guy. They just had to be true to themselves. Of course, I wasn't about to start promoting the return of UGGs or saggy Juicy track pants in public (I reserved my own for Saturday mornings in the apartment), but it also meant not everyone had to attempt to look perfect all the time—something I was finally learning about myself.

Bella met me on the set the following Wednesday morning—exactly a week after she'd first called. "I'm glad to see you did your own hair and makeup. We don't quite have the budget for that," she said with a laugh, but I smiled graciously and nodded.

"No problem."

"No wardrobe, either," she added, but I didn't mind. I had picked out the perfect grey and white tweed cami dress with back-zip black leather ankle-strap pumps. Besides, what kind of image consultant was I if I couldn't even put myself together? Bella led me out onto the set.

Even though the show was on community television, Bella's team had arranged for a live-studio format, with teens from various high schools in the audience, and some sitting on couches, MTV-style, as part of the show.

Bella adjusted the buckle on her belt, smoothed her blond bob and then took a seat in a green suede chair, indicating for me to sit on the slightly worn beige couch. "Are you ready?" she asked when we had three minutes to air. I nodded. I was ready.

For the first part of the show, everything went extremely well. I wasn't offending anybody, and everyone seemed to really agree with what I had to say.

Until Bella's co-producer, Kat, interrupted during the final commercial break. "We have our first caller."

Bella raised her eyebrows. "I didn't think we were going to take calls from viewers, Kat," she said and I panicked. It was the one thing we'd agreed on before I'd signed the waiver to appear on the show. For both our sakes. Hadn't they learned anything from watching me on *This Morning*? Unscreened calls from viewers with no tape delay + me = disaster.

But they weren't listening to my thoughts or watching as I, panic-stricken, shook my head furiously.

"Let's take it," Bella said as the cameraman gave us the signal that we had five seconds to air.

"Hi, we're here with image consultant Poppy Ross, and due to the high volume of callers eager for Poppy's advice, we're going to take a few calls."

I took a deep breath.

"Hi, who's this?" I said.

"Hi. I was wondering if you could help me."

I recognized the voice immediately.

"We'd love to," Bella said. "Talk to us. What seems to be the trouble?"

"I've been having some troubles with my . . . girlfriend," Parker said.

I couldn't find my voice. "What happened?" Bella asked, looking at me questioningly.

"I've been a real jerk. And I'm not saying that my girlfriend is going to win any awards for Girlfriend of the Year, either, but I've made a mess of our relationship."

"Go on," Bella said. I was too choked up to talk.

"I had a few too many drinks one night with a girl that I work with, and she kissed me. And I didn't stop her."

The audience—comprising mostly girls—booed. I stared at the monitor, wishing I could see Parker's face.

"It meant nothing—it really didn't. Which is why I didn't tell her. But she found out and I didn't know that she knew, so for months she's been having to deal with thinking that I liked the other girl, thinking that she meant something to me, when she didn't, and I totally regret it. I really love her and I want to make our relationship work, only I'm not sure how to do that."

"Have you heard from her at all to know that she wants to see you?" Bella asked.

"Not really. But she made me this really beautiful scrapbook, filled with pictures of us, and I was hoping that meant that she would give me a second chance."

"Poppy, what do you think?" Bella asked and gave me a look that, even though I didn't know her well, clearly meant *say something*. "Do you think the scrapbook is a sign she's giving him another shot?"

I could feel the tears building but I told myself to hold it together, at least until the cameras stopped rolling. "Yes," I managed. "I think so."

∿

After the show wrapped, Kat came right over. "You were fantastic!" she gushed. "So honest and emotional and obviously invested in the plight of the audience and callers. I definitely want to make call-ins a regular part of the show, don't you, Bella?" she said.

"Definitely." Bella nodded enthusiastically. "I don't think we have any doubt that we want you back every week. Still no pay . . ." She gave me a wink. "But you never know, down the road . . . What do you say?"

"It sounds great," I said, looking from Bella to Kat. "Thanks so much, to both of you. Now, if you'll excuse me there's something I really need to take care of." I brushed past them and rushed through the door to the street to call Parker. But there was no need: he was standing right out front, still holding his phone.

"Hi," he said quietly.

My heart was hammering in my chest. "Hi."

"You look so pretty," he said, touching my cheek.

My stomach was in knots. "You look good too." He was wearing a grey polo shirt and jeans I didn't recognize.

"You packed me a whack of boxer shorts, but not much else," he said and laughed lightly, then sobered. "I got the scrapbook." Then, as though remembering he'd just told me so on the show, he added, "Obviously."

I nodded.

"I loved it. Especially the part where you used chewing gum to attach the photos."

"I ran out of glue sticks for my glue gun and I couldn't find anything else to use. I guess I'm not very crafty."

He took my hands in his. "You're perfect."

I shook my head. "I'm not. That's just the problem."

"You're perfect for me. And the photos reminded me of that. But where did you get them?"

I shrugged. "I had them all tucked away."

"Why? Why didn't we put them into albums?"

"I didn't want them to get ruined." Even I knew how silly that sounded.

Then Parker reached into his bag and pulled out a beautiful scrapbook and handed it to me. "This is for you. I was going to give it to you on your birthday, but I thought you'd think it was cheesy."

I felt terrible that he thought he had to throw me a party rather than give me something personal, something he made. I opened the album, which made my own scrapbook look like something a second-grader had put together. I flipped through pages filled with photos of the two of us, including several he'd taken at my parents' cottage, but some of the moments I hadn't even realized he'd captured.

"When did you take all of these?"

"When you weren't watching," he said, almost sadly.

But what it told me was that I hadn't been paying attention. How did I not know that he was taking pictures of me? How had I become that self-absorbed?

"I'm not sure if you've already made up your mind about things, but I figured I should try for a chance to ask you to forgive me. I *am* your husband, and that pulls rank over whatever Colin is to you at this point."

"Colin?" I said, confused. "Nothing happened with him, I told you. It was one show, that I totally bombed by the way. Didn't you get my message?"

"I did. Though I wasn't sure if you were just saying that nothing happened to make me feel better," he said doubtfully. "And it doesn't really matter. I don't really want to know," he added, and I could see the worry in his eyes. I realized that he was finally experiencing a bit of what I'd felt when I found out about Sienna. But I didn't want him to feel that way. I loved him too much. But I was also still angry that he'd kissed someone else. And lied.

"Parker, what happened to us?"

He shook his head. "I'm not sure. Maybe we should start at the beginning."

"With the affair."

"Affair?" he said, blinking. "Poppy, it was just a kiss. The night of my accident. We had a client dinner at Frites—"

"But if it was a business dinner, why was Sienna there? Isn't she just an assistant?"

Parker nodded. "She'd dated one of the guys from the other company we were meeting with and given us the lead, so I brought her along because she really wanted to come. After dinner she said she'd convinced some of the guys to go for more drinks at Le Germain. I don't know if she really never asked them or we lost them along the way, but it ended up just being us. I should've come home to you but I wasn't even sure you'd be home and I really just wanted to have a few more drinks and try to forget how badly I'd screwed up at work. We got pretty wasted, and when we were leaving it was raining and she pulled me into an alley to hide under an awning, and then she kissed me. I'm not going to lie and say I pushed her away immediately. I'm a jerk, I'm not denying that, but I did stop her and was putting her into a cab when the lightning struck."

"Were you . . . were you holding her hand?"

Parker looked taken aback. "No. Of course not. I was holding the umbrella over her head as I helped her into the cab. The bolt hit the umbrella and went through me. She must have just gotten a shock from holding my arm, which was why I was knocked unconscious and she was fine."

"But if that's all that happened, I just don't understand why she referred to you as her *boyfriend*." I looked at Parker helplessly, searching for an answer.

Parker shook his head. "I don't know. I really don't. Maybe she wanted to legitimize flinging herself at me, or because she had a crush on me, but I wasn't interested . . ."

"So you *really* didn't have sex with her?"

Parker took my hands in his. "Of course not. I would never do that to you."

I knew that now, but I also knew that something had let him kiss another woman. I thought back to that night with Colin, when we met at the Hazelton. I supposed I could've easily let him kiss me. But I didn't. That was the difference.

"I'm *so* sorry, Poppy. I know it's no excuse but I was really drunk and I was feeling like shit from losing the account that day and I was upset that you wouldn't make time for me . . ."

"To come with you to a business dinner? Are you kidding

me?" I said, exasperated. "It's hardly quality time, Parker. And you don't cheat on your wife because she's busy. You *talk* to her. *You* talk to *me*. You don't kiss someone else."

He held my hands tighter. "I know. I know it's no excuse. I just felt alone and then Sienna started flirting with me, and it felt nice. I guess I sort of liked the attention. And for some reason, even though I barely knew her, I felt like I could just be myself."

"But why did you think you couldn't be yourself with me?"

"I don't know. Sometimes, and I don't want you to take this the wrong way, but sometimes I feel like I have to keep up with you." His blue eyes searched my face, as though he were looking for an indication whether he was saying too much, but I nodded. As much as I didn't want to hear the negative things he had to say about me, I knew I *needed* to hear it. "Like . . . you always had this expectation. We always had to eat in expensive restaurants and we couldn't just have friends over without it being a huge ordeal. I know it's going to sound ridiculous, but I felt like I couldn't even drink a beer without you judging me—that I was low-brow or something. Everything just got to be too much. And I wanted to stop it but I was worried if you knew I was changing you wouldn't want to be with me."

"I don't think making out with someone else is the better option. And besides, you were the one who introduced me to nice things. That's who you were when I met you. I was never like that, but I became the woman I thought you wanted me to be."

Parker closed his eyes. "You're right. I see that now. What a mess."

"Did you really think you couldn't drink a beer in front of me?"

"It wasn't just that. Even the basketball games when Ray left. Or the ball game I asked you to come to a few weeks ago."

"I honestly didn't realize it meant that much to you to have me there. I didn't know you loved sports so much."

"Poppy, how could you think I didn't like sports? I had season tickets for seven years. And we met in a *sports bar*."

"I just thought you worked there because it was your uncle's bar. I worked there and I didn't like sports," I pointed out.

He laughed softly. "I guess that's true."

"Okay, fine, but if you like sports, then I like camping."

"Huh?"

"It's true. But there have been lots of times when I've felt like I couldn't be myself. And *you* made me feel that way. Like work, for example. You made me feel like I had to be working as hard as you. So I did, and I'm not blaming you. But if it made me lose sight of *us*, then yes, I'm to blame, but so are you."

"I know." He fidgeted with my hands.

"And I really hate that Sienna had to be so sexy, you know that?" I said with a small smile.

"You know what she looks like?" he said, looking genuinely confused.

"Of course," I said. "You didn't know that?" But then I realized that he had no way of knowing. "If we're going to be honest with each other, you should know all of it." I told him everything. About the night of the accident, about Uhma, about the show.

Parker ran his hands softly up my arms, making my hair stand on end. "I can't believe you would go to those lengths to save our marriage. But what I don't understand is why you didn't just tell me that you knew."

"The same reason you didn't tell me. I thought that if I didn't tell you, and you didn't remember, we could just move on. That's why I tried to make myself over to look like her."

Parker stared at me in disbelief. "*That's* what you were trying to do—with the hair and the nails and—"

"Yes! But Elin said that it was stupid because it would just remind you of Sienna and then you'd go back to her."

Parker looked at me, bemused. "To be honest, you didn't really look like her at all."

I bit my lip and then smiled through my tears. "It was a pretty terrible look for me, wasn't it?"

Parker took my face in his hands and looked into my eyes. "You're just—you're so beautiful the way you are. I could never love anyone as much as I love you."

"So . . . when did you remember what had happened with Sienna?"

He dropped his hands back down to meet mine, his gaze never leaving mine. "Not right away. I guess maybe my subconscious was suppressing that part of my memory or something. But on my way home from your parents' place I had a lot of time to think. And then I remembered what she'd told me in the hospital, and it all started to come back to me."

"So did you always plan to tell me? Or was it just a mistake, at my birthday dinner?"

"Of course I planned to tell you, just not at Frites. The

last thing I wanted to do was ruin your birthday. I really did want it to be special. I knew I had to tell you, but I wanted to make sure it was the right time, and I wanted you to feel sure that Sienna was totally out of the picture—which she was. She was never even *in* the picture, but I knew what it might seem like, and I knew you might not believe me. But that night at Frites, I just got so upset when Colin showed up and then I had a bit too much to drink and it just slipped out that I'd been there before. I didn't mean for it to come out, but in hindsight, I'm glad it did. I didn't want to lie anymore—and that was the biggest one. I guess I was just so furious with you for the way you'd been acting, and then when I found out you'd been seeing Colin behind my back and that you did the show without telling me, I just felt like I had nothing to lose."

"So what do we do now?"

"I think we have a lot to talk about."

"Like cottages and babies."

"I know you don't want to have children. And it's not really fair that I changed my mind. It wasn't what we had planned, and just like the cottage, it wasn't fair of me to just throw my crazy wishlist at you and expect you to go along with it."

"It was just sort of . . . surprising. Especially the baby."

Parker squeezed my hand. "Just for the record, I think you'd make a great mom. But I don't want to force you to do anything you don't want to do."

I nodded. "I guess I just don't understand where all of this came from all of a sudden. I mean, I know you got hit by lightning, but it just sort of seemed like you became this totally different person."

Parker looked down at the ground and then back into my eyes. He stared at me for a long time, and then took my other hand in his and said quietly, "I almost died. And then I woke up and I realized that I had no idea how much longer I had with you. And I just wanted to make sure I didn't waste any time. I want to make the most of whatever time I have left. Whatever time *we* have left."

And for the first time since the accident, the truth of that hit me and I realized I had been so caught up in the affair I never really thought about the actual incident that set me on my own crazy course. He *had* almost died. I tried to consider what that would be like for me. Maybe I would act totally different too. Maybe I'd feel a sense of urgency to do all the things I'd thought I had a lot more time to do.

Almost as though reading my mind, Parker said, "I never thought I wanted a child, but after I almost died, I wondered if I'd regret not having a child. It's not like you get a do-over. But I sort of felt like I got a second chance." He blinked back tears. "And I kept thinking that if we had a baby, even if something happened to you or me, the other one would still have a piece of us." He paused and wiped away a streak of tears then held my hand again. "Even if that totally sounds like if I die, I'd be leaving you with dirty diapers." He forced out a laugh.

My eyes were so full of tears I could barely make out Parker's face. "Don't say stuff like that. I don't want to think about you dying. Even though leaving a piece of you behind is a really sweet thought."

"Let's not talk about dying anymore. We're both alive, and what I want most is for us to be together. Baby or no baby. Cottage or no cottage. We're a family. Besides—" he motioned to the building behind me "—now that you're a fancy TV star, maybe we should look into a bigger place right here in the city. We could spend the summer looking for a house—or, maybe a townhouse. Something big enough for you to have your own office."

"That's so sweet, but we won't have time this summer. Oh, and we won't be able to afford a new house in the city since they're not paying me to do the show. It's for charity."

"Really? That's really great," he said, nodding. "So I guess you'll be pretty busy with the show and work this summer . . ."

"Not really. It's just that we won't be in the city. We'll be at our cottage."

Parker looked at me in surprise, but shook his head again. "What cottage?"

"The one in the ad that you circled."

"Oh . . ." He looked confused. "It's not available. I wanted some time to think this past week so I rented a car and took a drive to the country. I ended up driving by it. I felt really sad because I thought maybe I'd never get a chance to be there with you. And that's all I really wanted . . ." His voice trailed off. "Anyway, someone already rented it."

"I know. I did. For us."

"You did?" He looked shocked.

I nodded. "If you'll spend the summer there with me. We can really talk, Parker. We can figure stuff out together."

He pulled me into him then wrapped his arms around me. "Really? But what about work?"

I wrapped my arms around his waist and looked up at him. "Work can wait. And I'll just drive in for the show once a week."

He looked into my eyes. "You're amazing, you know that?"

I smiled at the man I loved more than anything else in life. "So does that mean you want to spend the summer with me?"

He let go of my waist and cupped my face in his hands. He pressed his lips to mine and kissed me until I had to come up for air. "The summer and the fall and the winter . . . just you and me. I want to if you do," he said, wiping away my tears with his fingertips.

I nodded, as more tears—tears of happiness and love— streamed down my cheeks. "I do."

acknowledgements

This book was originally published in 2010 by the now-defunct Key Porter. I'm eternally indebted to ECW Press for putting *Love Struck* back on bookshelves. I'm basically love struck with the entire ECW crew, but especially Jack David, David Caron, Crissy Calhoun, Erin Creasey, Troy Cunningham, Jenna Illies, Carolyn McNeillie, Tania Craan and Laura Pastore.

Once again, I'm so grateful to my agent, Suzanne Brandreth, for your constant support and guidance, and for responding to my every impulsive email with wisdom, sincerity, perspective and wit. Also at The Cooke Agency, many thanks to Dean Cooke, Sally Harding and Mary Hu.

A thousand thanks to my incredibly talented editor, Jane Warren, for your kindness, critical eye and commitment.

Also at Key Porter, thank you to Jordan Fenn, Tom Best, Alison Carr, Jennifer Fox, Daniel Rondeau, Nina Paris and Kelly Ward for all your hard work.

To my experts and first readers: Suzanne Colmer (aka Your Shop Girl) and Erin Summer-Kibblewhite (aka Gift Shop Girls) for your image consulting savvy, and to Sammie Richards for letting me tag along on your shopping spree; my sister, Danielle Guertin, for the cycling consult; Mital Joshi, for sharing invaluable info on all things concerning lightning bolts and other medical emergencies; Sarah Hartley, for editing, encouragement (and dog breed smarts!); Suzanne Gardner, for research and cupcakes; and finally, for your help on love, marriage, faux-tans, author photo and all the rest: Lauren Baswick, Liz Bruckner, Christina Campbell, Emily Chaplin, Jacquie Clancy, Mandi Dama, Melissa Di Pasquale, Do My Hair (including Candice Best and Deborah McGrath), Jason Draho, Melanie Dulos, Kim Edwards, Claudia Infusino, Alicia McAuley, Aaron Michiels, Kathryn Prosciak, Chris Van Doorn and Denise Wild.

To the sole member of my writing circle (it's more of a writing teeter-totter): Marissa Stapley-Ponikowski, for reading every last version of the book, coming up with the title, and answering infinite emails within seconds to reassure me: "No, your book is not bad."

To my family: especially my Dad, Michel Guertin, for your love, support and enthusiasm; Susan Guertin; Grace and Gary Simmons; Danielle Guertin; Marcus Benesoczky; Janet and Terry Visser; Sarah Farmer; and Melissa, Andy and "mini-Melandy" Csaszar.

Finally, and forever, my love and infinite gratitude goes to Brent (aka The Hubs), for always believing in me and my dream, and for your endless support, encouragement, love, advice and glasses of wine, just when I needed them.